BLOOD SKIES

STEVEN MONTANO

Also by Steven Montano

BLOOD SKIES SERIES

Blood Skies
Black Scars
Soulrazor
Crown of Ash
The Witch's Eye
Chain of Shadows*
Vampire Down
The Ending Dream
Darker Sunset

* Coming Fall/Winter 2013

DEDICATION

To Liberty.
Queen of the Awesomesauce.

ACKNOWLEDGMENTS

Thank you Mom and Dad for believing in me.

Thank you Lib, Takenya and Sam for being on this adventure and sometimes letting me drive.

Thanks for Jen, Alan, Candice, Bruce and all of the other Indies out there for your support and inspiration. Rock on.

BLOOD SKIES

He sees the city. It stands beyond fields of broken sand and salt estuaries at the edge of a frozen sea, across from a forlorn tower made of black metal and razor protrusions.

It is a city of the living.

It looks unnatural. The city teeters at the edge of a frozen marsh. Transparent frost limes the outer walls, and strange insects like cursive figures lie petrified in ice colored dark with dirt and rust. The frozen sun illuminates the white-gray fields.

He feels like he's never seen it before. Cold and bitter wind curls off the surface of the frozen sea and carries the smells of corrosive salt and arcane steam. The sky is striated in alternating layers of dark and light, a cross-section like aerial soil. The horizon is both too close and too far away, and the debris-filled sky is two dimensional, a flat screen.

Nothing seems to belong. The world has been cleaved and fused back together by a blind hand. There is a sense of wrongness, a heavy and catastrophic air, a feel of the temporary. He feels and sees it, can almost taste it, though he isn't really there.

Is this a dream? A vision?

Does it matter?

He sees into the heart of Thornn: sees its angled towers and iron catwalks, the crenellated domes and flying bunkers. There are fields of half-built ships that will someday sail through the air. Farm fields protected by razorwire and automaton gun turrets made from sorcery-tainted steel. Dirigibles piloted by lightweight Gol aeronauts fly low in the sky – the Gol are un-people, dwarf and misshapen, bound by a shared knowledge they've been changed but forever unaware of what was done to them. In a way the Gol are representatives of the entire world.

Things were different before The Black, and everyone knows it. But no one knows how.

He soars over the rooftops, cognizant of the fact he is flying, but unable to feel the experience. He's an intangible: he sees and feels and smells the world as if through a ghostly lens.

He feels her there with him. He's never alone, and he's glad for it. She presses against him, her ethereal skin laced to his like a warm and sticky sheet. Her thoughts penetrate him, and her breath holds him in a warm vapor. He wears her like armor, like skin. Her form corrodes, reforms, comes together once more in a shimmering rain trailing him like a spectral wake.

He passes through twisted streets, over narrow lanes and between crooked houses. The city's architecture was fused together by need. It is ancient and medieval, but has been laced with things he knows are modern: streetlights powered by batteries, falafel vendors, percussive music created by programmable machines. Thick clouds of industrial smoke pour from tall brick chimneys and fill the sky. Windows spill yellow light as the pale sun descends. He hears voices and wagon wheels, horses and steam whistles. He feels currents of powerful magic, the crackle of arcane energies which provide the city with warmth. He smells fresh bread and hot cider, alcohol and smoked meat. He hears laughter, a baby crying, the clang of steel as it's hammered into armor or stakes.

There are crosses all over the city. They hang over doorways, are imprinted on buildings, have been drawn on the road in hexed chalk and blessed inks. The crosses are made of iron and bronze, hammered and hand-painted, tall and thin or fat and squat. Some resemble ankhs, and some look like blades. None of them do any good, and everyone knows it, but the crosses aren't there for practical purpose. They are symbols of the ongoing conflict.

The nearest Bonespire stands at the far end of the fields of ice and salt, past broken channels of sluggish dirt-filled water and shattered stone. From the walls of Thornn the Bonespire appears as little more than a black sliver, a malevolent needle surrounded by roaming shadows. The tower is only one of many, but it's from there most of the attacks against the city of Thornn are launched.

He wants to dream of a world where none of this has happened, of a place without The Black. He wants to dream of a place where his shattered memories of a peaceful childhood are untarnished, of a sky than doesn't darken, of a world that doesn't smell of rot. He wants to dream of a place where he can lay down and go to sleep without the fear of never waking up.

He doesn't know why, instead, he dreams of this place, this world he already knows, this world he wants to escape but wakes up to, inevitably, every single day.

All he wants is to dream of something different. He wants to dream of a place where he is not afraid.

APOTHEOSIS

Year 3 A.B. (After the Black)

Black noise hung in the air like a fog. Whispers slithered along the walls of the church in a dismal chant.

The halls seemed miles long, like dark tunnels of charcoal shadow. Dim beams of murky light cut through cracks in the mortar and the splintered wooden planks laid across the windows. The rooms were filled with frost and dust. The church was one of the last of its kind, a holdover from the world before The Black.

Knight desperately tried to take the sight of it all in before he died.

He stared at one of the angel's faces. Blood ran down her cheek, split along her nose and fell in twin rivulets of red rain to the floor. The statue's wings had been shattered in the battle.

The altar was at Knight's back, where it propped him up as he sat on the floor. He was barely able to feel anything below his waist.

The world outside the church was white. Harsh wind howled through the shattered windows, carrying the smell of death and the moans of undead. The air was cold and dry. Motes of dust dangled like drunken moths. Thick pools of blood covered the floor. Shell casings, broken blades and chunks of flesh were everywhere.

Knight tried to move. He could barely feel his arms and legs. A stabbing pain shot between his shoulder blades. Blood trickled down the holes in his chest.

No, he thought. *Not yet. Not yet.*

Knight lifted his head far enough to see the far doors. The shattered pews were covered with black vampire corpses still oozing blood. There were human bodies as well, smothered beneath the smoking ebon husks of the undead. Screams and the rapport of gunfire still echoed in his ears. The empty minigun sat smoking atop the altar.

The vampires had rained down nail shot and chemical bombs before they'd charged the doors. Smoke swirled and clung to the cracked walls. Dead winter wastes waited outside, a vast plain of ice and glacial drifts and graveyard cities interred in tombs of snow.

The stench of smoking meat filled Knight's nostrils and clogged his throat. He gagged and struggled to pull himself to his feet, slipped in his own blood and fell forward onto the altar. Knight sensed the looming twisted angels on the wall behind him, a fresco of black figures entwined in a vaguely profane dance of limbs and wings and shadow.

There were voices outside. He saw the air blacken from their breath.

"You have to move!" he shouted at himself, and he did, though clumsily. His legs were weak and his boots slipped on shells and blood, forcing him back to his knees. Blood trickled down Knight's mottled hair and ran over his face before it cut around his nose and fell to the floor. He was a reflection of the crying angel.

He could barely move. His muscles shook with effort as he clenched the altar with gloved hands and hauled himself to his feet once more.

The church doors shook. Motes of frost fell from the ceiling. Thick gusts of soiled snow blew through the windows and turned the air the color of ash. The cracked doors held steady, secured by bodies that had fallen against it in a grisly barricade, but Knight knew they wouldn't hold for long.

His left arm dangled uselessly at his side. His shirt and armor had been torn to shreds, and he was covered in thick cuts that ran down to the muscle. He wasn't sure how he hadn't passed out from blood loss.

He had to move. There was too much at stake, and too little time.

Teeth clenched with effort, Knight stumbled forward. He pulled his SIG Sauer from its holster, not even sure if it was loaded.

He stumbled one foot in front of the other to the back of the church. The doors buckled behind him. He heard a frenzied shout, a bodiless animal call over a chorus of humanoid screams. They'd use explosives soon.

Knight pushed through the doors leading to the center of the church, not wanting to wait around and see what was about to burst through the main doors.

The dark chamber he entered was decorated with wooden columns and a single flickering torch set in a wall sconce. Fumes of what he'd been told was magic lingered in the frozen air, an acrid haze that made his eyes water. Judging by the light spilling into the church behind him, it was just past dawn.

Time to do the deed, he thought. They'd almost been ready to complete the ritual when the vampires had attacked. The scholars had to make sure everything was ready. Most of the ritual had already been completed, and all that remained was the final stroke, the part of their task which had to wait until the sun was up. The vampires knew what they were up to, which was why they'd attacked just before first light.

I hope this works. I hope it was worth it.

Knight tripped and grimaced in pain. He set the pistol down and slammed the door shut behind him. Seconds later he heard the outer doors of the church buckle and shatter. His pursuers hadn't come through the windows because of the tripwires and holy oils, but that hadn't delayed them nearly as much as he'd hoped. He fumbled for the gun, nearly dropped it, and somehow made it to his feet again.

A shallow pit waited in a sunken space at the center of the wooden pillars, just at the bottom of a short set of stone steps. Knight had to step slowly, a difficult task with blood in his face and the room spinning. His feet felt like they'd been separated from his body. Knight managed to make it to the bottom of the steps, where he dodged a ring of candles set around a bundle of cloth at the exact center of the room.

The perfect center, Knight thought, recalling the priest's words. *The middle of the middle. There's something special about this place, some geo-religious significance: its fey lines, its orientation to the magnetic poles, a lot of faerie dust in the area, some fucking thing. This is the only place it can be done. The only place where we can save humanity.*

The vampires were coming. Knight stumbled to the cloth bedding he'd laid down for the child. Huge black eyes stared up at him. He looked into her face, and was reminded of his daughter.

Knight's heart froze.

I can't do this.

You can, he told himself. *You have to.*

Knight did his best to ignore the maelstrom of sounds behind him – whirring blades, mechanized weapons, hybrids of blood and bone shouting obscenities in some alien tongue. His arms shook.

He took a deep breath and pulled the trigger.

PART ONE
THORNS

Fields of snow and rivers of ice in reflective white and blue, steel and bone, a mirror a thousand miles long. A ghost train screams by in the distance, belching a stream of dark smoke. In the middle of this nowhere stands a massive mountain as black as coal. It pierces the sky.

He sees the forest glade at the base of the mountain. He knows she is there.

Something approaches. He senses it rather than feels it, a tremor, like electricity on his imaginary skin, a taste of unrest on his ethereal tongue. He hears dead whispers hidden in the frozen wind.

He is both vast and miniscule at once, an omniscient being squeezed into a bottle. The world plays out in his vision like a painting. He is flying.

His vision sweeps across the apocalypse landscape. He sees black waters and blood skies, skeleton trees in burning bogs, pale dancers on a distant vampire shore. He sees iron cities guarded by impossible weapons, threatened on all sides by living shadows taking the shape of wolves or ravens or emaciated men. He sees the dead lie in waiting, ready to assault what's left of humankind from scattered black towers of steel web and ossified bone.

All of it he sees, but cannot touch.

Soon, *she says.* You are closer than you think.

Closer to what?

To a part of the world you shouldn't be able to touch. A place that's in danger.

He knows her, and trusts her. She's a part of him.

He floats through aimless skies. The vapor of ages folds around him. He arrives back in his own dream, at the edge of unseen realities. He floats adrift in the folds of overlapping worlds.

ONE

WAR

Year 20 A.B. (After the Black)

Cross saw blood in the sky.

It was a trick of the dusk light. Thick rays of dying crimson sunshine cut through dark vapors hanging over the battlefield and drifts of white smoke spewed by crawling war machines. The air was a den of rumbling motors, heavy treads and great iron wheels crushing rock and shattered bones. Cross gagged on the taste of oil and exhaust.

I hate this place.

His entire body ached. Cross had slept maybe five hours in as many days, and that sleep had been more like scattered instances of half-slumber snatched in heaps of dirty blankets and piles of bandages left discarded outside the medical bivouacs. All of his sleep had been half-filled with nightmarish images of torn bodies and children drowning in burning fuel.

Grime and filth covered his skin. Cross's stomach ached. He was long tired of magically preserved rations and cheap wine. When he ate anything beyond a slice of bread his guts twisted and his urine burned. He normally didn't get sick thanks to his spirit, and that told him the problem wasn't an infection but his own inability to adjust to a military diet in the field.

He'd only been on the front lines of the war for two weeks.

He felt his spirit with him. She was a slippery electric skin hovering inches away from the next world, a wraith-like unguent against his flesh. The vapor of her spectral form turned his lungs cold as he breathed her in. She surrounded him, a weapon and a friend and a part of his own soul, intelligent but lost, cleaved to him and yet worlds distant. He knew her better than he knew his own sister, better than he knew himself.

Dark clouds twisted in the rot-tainted wind blowing in from the sodden wastes of Blackmarsh. Dismal fields of black mud stretched away in every direction. Dozens of dark tents lay like wounded across the torn landscape. Black smoke trailed in varicose lines up to a darkening sky the color of uncooked meat.

Cross tasted salt and soot in the cold dry air. He sat with a host of Southern Claw soldiers he didn't know, all except for Graves, whom he'd known since they were boys. Graves fit in better than Cross did with the regulars of Wolf Company. Of course, Graves was a soldier, not a warlock like Cross.

Warlocks. Weapons and freaks. The Claw's most valuable assets, and the closest humankind came to matching powers with the enemy.

All we have to do is burn our own souls for fuel and probably become cripples before we're thirty.

The tent walls shifted in the dank wind. A host of makeshift chairs wobbled in the unstable mud around a wide wooden stump used as a table. Cross sat with his cards clenched upside down in his hand, and he knew full and well he didn't stand a chance.

The soldiers of Wolf Company were a sullen and dirty bunch, nearly impossible to tell apart at the moment due to the black mud caked to their faces and uniforms. Shotguns, assault rifles, blades and bows hung from harnesses and stood propped against iron tent poles. Dozens of packs sat nearby in case an alarm went up.

"Why so grim?" Graves asked.

Graves's scars were barely visible beneath camouflage paint, mud and painted runes, which every soldier wore to prevent catching vampiric infections or arcane diseases.

"Are you serious?" Cross replied.

"Wow. Is your hand that bad?" As ever, it was difficult for Cross to tell whether or not Graves was being serious. He was something of a redneck bumpkin at heart, but he had plenty of field experience, having joined the front lines almost a year before Cross. "You might as well just fold," he added after he stared at the back of Cross's cards, like he possessed x-ray vision.

"You should listen to him," Malone smiled. "In fact, you should both probably just give up now." Malone was tall and broad of shoulder, with a chiseled face and short dark hair. Graves had once joked Malone looked like the lovechild of Superman and Frankenstein's monster. "Full house."

"That's not possible," Cala said. It was well known she was the only card shark in the squad. "You can't even *spell*. How do you expect us to believe you were able to put together a full house?"

"He thinks we're playing Go Fish," Graves laughed.

There were fewer than thirty soldiers in the camp. Most were Southern Claw, but there were also a half-dozen mages and a lonely Doj engineer named Zender. All of them lived a cramped existence in the scattered tents, which were as full with equipment as they were with personnel. Sacks of blessed soil stacked high like sandbags surrounded each tent, and the rest of the camp was littered with bundles of black iron rods bundled together with wire, barrels of ash, boxes of pellet, ammunition, raw moon rock and sacks of hexed salt. Little of the equipment was for the soldiers, and instead belonged to the mages. There was work to be done in the Blackmarsh, work that was too important, Cross thought, to be handed to a bunch of young warlocks.

What the hell am I doing here?

His spirit pushed against him as if in answer. The breath of her form floated across his skin and filled him with living smoke. His fingers tingled, and he licked his lips to taste her electric form. He unfolded his cards onto the table. Graves, Malone, Cala, Locke and Gage all nodded their appreciation when Cross conceded the game, since he was just holding them up with his indecisiveness.

Cross knew Gage and Cala also felt on edge. A mage's spirit was attenuated to subtle fluctuations in the living world. They existed in the space between the living and the dead, and it was a witch's or warlock's spirit who granted them sight that pierced illusion, who could scout out over a score of miles, and who detected unseen threats both mundane and magical. Being anchored to his spirit allowed Cross to cull bits of her shadowy essence and transform it into potent energy and create effects humans had come to know as magic. It also meant he was constantly exposed to the world of the dead, and that he walked with one foot perpetually in the grave.

Cross had lived with her since adolescence. He'd first known of his spirit's existence after he'd nearly died of smallpox. Even though she'd saved his live, he was still destined to die young. No one could survive for long tied to an arcane spirit. By their very nature spirits were emotionally volatile and dangerous, lest they'd be unable to produce the energies they did.

He sat back and looked at the dark tree line marking the border of Blackmarsh. It was difficult to tell how deep the marsh was, but with any luck Wolf Company wouldn't have to press in any deeper than the outer perimeter, if and when air support finally arrived. In order to get close enough to set the hex rods and initiate the detonation sequence that would clear out the vampire garrison located deeper in the marsh they'd have to contend with acid drakes and hellwyrms, and that was where the airships came in.

Too bad they're about three hours late. It would have been nice to have done this before dark.

In a sane world they would have just postponed the mission and evacuated rather than camp so close to enemy territory, but the Company had solid intelligence that a shipment of corpses set for reanimation would be delivered to the Blackmarsh by dawn, and the garrison had to be destroyed before that happened.

"I'm out next hand," Cross said, and he stood up to walk around.

"Cross," Cala said. She was a short and stocky woman with a thin scar on one side of her face. Her dark hair was pulled back so tight it made her face seem paler than it actually was. "Are you all right?"

"Don't you feel it?" he asked.

"Love?" Graves laughed.

"They're both on their period," Malone said with a laugh.

"Magic," Gage interjected. The dark-skinned man wasn't known for his sense of humor. "Weapons." He turned and looked at the Blackmarsh. "They're getting...."

He never finished his sentence. The first blast ignited the stagnant sky. Fire rippled across the mud in an explosive wave. Heat pushed against them. Cross felt a swelling chorus of screams tear at the tent and whip mud across the ground. Panic welled up. His spirit shrouded him with an ethereal glaze.

Cross leapt back as shrapnel and explosive blades whipped the air. Gage was lifted up by the blast, his body shredded by a phalanx of steaming razors. Shadows leapt at the Company from nowhere, liquid darkness made humanoid, unfolding out of two-dimensionality. Shouts and gunfire echoed across the camp. Another chain of explosions sounded as exploding dark blades cut the mages apart.

The mages are the targets, Cross thought as the concussive force from the explosions threw him onto his back. *They know why we're here.*

His vision swam. Another blast made everything go black.

Shadows move in the trees beneath the mountain, female forms dancing in ghostly silhouette against a driving wind screaming across the plains. He sees black smoke stream off into the distance, the arcane pollution from a distant train. Equine shadows and jagged blades move around the edge of the forest, unsleeping sentries who hedge in the tired and withered looking humanoids standing wet and alone in the prison of dark trees. The mountain is a massive knife probing the crimson sky.

He looks on this and knows he's not supposed to see it, this forbidden place, this secret. It's the shape of things past and buried, and things still yet to come.

Cross woke to chaos. Gunfire erupted all around him. Blood and mud covered his eyes with a greasy film. His sense of direction was gone. Shaking limbs slipped in the mud as he struggled to rise. He smelled thaumaturgy in the air, a burning cloud of caustic fumes.

He struggled up to his knees, pulled slime and effluvia away from his face, and looked at the Blackmarsh.

The Ebon Cities regulars – the vampires – were coming.

The lead war machine was a shrieking monstrosity, a steamrolling juggernaut covered with chitin plates and bladed chains dangling from the deck. The vehicle plowed through bloody black earth. Massive red wolves and their masked vampire riders fell in line behind the vampire tank. The riders held serrated swords and axes, and the wolf's howls echoed into the darkening skies.

The camp was in disarray. They still had no air support, and its delayed arrival had given the Ebon Cities regulars stationed there in the Blackmarsh plenty of time to mount an offensive. Bodies lay in bloody heaps, and thick red smoke billowed across Cross's field of vision. Soldiers and mages shouted as they desperately tried to rally.

Cross's spirit swam around him, dizzy and angry, and through her he felt the onslaught of dire energies launched at the Company, he sensed the presence of rebuilt Crujian war machines and dismal undead weapons fueled with stolen blood. Southern Claw cannons fired from behind him, and the cold iron shells detonated with thunderous force against the dreadnaught and the wolf riders in great explosions of fur, metal and undead flesh. Adrenaline coursed through the air, so thick it seemed to fall like rain.

Cross picked up his pistol. He found Graves in the crowd and made sure he was all right. They both joined the rank of Wolf Company soldiers and charged ahead.

He wasn't ready to die. He was even less ready to die alone.

TWO

WHITE

Year 22 A.B. (After the Black)

A single white apple hung from the tree, an orb of frozen snow, and a tiny ice-white spider crawled across the face of the fruit. The small and withered tree sat in a shallow river bank filled with muddy water and foul runoff from the Reach. Wind blew in from the vast eastern tundra and whispered through the reeds like a sad and distant song.

The sky was low and oppressive, and the air was raw with cold. Cross stared out past the dense skeletal foliage beyond the tree into the Reach, a colorless wasteland of ice floes, snow-covered hills, arctic waters and drifts of snow deep enough to drown in. The harsh white of the Reach marked the end of civilization, for it was where Thornn's sphere of influence ended and where the deadly hostility of the wilderness began. There were no other cities of the Southern Claw Alliance this far north – the closest, Ath, was several days travel – so in many ways Thornn truly did stand alone.

"Eric? Are you okay?"

His sister, Snow, stood off near the gravestones. The long and thin cemetery stretched all of the way back to Thornn's reinforced red stone walls, which stood beneath layers of arcane ice and enchanted concertina wire. The city was squat and ugly, a troglodyte atop a twisted snowbound hill. Thick plumes of dark smoke slithered like serpents into the dead white sky. Cross heard the distant wail of klaxons and machinery.

His sister wore a pale cloak. The cemetery, in contrast, was dirty and dark, and the grave markers were just low plates of steel etched with the names of the departed. Thornn's citizens couldn't actually be buried, as the danger of the dead being reanimated was too great, so instead they were cremated. Cross understood reanimation had been a bigger problem some fifteen years ago, back in the early days of the war. Now the melting down of the deceased was so standard a practice no one even thought twice about it.

"I'm fine," he said. "Come look at this."

Cross glimpsed sentry gargoyles hovering over Thornn like a murder of grey crows. Arcane storms invisible to the naked eye formed a quiet cyclone of protective magical energies over the city. Those energies emitted a constantly collapsing field of destructive power specially attuned to necrotic flesh.

Cross's spirit drifted out and away, floated near the edge of the grave field before coming back to him. There was no danger in the cemetery, so his spirit was at peace, and her calm filled him. She fell around him like warm vapor. She'd been with him since he was eight, when it had been discovered he was a warlock. He could barely remember being without her.

"What is that?" Snow asked. She was shorter than Cross by several inches. There was little mistaking their relation, since they had the same coal black hair and large green eyes, and both of them were exceptionally pale. Her hair was cut short along the sides and on the back but was long on top, and a single white streak ran down from the center of her temple. Her choker was black leather set with a black cross. "Is that an apple? God, it must be rotten to the core."

"I don't think so," Cross said. "Look at it. I think it's fresh. It's just...white. Maybe it was drained of its color by this place." It was possible. Entire crops had been leeched lifeless near inhospitable regions. Cross had heard of whole forests in the Bone March rendered bone white by the unnatural landscape, and the Wormwood was so corrupt even vampires feared the vegetation. There was the Reach, a vast tundra, and the Ebonsand Sea, with its intelligent crabs who muttered arcane curses and Vuul pirates claiming control over waters infused with occult blood. The world was a diseased and broken place. Cross knew it had been better once, back in his youth, but it was growing harder and harder to remember it.

"It's beautiful," Snow said.

"Yeah," Cross said. "I guess it is."

She and Cross stood shoulder to shoulder. Baleful winter breeze pushed at their cloaks. The arctic sun was rapidly setting. Behind them, well past Thornn and on towards the lowlands, lay a brittle landscape filled with loose stones and shallow riverbeds, salt marshes and estuaries, cliffs of dark clay and low-rolling mists. If one took too long to cross the plains it became difficult to remove the smell of decay and rotting vegetation from the clothing or skin. It was a few days travel from Thornn to the northeastern tip of Rimefang Loch, where armored boats sailed south to other Southern Claw cities on the coast.

The chill grew worse. Cross estimated they had less than an hour before sundown, by which point they had to be inside the city walls. His spirit drifted close, passed between he and Snow (she pressed tight against him, as if jealous of his flesh and blood sister) and circled out and away, cognizant of their surroundings, always on watch for anything which might do them harm.

"Do you think Mom is doing well?" Snow asked.

They stared at the apple, and into the Reach. Snow didn't like to look west, towards the Bonespire, even though it was difficult to see it from there in the grave field. The western plains were level with Thornn, while the markers were lower by a good hundred feet. A winding path led up the hillside and back to the eastern city gates, through the barbican and into the guardhouse. It had been some time since Thornn had actually seen a Gorgoloth attack from out of the Reach, but the ebon-skinned barbarians had historically wrought so much devastation that hostility from that direction was considered inevitable, just as everyone expected an attack from the Bonespire to the west. Thornn was prepared for the next assault, regardless of which direction it came from.

"I don't know," Cross said with a shake of his head. "I hope so."

Snow was nineteen now. Cross hated seeing her grow older, but he was glad, at least, that she'd stopped asking if he could see their mother's ghost, if she'd be able to communicate with it like she and Cross did with their own spirits. It had been so hard to explain to her it didn't work that way, that what a mage and his spirit shared was a bond, a melding of souls. Besides, a mage's spirit was an entirely different type of creature, and while Cross's spirit could sense the souls of the recently dead there was no communication with the deceased, no way of interacting. The spirit of their dead mother, like all dead spirits, was mindless. It would be like trying to talk to a wolf.

"I miss her," Snow said quietly. "And I miss you."

"I'm here now," he said.

"You haven't been around very much," Snow said. "You're not in the city very often. And on the rare occasion you are here it would be nice to actually *see* you." Snow put her arms around his waist. He remembered her when she was young, when he used to take away her toys and hide them, and even after their mother took *his* toys he still wouldn't tell where he'd stashed them. Now she was almost grown up, and a stronger person than he was.

And she was a witch, just as he was a warlock. They were both cursed with that power. They had a great deal of natural talent between them, they'd been told, maybe the most of any brother and sister who'd ever served the Southern Claw.

One mage in the family was enough, he thought. *One was probably too much. Why did you have to be one, too, little Sister?*

He didn't want to delude himself. He knew Snow would have to serve in the military someday. It was the price you paid for having the gift of magic.

"How've you been?" he asked. He returned her hug and slowly led her back towards the city. "We didn't get much of a chance to talk before we came down here."

"I'm fine," she said, the note of sadness in her voice unmistakable.

"How's the job?"

"Librarians are all the rage now," she said. "All of the boys want to talk to us, and we get to play with the latest, most amazing technology."

"Right. So really, how is it?"

"Boring. Much more boring than what you do."

"I doubt that," he smiled. He knew she knew better, but he always tried not to worry her. As it was he'd made clear he wouldn't tell her any details of being a Hunter. The life expectancy of personnel in the military wasn't very long, even less for members of vampire Hunter squads. At two years spent in the service, Cross was halfway to the average.

I hope you're different, he thought as he looked at Snow. *I hope to God you don't choose to do this, too.*

They paused by their mother's gravestone, covered with a thin trace of frost. The hammered bronze plate on the cracked marble read ALICE CROSS. There was no matching plate for their father, as he had died before The Black, so his name had instead been chiseled on the obelisk memorial on Ghostborne Island. Cross tried to get out and see the monument at least once a year. Snow had never been there. Rimefang Loch was just too dangerous to navigate lightly.

That's okay. You're safer here than anywhere else. There isn't much out there worth seeing.

There were hundreds of gravestones. Ice and gravel crunched under their boots as they slowly walked through the neatly spaced rows. Some of the older stones had fallen apart, or their copper and iron face plates were covered in grime or frost or had been worn away by the unnatural lightning storms that sometimes ripped out of the Reach, storms summoned by Gorgoloth shamans years ago, back before the barbaric race had given up its magic to the Cruj in exchange for weapons. Cross glanced back at the glacial horizon and saw endless fields of white, icy canyons filled with swirls of windblown snow, low clouds as thick as iron. Somewhere out there, hidden deep in the clefts of cracked ice and valleys of dark rime, were the subterranean homes of the Gorgoloth, barbaric humanoid creatures with black skin and stark white hair, a race driven by a need to destroy. They were just one of the many non-human races that so far as anyone knew hadn't existed on earth prior to The Black, but human memory was by and large incapable of recreating the time before. Everything had changed, but no one remembered how things had once been.

As terrible as battles against the Gorgoloth had been, they were hardly the greatest threat facing Thornn or the Southern Claw. That was the vampires of the Ebon Cities.

Cross's chest seized up at the notion of returning to the field. He had only three days of leave left, and he anticipated it was going to be cut short any day now since the search for the outlaw called Red hadn't made much progress.

Being a Southern Claw war mage for two years hadn't done much to quell Cross's nerves. Even with his spirit doing her best to keep him calm and protected, Cross still hadn't learned to sleep very well. The thought of what he might face in his nightmares made him shudder.

"Are you sure you're okay?" Snow asked. They held each other close as they walked across the field and up towards the hill.

"Yeah," Cross smiled. "I'm just cold."

"What are you doing tonight?" Snow asked after a long pause.

"I'm going to The Black Hag with Sam. You want to come?" He knew she wouldn't. Snow was a bigger drinker and socialite than he was, by far – last he heard she was still capable of drinking almost any member of Viper Squad under the table – but for some reason she preferred to keep her brother in quiet company. That was fine with Cross, who liked to delude himself into thinking she was still eight years old. To see her drinking, dancing and flirting with local industry workers and city guards would probably make his blood boil and cause his spirit to lash out in anger.

"Not tonight," she said. "But I expect you over for dinner tomorrow. How many days of leave do you have left?"

"Three. I hope."

"You can't leave without me making you dinner at least once."

"It's a deal."

A lone building stood elevated over a narrow stream running the length of the grave field. The structure was badly in need of repair, and looked to be a refugee from the older and smaller city which had stood in the area before Thornn was built back in A.B. 9. All but one of the windows had been boarded up, and various machinery parts, iron sheets, metalworking tools and broken weapons lay scattered on the petrified grass in the front yard.

The debris surrounded another lone and dead tree. A humanoid doll maybe a foot tall and made from tin cans and funnels bound together by wire and glue dangled from the branches like a piece of metallic fruit. Eyes made from buttons and a mouth made of discarded cable formed the semblance of a face, and the tiny figure dangled by a string noose tied around its neck. It swung back and forth in the dry wind, clanging against the tree, its infantile face frozen in happy grimace. It looked like the Tin Man, hanged.

The grey sky groaned with something that sounded like thunder, but wasn't. It hadn't rained much since The Black. Storms were unnatural and filled with hateful energies, sometimes even the screams of the dead. Growing up, Cross had wondered why more people weren't completely mad.

Maybe they are. Maybe we're all insane.

"'But I don't want to go among mad people,' Alice remarked.

'Oh, you can't help that,' said the Cat. 'We're all mad here. I'm mad. You're mad.'

'How do you know I'm mad?' said Alice.

'You must be,' said the Cat. 'or you wouldn't have come here.'"

"Can you get me a copy of *Through the Looking Glass?*" he asked Snow.

"Wow. Random," Snow smiled. "You want 'Alice', too?"

"Sure."

"I will. But you can only have it if you come to dinner tomorrow."

"Are you going to make me meet your boyfriend?" he asked with a mawkish groan. "Groff?"

"Geoff," Snow said curtly. "And the answer is 'yes'. Probably."

"Can I think about it?"

"No."

"All right, then. Just bring the books, and nobody has to get hurt."

They walked in silence for a time.

"We're in the looking glass," Snow said softly. "I feel like that most days. Like we're on the wrong side of some broken mirror."

"Yeah," Cross said. He didn't know what else to say.

The siblings drew close to the city. Flame cannons sputtered hot white flames and bled the smell of burning fuel as they swiveled on rusted iron mounts at the southeast barbican. Electric currents ran up and down the black iron poles on either side of the steep dirt path leading up from the grave fields to the rear city gates. Cross and Snow passed hexed concertina wire hung with what looked like voodoo implements rattling in the chill breeze. Masked sentries in heavy armored coats regarded them from behind sandbags atop the barbican. The guards held assault rifles and sabers and wore black grenades on bandoliers.

Cross carefully positioned himself to Snow's left as they advanced the last few meters up the trail, which leveled out with the ground at Thornn's base just before it reached the city gates. There was no way to avoid seeing the Bonespire on the far side of the frozen fields, but Cross always did his best to shield her from the site, out of habit if for no other reason.

Estuaries of salt and brine lay west of Thornn's cone-shaped outer walls, a massive expanse of broken white and grey earth torn apart by mortar blasts, trenches, dried-up riverbeds and the grind of now abandoned vehicles. Soldiers milled about in small groups, keeping low in spite of the absence of any visible enemy, their feet stuck in the white mud and cold water. The fields were miles wide and littered with bunkers, bivouacs and half-shattered stone and iron walls. The air smelled of rust and dead fish.

Far in the distance was the nearest of the Bonespires: a dark ebon needle shrouded in shadow. The tower was a tower made of black steel and blacker stone, a barbed protrusion jutting from the earth like an obscene razor blade. Jagged crenellations and nail-like barbs covered the structure like a porcupine's quills, and at its base moved dark vehicles covered in clouds of black steam. Occasional bursts of lightning cast the Bonespire in eerie silhouette.

Cross wondered how many Ebon Cities vampires were stationed inside. It had been some time since fighting had taken place between Thornn and the Bonespire, but everyone remained vigilant. The war raged on elsewhere, but for the moment the battle for Thornn had drawn to a stalemate.

Because you bastards are busy waiting for Red, he thought bitterly. *Why waste your resources fighting when the key to killing all of us is about to be delivered right into your hands?*

"Please tell me you won't be going back there," Snow said. Cross hadn't realized they'd stopped walking.

"I'm not," he said. "I'm not going back there."

"Are you going to be sent to look for Red?"

"You know I can't talk about that." He said it more for the benefit of the sentries posted there at the gate: he'd tell Snow later, maybe when they met for dinner.

He looked at his sister, and found himself at a loss for words. There she was, nearly a woman grown, and for some reason it struck him as so odd, so strange she should be standing there, this old, this mature, when in his mind he still saw the lanky and long-haired little girl who only referred to him as "My Eric", who'd walk around the house in one of his old shirts that fit her like a sack, who as a toddler told their mother "I don't think so" and nothing else for almost a month, who he'd grown up being taught he had to protect. Seeing her there now, so tall and beautiful and confident and grown, filled him with worry and nearly brought tears to his eyes. His spirit felt it too, and she held him tight, drew him close and slid across his skin like a warm shroud.

"Eric?" she said.

"Yeah," he smiled. He wouldn't tell her about the ache he felt in his chest when he thought about how young they'd once been, or why the reason he'd volunteered for the military in the first place in spite of his fear was because he'd always been driven by the need to keep her safe. "Let's get you indoors," he said. "It's getting cold."

THREE

KNIVES

Samuel Graves was Cross's only friend aside from Snow, and they'd known each other for as long as either of them could remember. Graves was an experienced soldier and Hunter. He was also an admitted social deviant who insisted on getting Cross into as much trouble as humanly possible.

Before Cross could meet Graves he had a number of errands to run. He wasn't looking forward to any of them.

First he walked Snow home, where she would doubtlessly await the arrival of Geoff. As much as Cross hated thinking about his sister being involved in a relationship he liked the idea of someone watching out for her when he wasn't around...which, as Snow had accurately pointed out, was often. The fact that Geoff was looking out for Snow was really the only reason he and Graves had let the faceless boyfriend keep breathing, or so Graves liked to claim.

Lengths of transparent cable filled with viscous colors stretched out over the streets, conveying messages, hex currents and fluids racing back and forth across the city. There were so many of the lines the city appeared stitched.

Dust and gravel filled the air with gritty haze. Thornn was round and sinuous, made from sandstone and brick and reinforced with cold steel plates and black iron meant to ward off incorporeal threats. The buildings were tall and tightly clustered together, lending the narrow streets the semblance of valleys running through urban canyons. Parts of Thornn rarely saw sunlight, but steam vents and green-fire street lamps prevented the accumulation of ice on the roads. Narrow windows spilled light into the heart of the city, an area filled with fountains, statues, or replicas of the obelisk monument on Ghostborne Island. Children played beneath the protective canopy of spirit shields and armed nannies, and there in the Centertown district Cross was always struck by the smell of bakeries and bars, a strangely delectable blend of cardamom, hazelnut, sweet liqueur and cigarillos.

Snow lived in a small apartment across from the library, a columnar red and white stone building hedged in by leering gargoyles. The bruise-pink sky was slowly fading to purple and black.

"Tomorrow night, then," she said, knowing full and well if she made it a question Cross would find some way to become unavailable. "I'll make you something tasty."

"So we're ordering out," Cross said with a nod. He smiled and dodged Snow's attempt to push him down the stairs. "Am I seriously going to have to meet Geoff?"

"Yes."

"Fine. I'll see you then."

"Be good."

"I'll try."

Cross went north and out of the Centertown district, and he didn't have to go far before he was in the seedier side of the city. Lesser used streets, even narrower than elsewhere in the city, wove like veins between unnamed bars and hashish houses, brothels, unregistered doctors and soothsayers. Before long the roads were filled with refuse, and the normally radiant gas and thaumaturgy-powered street torches cast ghostly flickering glows dancing in feeble luminescence off the dark buildings. Scantily clad whores slithered along the brick and mortar lanes like drugged serpents, and the harsh scent of arcane hash and sex clung to everything. Cross heard shouts from behind closed wooden doors, some of them raucous and fun, others violent and angry. People with blistered feet and unclean faces slept in the gutters. Money changed hands. Cross saw an occasional mugging, over and done with before it was even clear what had happened. There were fewer people there in The Dregs than in Centertown, but they were made legion by the murky light.

His spirit hovered close and clung to his skin like a sail to a ship. They were both calm – they'd been in worse places, but it was still difficult for her to sift through the clouds of emotion there in The Dregs so she could help Cross keep clear sight of what lie ahead. Illegal dealers and unscrupulous merchants made heavy use of arcane locks and wards, which meant the streets in The Dregs were more packed with spirits than with people. Cross couldn't see those spirits so much as feel them, just as he could never truly see his own, at least not with the physical eye. Of her he had a sense, an imprint in his mind of how he thought she appeared which, in turn, crafted her actual form. If ever there was a way to actually lay eyes on her he knew he'd know her on sight. She was quite literally a part of him.

Cross eventually came to a narrow alley marked by silver runes etched on the enameled black stone. The alley dipped at a sharp angle down to a single black door marked by more silver runes. The sky overhead had grown red and dark. Cross heard carousing and drunken laughter in the open doorways of nearby bars, and dim green streetlamps feebly sputtered light against the grit and shadow.

"You want something?" a dark man asked. His skin was pure black, and his bare chest and arms were covered by more of the concentric silver runes. Even more adorned his face, highlighting his angular cheekbones, thick lips and lack of eyes.

"Yeah," Cross said with a nod. "She's expecting me. This is the right hour, so she should be ready."

"I know." The man's voice was deep and hollow, like he stood at the bottom of a well. "But the question is, are *you* ready for *her*?" He laughed evilly and motioned Cross to go ahead.

I hate that guy.

The door was unlocked, but because it was so heavy and its hinges were so rusted and old it still took considerable effort on Cross's part to actually force it open. A subtle air filled with incense and musk enveloped him as he squeezed his way through. The room was lit by golden candles, and strangely-angled mirrors seemed to float on the onyx walls. Dark chairs and black curtains lent the room a claustrophobic air. Cross pushed the door shut behind him.

"There you are."

Warfield walked out from behind the curtain. Her black dress was loose and flowing and looked like it had been clawed or chewed on at least twice. The sleeves hooked around long fingers tipped with stark black polish. Tall boots made from black leather and fastened by silver buckles clacked loudly on the floor. Warfield's dark red hair was cut short, allowing Cross to see the runic tattoos on her neck and what of her chest her dress left exposed, which was quite a bit. Warfield was almost as tall as Cross (impressive given he stood just over six feet), and her body was lithe and thin. Painted black lips curled in mock smile.

"Here I am," he said.

"Did you bring it?"

"I wouldn't be here if I hadn't."

"Then step into my office." She led him back behind the curtain and into a dank and cluttered room piled high with arcane detritus, broken magical components, empty alchemy vials, used batteries, spare wires, a variety of clamps and pliers and shreds of parchment and dried wax. Warfield's desk was a tiny table which walked on its own accord. What appeared to be gargoyle's claws on the table's surface held an iron lockbox.

But what really drew Cross's attention were the knives displayed high on the back wall, illuminated by cold silver light emanating from a number of crevices in the ceiling. The knives were curved, with thin bone-white handles and utterly black blades, the metal so dark it seemed to suck the light in. Runes had been cast on the blade's faces, and the edges were honed to such fine points Cross could practically taste how sharp they were.

"Wow," he said.

"You like?" Warfield smiled.

"I'm not sure," he answered. "I think I'm just intimidated."

"I'm talking about the knives," Warfield said with a wry grin.

"Oh," Cross laughed. "In that case...yes."

As far as Cross was concerned, Warfield was so far out of his league even fantasizing about her was a waste of time. He'd had very little skill or luck with women, and, perhaps more importantly, he found he rarely had the time to even worry about it...which was why most of his relations only took place at the Grey Angel, or, on occasion, the Red Scarab, the only two barely reputable brothels in Thornn.

Cross dropped a small black bag on Warfield's table with an audible clink. His spirit recoiled as Warfield approached. Warfield's male spirit oozed with power, doubtlessly tied in one way or another to the arcane generators Cross had detected behind the curtains. Warfield had enough energy surging through the place to detonate the entire block, which was why she kept everything so well hidden under the dampeners.

Warfield opened the bag. Cross had collected a good number of wight canines over the course of his two years in the service. The dark iron teeth had been filed to sharpened points, and they were decorated with ritual markings to denote kills, standing, rank, or place of origin. They exuded cold steam, but the effects were harmless and cosmetic, as they lost their poison and arcane qualities when removed from the corpse that had once bore them. Warfield smiled and opened the small box on the table. It was very plain, unpolished and old. The lock had been visibly broken, and the darkened wood looked to have been exposed to a fire. Cross pushed his hand against the lid and checked for wards or traps. He had no reason to distrust Warfield, but it never hurt to be careful.

You don't live too long if you're a trusting soul. That was a lesson Cross had learned early. *Never trust a beautiful woman* was another.

The pyrojack gauntlet was in the box, as promised. It was an older and less attractive design than the gauntlets he used now, black leather and iron devices bound with wires hooked to a belt-mounted battery pack. Those gauntlets provided assurance he could properly channel his spirit, and that doing so wouldn't consume his mind or his body. The pyrojack was different – it was an independent arcane item rather than an implement, and the lone remaining red gem set between the knuckles of the first and second fingers of the gauntlet was a self-contained weapon. Only a mage could activate the missile which, so far as Cross knew and so far as Warfield had promised, would launch out to a range of nearly 500 yards and explode with the force of three grenades. Best of all, using the missile wouldn't exert any actual pressure on *his* spirit. The pyrojack would come in handy, he thought, for times when his spirit's energies had been too far extended, or if he needed to use her for defensive purposes and a pistol just wouldn't provide enough firepower. Cross's spirit helped him sense the power and potential in the device.

"What are you going to use it for? A little stress relief while you're on leave?" Warfield smiled. Blowing something up for kicks was pretty much what he expected *she* would do with the pyrojack if it stayed in her possession...destroying things seemed to be something Warfield liked, along with sleeping with men twice her age and getting as stone dead drunk as she could on a regular basis.

"I'm saving it for a rainy day," he said with a shake of his head. He put the case into his pack. His eyes were again drawn to the ebon blades. Their silver slashes looked like scars. "What's up with the black knives?"

"They're Necroblades," Warfield said with a strangely proud smile. "Undead use them. Rathian assassins. They're harmful to spirits."

"They target the spirit?" Cross asked with a nervous laugh.

Warfield shook her head.

"They sever the bond," she said. "Cut the spirit loose."

It was every mage's worse nightmare. While there were theories about such scenarios, no mage had ever been known to lose their spirit and survive the experience. The pain and shock of the separation was too much, like having your skin removed, but instead of a lengthy period of suffering the experience would be shaved into just a moment of intense agony. The spirit, if indeed it survived the separation, would in all likelihood be devoured by malevolent incorporeal predators from the world of the dead.

"Where the hell did you get those?" Cross asked. *And should I report them?*

"Come on, Eric," Warfield smiled. "You can't expect me to tell you where I shop for my toys. You might not come back."

It was hard not to focus on her perfect skin, her pursed lips and her large and expressive green eyes.

"You're right. I might not."

Cross took his leave and returned to the soiled night. It wasn't the image of the knives that burned in his memory as much as the notion of losing his spirit.

He had some time to kill before he was supposed to meet Graves at The Black Hag, so he briefly stopped by his home, an apartment at the edge of The Grange, a secluded neighborhood known for its briars, antiquated wooden houses and incredibly steep dirt roads. Thick iron fences sealed The Grange off from the surrounding neighborhoods, but the prevalence of twisted trees and shadow-drenched corridors of brick and foliage gave the area a vaguely threatening air. Even with armed patrols and magically reinforced locks set on most of the quaint looking cottage-style houses, Cross usually sensed something malevolent in the shadows, just out of sight.

Cross's apartment was located on the upper level of a small brown building. The lower floor was an abandoned book shop which had been boarded up some months before when the owner had been found drained of blood outside the city walls. With no heir apparent, Hobb's Books was claimed by the city. The inventory was sold off and the funds were used to help rebuild some of the outlying homes destroyed in the Gorgoloth assault from the previous winter.

The door to Cross's abode stood at the top of a short set of cracked stone steps. He purposefully avoided the thirteenth step, as he was highly suspicious it was waiting to one day crack loose and send him into a neck-breaking fall down the previous twelve.

The inside of his apartment was a single dark room layered in brown and black rugs and decorated with maps of the known world, illustrations of the Ebon Cities, and lists of arcane maladies, inhuman creatures and known vampire champions. It looked less like a habituated living space than it did a poorly organized ready room. A single table and chair bore stacks of books, unwashed cups and mugs; the bed, which had no legs and lay flat against the far wall, hadn't been made in months. Snow avoided his apartment as if it were infested, and Cross didn't blame her. The air smelled musky, and the lone window only let in a feeble amount of light, largely because the glass was dirty beyond the capacity of even flame cannons to clean.

Cross lay down, and before long he slept.

He dreams of knives. They hold him in like a bladed cage. He stands on the deck of a black ship in a black sea, softly floating through laggard waters.

Behind him stands a dead city in the cold mist, and on the far shore is a black mountain and a forest filled with women as terrified and alone as he is. He knows who one of them is, and he knows he has to save her.

Cross woke just after dark, feeling even more lost and uneasy than he had before he'd slept. He spent a few minutes getting ready before he went to join Graves at The Black Hag.

He couldn't get the image of those black knives out of his mind.

The Black Hag was one of the only establishments in Thornn Cross enjoyed spending time in outside of his apartment. The subterranean tavern doubled as a gaming pit and a meeting spot for mercenaries, soldiers, criminals and other luminaries of the seedier side of Thornn's populace.

Thorn was the most remote city of the Southern Claw Alliance, a center for repopulation after creatures released by The Black had wiped out so much of the human race. At first it had just been the vampires, pale-skinned fiends who'd come in waves like barbarians, unorganized and hungry, seemingly as shocked by this new apocalypse world as the humans were. After a time the vampires slowed down, grew organized, and built the Ebon Cities, at which point they settled into control over much of what was left of the world. But there were other creatures out there in the wastelands, some worse than the "suckheads": the monstrous Gorgoloth, the giant and enigmatic Cruj, the black-hearted Sorn, the Vuul, the Eidolos, and the undead, scores of zombies and wights and lich and ghouls and other things that should have existed only in nightmares. But nightmares had become real, or else they'd always been real and humankind had been ignorant about it until The Black came along and woke them up.

Cross wondered about that, sometimes – if the world had always been this way, Earth convergent with other realities, and if humans had just been cut off somehow, ignorant, adrift in the sea of their own isolation. Everything was different after The Black, but very few could remember what things had been like before the catastrophes and the vampire invasion, before the existence of magic and caustic seas. It was hard to remember what the world had been like before half of its people had died, before giant wolves and killer trees roamed the poisonous wilderness, before abandoned and ancient cities had appeared out of nowhere, sometimes shattering other cities in the process. Multiple worlds, squeezed into one.

The frightening truth was there was a time before The Black, and a time after, but as the years stretched on it grew harder and harder to separate the two.

Humankind had banded together under the guidance of the White Mother to build fortress city-states like Thornn. There had been many more cities in the beginning, but most of them hadn't lasted long. Those that endured formed the Southern Claw Alliance, a confederacy of humans working together to survive in a brutal new world. Most of the power in the Southern Claw resided in the hands of the military, which fought off constant attacks staged by vampires of the Ebon Cities and other creatures from the wastelands. Most of the Ebon Cities attacks directed at Thornn were guided by an extremely old vampire known as The Grim Father, ruler of the Ebon City of Rath, a remote place in many ways an undead equivalent to Thornn. Cross had never seen Rath. It was doubtful he ever would.

The music in The Hag – old world stuff, tinny, heavy with drums and electronics, music meant to be danced to by tribal people and arcane natives – blared from mystic gramophones mounted high on the dirty stone walls. Iron gates sealed the large dungeon-like room off from the rest of the world. The poor lighting came from smoking lamps bolted to the tables, miniature chimneys releasing an acrid blend of tobacco and cinnamon that filled the room with an eye-burning haze.

Cross and Graves grabbed a table near the back, where they met up with Graves's friend Jonas, a warrior-priest who could hold more liquor and stir up more trouble than Cross and Graves combined. The long-haired priest still wore his cross-emblazoned armor and his crimson cape, which made him strangely fit in well with the chamber full of mercenaries, drug addicts and slinky women.

Cross sucked on the cigarillo Jonas gave him. He regretted ever having quit, and he knew he'd feel different if he actually survived to see morning. Despite having spent the better part of two years in the presence of soldiers and other vampire hunters – a class of people known to play even harder than they worked, for it was never assumed another chance to play would come again – Cross had a surprisingly low tolerance for alcohol, due mainly to his thin frame and high metabolism. Regardless, Graves and Jonas kept buying rounds, and before long Cross was just barely coherent enough to realize how lucky he was to still be *at* the table instead of *under* it.

But it felt good – burning eyes and lungs and struggles to stay conscious notwithstanding – to not be worrying about anything for a while, to not be thinking about Snow, about how he wanted to get them both away from everything, away from the vampires, away from war, away from arcane diseases and nightmares and pain. Away from all of the death. No such place existed, and he knew it, but it was good to dream.

Cross wandered (carefully balanced) around the game tables, put some coins in and threw the dice, won some money back, played cards, lost, shuffled his feet to the music like he knew how to dance, watched some pretty ladies, bumped into people, drank something Jonas gave him, smoked some cigarillos, swam through the haze, his mind adrift and scattered, awash on the tide of energy, his body and being turned molten, suffused in that place, lost adrift for a night, not his, not anyone's, part of the crowd.

But he came back to earth. He wasn't sure when he'd first seen her. In his near stupor he must have been up close when it happened, because there was no way his watery eyes could have made her out from more than about ten feet away. She was tall and thin, with medium-length dark hair and a tight and revealing dress. She was unquestionably overdressed for The Black Hag, but he doubted anyone who saw her minded. He was frankly unsure if he'd ever beheld anyone so beautiful. He also understood she likely looked much better to him at that particular moment than she normally would, courtesy of the uncounted drinks he'd imbibed, but he didn't really care. She was at the edge of the room, close to the wall and away from the main throng of people, looking about, as if for someone specific.

Of course she's looking for someone, you moron. You think a girl looking like that would be here alone?

And yet he walked right up to her. In his right and sober mind Cross would've watched her for a moment from across the chamber, contemplated what he might say, counted down in his mind, and never gone to talk to her at all.

But you're not in your right and sober mind.

"Excuse me, Miss," he said. He nearly had to shout to be heard over the noise. "I couldn't help but notice...you look lonely."

"Well," she smiled. "No. Not really. I *am* from out of town, and I don't really know anyone." She gave him a look. Her skin was flawless and pale, her eyes cold feline and very sharp, her lips full. When she smiled her face glowed. "Listen...I'm in a relationship. Long term, actually. Not that you...well, you know. In case that's what you're looking for..."

"No, no," Cross said, fairly certain he wasn't lying. "No, I don't...I don't think so," he laughed. "No, I'm not looking for anything. I don't think." He laughed. "Sorry, I...really just thought you looked like you could use someone to talk to."

She smiled. People passed by, the light shifted, a roar erupted from a nearby dice table, and the strange music played on.

"Yeah, I guess I could," she smiled. "I'm Cristena."

"Eric," he smiled. "But everyone just calls me Cross. It's very nice to meet you."

"Why does everyone call you 'Cross?'" she asked. "Are you a priest?"

"No. It just happens to be my last name."

"Good of people to call you that, then," she smiled.

"*I* think so."

Most of the rest of the evening passed in an even stronger blur than what had come before. He uncovered only the barest details about Cristena. She was from an Alliance city called Fane, and she was in Thornn to see if she'd like to relocate there. She was having relationship issues and was contemplating forging a path alone, but no decisions had been made. She liked wine, scarce as it was.

He was captivated by her. Maybe it was because Cristena was a stranger to him or maybe it was because he'd consumed enough alcohol to slay a mule, but Cross couldn't look away, even when he couldn't really hear what she was saying thanks to the noise.

"Is employment here steady?"

"It is," he said with a nod. "Best anywhere, actually."

"Right," she smiled.

"What do you do?" he asked.

"I'm a tracker," she said.

"A witch?"

"Yes. And you're a warlock."

"Right." If he hadn't have been so drunk he would've detected her spirit through his own. As it was, he was lucky to detect his own feet. Out of a mix of fear and confusion, Cross reached out and tried to find his spirit, and there she was, lingering just out his reach, the vapors of her ghostly self disheveled and twisted, curled into a form as unstable as Cross's alcohol-induced mind.

"There you are." Graves came up and took Cross by the shoulder. He looked entirely too sober considering how much Cross had seen him drink. Graves was short and stocky, with messy blonde hair and a number of facial scars mostly hidden by his trim beard. His black shirt hung loose so the tattoos on his neck and arm were easy to see, especially the barbed snake running the length of his well-muscled left arm and the fanged snake skull symbol of Viper Squad on his right shoulder. "There's some trouble." He smiled at Cristena. "Well...hello there."

"Hello," Cristena said with apparent disinterest. "Thanks for interrupting."

"What 'trouble'?" Cross said in a panic.

"An attack. Sorry, Romeo, time to go." He gave Cristena a curt nod. "Miss." She looked ready to say something, maybe even invite herself along, but Graves hauled Cross away. The room spun.

"Graves, I am seriously drunk..."

"Sober up, then," Graves said. He didn't sound like someone who'd consumed half a dozen black guavas. Graves grabbed their flak jackets and hauled Cross along behind him. They both wore their Southern Claw fatigues and steel-toed boots. No one ever really dressed down from armor in Thornn – if you did, you weren't going to live very long.

They launched up the stairs leading from the gambling pits to the elevated drinking floor, and from there they followed more steps to the main doors. The air was a cloud of smoke and darkness generously flavored with whiskey. Cross's eyes stung until they finally reached the street.

They emerged with pistols in hand. Cross struggled with his standard issue warlock's gauntlet, hooked by electric wiring to a portable battery pack on his belt. He nearly tripped on the top step.

Cross's spirit surged and curl against him. He tasted the hot hex of her power in his blood as she purged the alcohol from his system. Sweat beaded on his forehead, and his stomach lurched.

"Wait."

Thornn's streets were tall and drenched with shadow. A dank yellow moon hung like a sulfur stain in the blue-black sky. Cross felt his guts explode as he vomited toxic yellow sludge against the side of the building. He threw up so hard it ached down to his groin.

"That's beautiful, man," Graves laughed. Graves never had any trouble holding his liquor. Chances were he was already sober, and *he* hadn't needed his spirit to force the booze from his system.

"Shut up," Cross stammered. The shivering night was fish blue, tremulous and thin. Thornn's buildings were so dark they might have been splashed in ink. "Where are we going?"

"I got a message from Morg," Graves said. Cross saw the sending stone in Graves's fist. "There was an attack in the Hightower district. Nasty stuff."

"And we're supposed to help?" Cross asked hesitantly. "Unarmored and half-inebriated?"

"Maybe," Graves laughed. "Let's go."

Klaxon alarms sounded through the night. There weren't many people on the streets: Thornn's citizens were smart enough to observe the loosely enforced nighttime curfew, and those few who were about appeared only long enough to peer up the hill towards Hightower, a richer part of town marked by tower-like buildings.

Cross sent his spirit ahead. He felt her race through the thin air, twisting and dancing across the city in search of danger. Normally he only allowed her to roam a few hundred feet away, as their connection grew tenuous and the information he received from her was less reliable the further from him she was. Only witches had the talent to send their spirits out for long range reconnaissance. Cross's spirit flowed in and out of buildings and shadows like a racing raven. She found the source of the danger, but by the time Cross and Graves caught up with her, sweat-laced and out of breath from a mostly uphill run over the course of fifteen blocks, it was all over.

The area near the tower where the disturbance had taken place was spare, just a few brick and mortar buildings, a small stables and an old well. The air was quiet and still. Cross looked up. The tower was ebon, and every window had long since been boarded up. The entry door stood ajar at the top of a short set of stairs. A dozen or so city guards led by the enigmatic Moone were in the process of securing the area. Arcane currents had been laid out in a fence-like pattern, weaved together so no undead spirit could possibly escape. Green flames in iron sconces had been wedged into the ground, painting the air an eerie jade. Thornn citizens stood at the outskirts of the iron poles, huddled together and staring in at the scene of what had been a grisly slaughter.

"There," Graves pointed, and he led them into the throng of city guards. They were almost stopped, but Morg spotted them and motioned they be let through.

"You missed the fun," he said in his baritone voice. Morg was a tower of a man, standing a full head taller than Cross, intimidating even in his loose shirt and sweat pants. He'd either been home relaxing or out for a jog. "This one was bad."

"This is weird for the attack to come in the middle of the city," Graves said. Cross could only nod.

Moone, the leader of Scorpion Squad, was a gaunt and bearded man with grey hair and steely blue eyes. He was one of the senior Southern Claw officers in Thornn – only Cross's mentor, Winter, had anywhere near as many years of service as Moone did. He approached them with a grim expression.

"We were just talking about that," Morg said. "Strange for a suckhead to attack this deep in."

"It had been in hiding," Moone said in his gravelly voice. "The White Mother isn't going to like this."

"You mind if we take a look?" Morg asked.

"I was hoping you would," Moone said. "I think you'll find what's inside...interesting."

The bottom level of the bell tower was a single open space. There were a few chairs where people could sit and rest, and a table for meals and games. Now everything was covered in knives: thousands of blades, covering every visible surface like a sea of razor quills. There couldn't have been more than an inch of space left between the jagged edges. Some ten thousand points had been jabbed into the walls, floor, ceiling and bodies and broken off. Morg had to kick some out of his path just so he could step into the room.

Three corpses lay in unrecognizable heaps on the ground, their bodies perforated head to toe by the rusty weapons. Shreds of clothing clung to their decimated bodies. Bloody messes of hair and skin had spread like grisly jam.

"Wow." Cross gagged and covered his mouth with a gloved hand. The smell of opened intestines and spilled bowels was thick, an outhouse in summer. Neither Morg nor Graves showed any signs of being repulsed. They moved slow in an effort to avoid the pools of blood. "The vampire that did this was *pissed*."

"He definitely had a crabby night," Morg said.

"We think," Moone said from behind them, "that the Suckhead had been hiding out here in the tower. This building was condemned for safety reasons a month or so ago."

"Sir, who are the victims?" Graves asked Moone, but it was Cross who answered.

"Two girls, one boy," Cross said. His spirit clung to him as if for dear life. The spirits of the victims, severed from the human hosts, were close by. Their presence made the air heavy and sick. They were lost and confused, and they'd try to take Cross's spirit with them, or else attack her in their rage and confusion. "They were just having fun," he said as the information came to him. "They were going to do some drinking, maybe some black powder." He swallowed. His skin was frozen, and his fingers shook. It took everything he had to keep her close, to hold her back from those lost and tormented souls. They'd be gone soon, and she'd be safe.

"There," Moone said, and he indicated the other side of the room. "That's what I wanted you to see."

Scrawled markings covered the wall. Runes had been drawn over a rough map, and coded notes, arrows and cross-marks connected dots and triangles and pictures of what looked like eyes. The entire wall had been hidden behind a sliding panel, a removable plate secured by old magic the vampire had apparently torn away. The map was of the northwest part of the country, and it bore location markers for the Wormwood, the Bone March and even the Carrion Rift. The markings were coded, but from what Cross could determine they seemed to be arcane calculations, geo-empathic equations and carto-thaumaturgic drawings. Someone had worked out a location, a place where they wanted to go.

"What happened here?" Morg asked.

"From what we can tell the vampire came here for this map," Moone said. "Either he meant to read it, or destroy it. Then these young people came along..." They stood in silence for a moment. Soldiers barked outside at bystanders to back away. "My squad got the bastard."

"This map," Cross said. "I'll need some time to decode it, but at a glance...it looks like directions."

"To where?" Graves asked. "And who made it?"

Cross stepped closer. It would have taken an extremely experienced mage to make those calculations, to work out the geometry and arcane algorithms. He had no idea where the raw data had come from, but the work itself was complex. Only a few mages could have done it.

"The Wormwood," he said. "Red made this map. And if it leads where I think it does, she's headed for the Wormwood."

FOUR

WHISPERS

Cross woke to a knock on his door.

It was difficult for him to rise from the blankets since his head felt like it had been filled with lead before being rammed against the wall and then left out in the sun to dry like a piece of fruit.

Light fell into his apartment in broken shards. Judging by the dull red color of the air and the cloying chill it was just past dawn. Cross had fallen asleep face down and completely nude, which was one of the normal side effects of his drinking too much.

Too bad I always wake up alone.

His mouth was filled with dry mucus, and when he coughed he felt like he was ready to spew a mouthful of nails. His muscles were locked, and when he tried to move he almost fell off the bed.

This is why I don't drink.

Cross's spirit drifted just at the edge of his thoughts. Power churned like boiling hot liquid in his gut as she tried to flush the toxins out of his system, working so fast he almost vomited.

The knock on the door came again.

Damn.

"What?!" he shouted. He didn't know any of his neighbors, and it was rare anyone who came to his apartment to summon him to duty actually bothered to knock. He never locked the door – the runic wards over the doorway made it very clear a warlock lived there, which was usually enough to deter most would-be human intruders. Non-human intruders actually brave enough to hunt down a warlock weren't likely to be dissuaded by a mere door.

Whoever it was, they didn't respond to his question. But the knock came again.

Cross blinked, let his spirit's energies pulse through his body, quickly pulled on his pants and picked up his HK45 from the desk. The pistol felt heavy in his hand, and the runes carved into the grip were cold against his skin. Cross walked along the rugs, waited at the door for a moment, and opened it.

A homunculus stood in the doorway with a stupid grin, a disturbing parody of a human face. The golem was made of red clay and black brick, its eyes were slits cut over the mawkish grin, and its nose was an ill-constructed protrusion filled with arcane powders which allowed the brute to use scent to find its way around the city, since it was generally considered too expensive to provide the constructs with vision or hearing since they were so short-lived. They were a lesser construct, among the simpler implements a mage could create.

"Deliver," Cross said. He wasn't sure if he really wanted a message sent to him so early in the day.

When a homunculus spoke, it was a magical audio recording, a reproduction of the voice of whoever sent it in the first place. Normally it was the crafter, but Cross knew there were a few mages in Thornn who had a surplus of prefabricated golems they sold for use by whoever was willing to pay their sometimes inordinate fees.

It spoke with a woman's voice. Cristena's voice.

"Sorry to track you down like this. I was wondering...well, I need to ask you something. If you're interested, I'd like to meet with you...do you know a good place for breakfast?"

After Cross recovered from the initial shock of hearing her voice, he gave the golem a return message and sent it on its way. He was ready in just a few minutes, and without even really thinking about it he was out the door and on his way to the other side of town, unaffected by the bitter morning air.

Krugen's was a spacious and well-lit establishment, which made it somewhat different from nine out of ten of Thornn's other watering holes. Krugen's had wide booths and a round bar in the middle of the alabaster stone room. The air smelled of whiskey and fresh bacon. Heavy curtains covered the exits, and at that early hour Cross was alone save for the serving ladies, all of who wore solid white dresses made to look like they'd come off a movie set from the 1940's. The place felt like it was made from milk, and the color scheme made Cross (and, when she arrived, Cristena) stand out in stark contrast.

Cross was there a short time by himself. He drank strong black coffee and nibbled on black bread and white cheese. Most of Thorn's food was grown in arcane greenhouses, where foods natural to the region – potatoes, greens, flax, turnips and carrots, milk and meat and cheese from safely guarded chickens and goats, honey and rhubarb – were given magically prepared serums and hormones and were bedded in arcane soil to promote their growth. Krugen's, however, maintained its own plot of well-protected land right there in the city, and if their prices were a bit steep it was because they offered some of the only fresh beef, cheese and home-ground bread in the city, and maybe in the all of the Southern Claw Alliance.

Cristena arrived a short while after, but still well before any other customers. She wore a loose black dress which hung over her flexible leather armor, and her dark hair was pulled back tight save for a single lock that dangled down over the left side of her face.

Cross tried not to stare. For a moment he forgot how to breathe.

"Hi," she smiled, and she set a weapons harness laced with knives and guns on the table.

"You look lovely," Cross said, and he was sorry he'd said it moments later, but if Cristena took any offense she gave no indication. Instead she stood there and looked at him quizzically.

"Is that the same outfit you wore yesterday?" she said with a grin.

"It may look eerily similar to what I wore to the Black Hag last night, yes...but it's not."

Cristena sat down and pulled out a pack of cigarillos. They were Raams, a brand of smokes out of Fane, one of the few places that could afford to grow its own tobacco and not have it taste, as Graves liked to say, "like weeds soaked in yesterday's piss". Cristena lit two and handed one to Cross. Normally he would have been reluctant, but he took it without hesitation and pulled the sharp licorice and herb infused smoke into his lungs, which he practically felt crack and shrivel as he inhaled. They ordered breakfast – Cross had Egg-in-the-Hole, Cristena ordered a salad and fresh local eggs – and they drank coffee.

"How do you like Thornn?" he asked after they'd finished. There was a palpable tension in the air. Cross pushed his plate aside. He had eaten the egg and thick toast, but there were enough hash browns left on his plate to choke a warhorse. As it was he was so full he felt he'd sink like a stone if thrown naked in a river.

"I like it a lot," she said after some hesitation. "But I'm not sure if it's for me." She lit another cigarillo. "Cross...I need to ask you something. And I want you to know it's...perfectly all right if you don't want to answer."

"Ok," he said. Cross knew that in a perfect world she would have been coming on to him. He also knew it was far from a perfect world. "What is it?"

"I need to know what's happening with the hunt for Red."

Cross took a deep breath. His pistol suddenly felt heavy in the holster inside his coat. His spirit tensed and collected near him, and he sensed Cristena's do the same. They pushed and tested against one another, not quite angry but tense and brimming with potential violence.

"And why would I tell you anything about that?" he asked. "What makes you think I even know?"

"Your eyes just confirmed that you do," Cristena said with a nod. "And I don't expect you to tell me anything, Cross...but I'm asking you anyways. I'm asking because I need to know..." Something in her manner, in her sudden change of demeanor, took Cross off guard. He hadn't seen her look at all vulnerable up to that point, and it was disarming.

Careful, he told himself. *She could be setting you up.*

His hands shook, but he did his best to keep them steady as he pressed them flat against the table. Slowly he pushed his left hand into his coat and felt the gun handle. Both of their spirits were poised, coiled like snakes.

Please don't be an agent for the Ebon Cities. That would be just my luck.

"Renaad," she said. "My husband. His name...was Renaad. He was a member of Talon Squad."

Cross swallowed, nodded, and pulled his hand away from his jacket.

"I don't know," he said quietly. "I doubt I've heard anything you haven't."

"Please," Cristena said quietly. Her transformation was startling. She seemed just a shadow of the strong and charismatic woman he'd met the night before. "Anything...anything you can tell me." The air was suddenly colder than before. "I *hear* him," she said quietly. "I hear him whispering to me." Her voice was broken. Cross thought he saw tears in her eyes. "That's not how it's supposed to work. If he's dead, I shouldn't be able to hear him. He should just be...gone."

Cross didn't know what to say. There was very little he *could* say. When the criminal witch Red – Cross would think of her as nothing else, regardless of who she'd once been or what she'd once meant to the Southern Claw – had taken flight with vital information in her possession, the White Mother ordered that she be hunted down and eliminated. Ebon Squad, an elite team out of Glaive, had been the first to be sent after her.

After it set off after Red Ebon Squad was never seen alive again. Their remains were found east of Thornn, in the white wastes of the Reach. It hadn't been Red who'd killed them – powerful though she was, she couldn't take on an entire Hunter squad on her own – but the team had been ambushed by a powerful Ebon Cities kick murder squad out of Rath. The Ebon Cities, it seemed, were also tracking Red. Prior to the destruction of Ebon Squad, it had been assumed Red was bound for one of the Ebon Cities to give the vampires her stolen information. Intelligence gathered since her disappearance, however, hinted that while her actions would ultimately help the vampires it was not the Ebon Cities who she planned to sell the Southern Claw's secrets to.

Unaware and afraid, the White Council dispatched more teams to find Red and stop her, among them Talon Squad. On those rare occasions when members of the squads were actually found there was usually not much left. The Southern Claw was suddenly running short on elite squads. There were plenty of soldiers, but the Hunter squads were the Southern Claw's elite weapons in the war against the Ebon Cities. Losing even one Squad was a serious blow to the Alliance. Losing five had been devastating.

"I'm sorry," he said. "I can't imagine..."

"No. You can't." Cristena finished her cigarette, stared at Cross for a moment, and stood up. "I'm sorry. I think maybe you had a different idea of why I wanted to meet with you."

"Maybe," Cross said. "But that's not important. Cristena..." He stood up and looked her in the eye. "I'm sorry. I wish I had good news for you, or *any* news for you. I don't know anything about the missing Squads." There was no need to explain that most of them were presumed dead. Cristena's cool demeanor and self-control were all but gone.

"Are *you* going after her?" she asked him. Something froze in Cross's gut. He'd been trying not to think about that.

"Yes," he said. "I am."

"Then do me a favor," she said. "Kill her." There were tears on her face. "Kill that bitch for me. Maybe then I'll stop hearing Renaad's voice every time I touch my spirit. Maybe then I'll actually believe he's not out there somewhere, suffering. Maybe then I'll be able to sleep again."

She turned to leave, but Cross stepped out to stop her.

"We need a tracker," he said. "My squad...I mean, the squad I'm in, Viper Squad, needs a tracker. I'm sure given the circumstances..."

"No," Cristena said. She kept her eyes down. She wouldn't say yes. He knew she wouldn't, and she was right not to. She left without another word.

Cross sat back down and drank more coffee, wondering all the while if he shouldn't drink something stronger. He checked the clock on the far wall, a pale and monstrous thing like a ghostly whale. The briefing was at 0900. Cross had just enough time to finish his coffee.

He watched a spider cross the floor. It was out of place there in Krugen's, a place known for being so immaculate. The spider was ashen pale, like it was made of ice. It scurried towards the door.

Cross had lied when he'd told Snow he'd never heard their mother after she'd died. For a while, he'd heard her all the time. He wasn't sure if she'd finally stopped, or if after so long he'd just learned to ignore her.

FIVE

SHIELD

The briefing rooms for Southern Claw military personnel were located in a massive old hospital which had been converted to double as the military headquarters there in Thornn. The building was also a prison, a church, an arcane workshop, and as an asylum for people whose minds had succumbed to the horrors and madness of living in a world filled with undead, magic, and post-apocalyptic abominations. The gothic structure was all tall arches and pedestals, smooth columns and bladed promenades, arched halls and ancient oak doors. The dark stone lent the hospital an exceedingly ominous atmosphere, and the improper lighting throughout the structure made it seem like some ancient European castle.

Not exactly the feel I'd have gone for, Cross thought. He'd always hated the place, but he'd be the first to admit it was extremely defensible. The hospital hung directly over the churning waters of the Bloodnight, a sharp and cold river running southwest into Rimefang Loch, and the only way to get inside apart from using the heavily guarded gate was to scale one of the sheer forty-foot steel walls. Those walls were perfectly positioned to douse intruders with generous doses of gunfire, arcane missiles and vats filled with caustic substances.

Vampires, of course, had little need to climb thanks to their Razorwing mounts, but those who'd redesigned the hospital had taken care of that through the strategic placement of warlock marksmen and carefully woven ethereal nets cast by expert trackers. Anything, living or undead, that even attempted to fly close to the hospital's walls would be detected, incinerated and shot down. To date, not a single Razorwing or undead flier had made it close.

Cross waited in the main hall, a wide chamber carved from dark and dirty stone. The windows in the hall let in scant traces of muted light. Oversized lanterns dangled from the vaulted ceiling. Cross stood with one boot planted against the wall behind him, nervously rubbing his fingernails together. He hadn't shaved in days, and he imagined he looked like a ruffian.

Cross was pale, tall and thin. He dressed in black fatigues and wore a heavy black armored coat that added nearly forty pounds to his weight. In spite of not having shaved Cross's face still felt mostly clean, since he'd never been good at growing a beard. Snow said he had a baby face, that he looked even younger than twenty-six.

His spirit swirled around him, as agitated as he was. He'd been asked to wait while Morg and Winter conferred with others whose identities Cross could only guess at. Based on the nature and sensitivity of their mission Cross guessed most of the senior officers would be present, which meant Pike, Argus, and maybe even Jericho, the ranking senior officer in Thornn. So far as the whereabouts of the rest of Viper Squad – Graves, Kray and Stone – Cross had no idea. As far as he knew they were supposed to be there for the briefing along with him.

Something's wrong. The thought gnawed at him. There was so much at stake – the lives of everyone, really, and the future of not only Thornn but perhaps the entire Southern Claw Alliance. The White Mother and her advisors were taking no chances. Cross hated not knowing what was going on. He hated being kept there, waiting.

The air seemed to grow colder the longer he waited. He heard moans from the medical wing: soldiers felled in recent skirmishes, sent back to Thornn by airship to receive the best medical support in all of the Southern Claw. A dying patient screamed somewhere beyond the massive oak doors. Cross wondered if it was someone he knew.

Thornn was one of the largest cities in the Southern Claw, with ample natural resources and a stockpile of experts, from arcanists and historians to engineers, doctors and scientists. After The Black, when the world was falling to pieces and scattered refugees were forced to do everything they could just to stay alive, the enigmatic creature who'd later come to be known as The White Mother scoured the world. She'd searched not only for survivors, but for the *right* survivors: people who could help remake civilization, people whose knowledge and abilities could carve some sort of future out of a place that had become a cesspool of nightmares, mutants and death. There was no telling how the White Mother had known who to select or how to find them, but it was a known and accepted fact she herself wasn't human, but a creature who'd come over from another world during The Black. She was as formidable, as ancient and as powerful as her opposite, the Grim Father, Lord of the Ebon Cities and the enemy of all humankind.

No one ever met the White Mother. She worked through intermediaries like the White Council, and she left the governing and direct leadership of the Southern Claw Alliance to its own.

To people like Red.

The nearest door opened. Cross caught a glimpse of the massive hospital chamber, a vault of columns taken up by beds, sheets and curtains, surgical tables and tubes, medical engines and healing turbines, and row upon row of the injured. They were victims of the vampires of Rath, casualties in the field skirmishes and small-scale battles that took place far to the south. Most of the wounded in those battles were sent to Ath, but when Ath's hospitals began to run out of beds they were re-routed to Thornn. A glimpse was all it took to see why Phil Rikeman, the head surgeon, rarely got any sleep.

Cross saw him limp into the hall. Rikeman was a gaunt man in gray fatigues; he wore a thin beard and had surprisingly muscular arms. His surgical gloves were stained with blood, and he looked bone weary with exhaustion. Rikeman's limp came from the magical brace he was forced to wear over his left leg, an uncomfortable looking hunk of cold iron set with switches, dials, gauges and heavy leather and chain straps holding it in place. Thin trails of ice-cold steam escaped from the joints of the leg brace, exhaust from the arcane engine which kept a magical disease in Rikeman's leg stable so it wouldn't spread and destroy the rest of his body. Cross didn't know how that had happened to him, and didn't really want to.

"Cross," the surgeon said. "Are you feeling okay?"

"Yeah," he said. "Just waiting."

"I mean...you're all right? No more headaches or anything like that?"

Warlocks tended to be a sickly lot – channeling one's arcane spirit to produce magical effects took a heavy toll on the body. It was a surprise when some lasted as long as they did. In the end, the ones who lived wound up something like Cross's mentor, Winter: harnessed to bio-charged battery packs or with chemical wires hooked into their veins so they could maintain contact with and channel magic through their spirits without burning their bodies dry. While every warlock had to channel through some sort of an implement, it wasn't until they grew older that they needed them just to keep breathing. Luckily for Cross, he and Snow were both considered more powerful than most other mages their age. If he was lucky he'd be able to wait a while before he had to rely on his arcane gauntlets for day-to-day survival.

"No headaches," he said with a friendly shake of his head. "I'm fine. Snow is good, too."

"Yeah, I just saw her."

Cross thought about that for a moment. "What? Wait, when? Why?"

The opposite door opened, and several Southern Claw officers stepped out. Cross saw Winter, Pike, Moone, Argus, Jericho, Zelestine and King. The meeting chamber was filled with maps and charts, empty mugs and plates and sweet cigarillo smoke. Morg and Winter remained inside, along with Snow.

Oh, no. No.

"Cross," Morgan said. Snow looked up, caught his eye, and nervously looked away.

"Sir..."

"Now hold on. Before you jump to conclusions..."

"She's joined Viper Squad, hasn't she?" Cross said. "Sir, she's my *sister*. There are protocols about siblings serving in the same unit..."

"I said *hold on*," Morgan said, quiet but stern. The other officers looked back as they filed down the hall. "This is a matter to be discussed behind closed doors." Morgan's voice was a near growl, especially when he was angry. He never raised his voice: it just got deeper. "So move it."

Winter nodded as Cross briskly entered the meeting chamber. Cross glowered. He was shaking, racked with anger so hard it made his gums ache and his eyes burn. His spirit was caught up in his emotions, and she focused the rage into the effort of stabilizing her own cyclonic form. Arcane safe-guards spread throughout the hospital would prevent her from manifesting in any harmful fashion, as doing so would cause both she and Cross a great deal of pain. Managing both of their emotional states was exhausting. Cross was suddenly short of breath, and it was difficult for him to raise his eyes and look at Snow, who sat in a plain black dress and black tights and the tall black leather boots he'd bought her for Giving Day.

"Take it easy," Winter advised. "I'd have preferred *she'd* told you, but she had her reasons..."

"Telling me would have been *great*," Cross said. He looked at his sister.

Morgan closed the door harder than he normally would. Morg rarely lost his temper, and when he did it was downright frightening.

"All right," he said. All Morgan needed was a breath to regain his composure, and he was once again the cool and intimidating leader of Viper Squad, the one whose very name was practically a legend. "It's time for some family drama. Let's get this over with." He looked at Snow for a moment, and then at Cross. "Southern Claw protocol is being overruled in the case of Cynthia Cross joining Viper Squad even though her brother, Eric, is already a member. My squad has been in need of a tracker ever since we lost Cala. If not for the recent uncovering of Red's destination, finding Cala's replacement could have waited. As it stands we're one of the few available teams left qualified to hunt Red down, so finding a new tracker has become a matter of great import. Winter?"

The old man nodded.

"Cynthia..." Winter began.

"Snow," she interrupted. "I haven't been called 'Cynthia' since I was five."

"Snow," Winter said, "is, bar none, the best candidate for the position. In fact...and this seems to run in the Cross family...she's the most naturally talented witch I've seen in a long, long time..."

"She's my *sister*," Cross said coldly. "She's not a soldier."

"I'm right here, Eric," Snow said quietly. "And it's not like I'm coming straight out of the library. I've been training for months, while you've been away."

Of course you have, Cross realized. *You'd never walk into something like this unprepared: we both got that from Mom. You've been training, probably learning to focus your skills and control your spirit, and I wouldn't know a thing about it because I haven't been here. Even when I am...I'm not here.*

"The fact of the matter is," Morg said when the silence drew long, "what's done is done. A protocol override has been voted on and approved by the senior officers in Thornn, as has your sister's inclusion as a member of Viper Squad. You two need to sort this out."

Cross stared at his sister, she stared at the floor, and both of them were near tears.

Morg waited. For a moment Cross wondered if threatening to quit would change their minds, but the notion passed quickly. He knew he couldn't quit, especially not now. His anger was gone. His spirit clung to him, embraced him. She was desperate to keep the cold of his sadness at bay. It didn't work.

Morg and Winter left the room, promising to return for the briefing in a few minutes. Cross and Snow were alone.

He looked at her and saw her at eight years old, dressed in a frumpy shirt dangling down to her ankles, always refusing to wear pants; he saw her at twelve, building snow forts with him after dark, as unafraid as he of the terrors in the night; he saw her at fifteen, looking at boys, but he never saw her much because she read so many books and always hid in her room, and all he ever did when she emerged was tell her to go away and leave him alone. He'd never understood what his mother meant when she'd said they were growing up too fast until that moment.

"Eric..." Snow began, but she fumbled her words, and her mouth moved with an empty rhythm. "I'm sorry...I want to help...and I knew you..."

Cross shook his head and reached out his hand. She gave him hers in return, and he pulled her into his trembling arms.

I can't stop you, he wanted to say. *I want to, but I can't. All I can do now is everything in my power to keep you safe. I'll be a shield for you, little sister. I'll protect you.*

"I can't wait," he said quietly, "to come over for dinner tonight."

He felt Snow smile. Inside, his heart cracked. Their spirits danced a lonely dance, soft and slow, not quite touching, circling their human anchors like it was a child's game. Cross held Snow for a time before the rest of Viper Squad arrived, and the briefing began.

PART TWO
HUNTERS

He sees the mountain, a grim edifice of black rock embalmed in hoarfrost, so immense it penetrates the pale sky like a blade. Ice winter clouds float over its onyx face. Iron mist hovers inches above the sluggish crystal waters of the silver marsh at the mountain's base.

Women sit on the brittle grass and dip their bare feet into an ice-laden stream. They are fair and pale, their skin the color of milk. They live in this prison of sleeping trees, whose branches lay across the ground like spent lovers. The scents of dying lilacs and corroding hyacinths drift up to heaven on a chill wind. The jet mountain looms over the glade. The wind blows through the clearing and ripples their dresses and hair. When they speak he can't hear them, but he sees their words like platinum ghosts. Leaves float over the ground. The trees stir like skeletons.

The women share memories of home. They recall dark buildings slick with rainfall and streets filled with armor and smoke. Statues of tall men eclipse the city with their shadows. The air is heavy with fear.

But this, this glade, is a better place for them. They sit near the waters and quietly laugh, knowing their presence is ever in flux. They dream of the present, and though he knows they must be freezing they look comfortable and at ease. Gossamer branches sway behind them. Beyond the lavender trees hangs a cold and empty moon, a portal through the clouds.

A sound like thunder approaches. The unicorn's hooves splash in the water. Their whinnies echo through the mists.

The women run. Their wool dresses have been made heavy with moisture, and the marshy forest slows them with its sodden earth and tendrils of silver smoke.

He tries to help them, but he isn't really there.

The unicorns emerge from the silver fog like a chain of nightmares. Their skin is black and coarse, and thick dark blood oozes from their nostrils and hooves. Their eyes are white and their horns are jagged and covered in scratches. Their teeth are fanged.

They descend on the girls and kill one of them almost instantly. Her terrified face reflects in the unicorn's eyes as their horns rend her fragile body apart. Mangled remains fall up into the sky, where she's swallowed by rain falling like inverted tears.

The other girls run through the marsh, hindered by thick vines and walls of foliage. Fog cages them.

Again he sees their memories of the place they once called home. Black rain falls onto steep stone steps ascending to a grim palace, the heart of the black city. Silhouettes of soldiers surround them, men and women determined to keep their realm safe from the faceless advance of a distant enemy. White fires burn in great pits, dank beacons to light the soldier's return. Armor grinds against stone as they march onto fields of blood and rain. The soldiers die in battle and fall in waves, face down in the mud, the life crushed from their bodies.

The unicorns are persistent hunters. They show no mercy. The women are exhausted, their bodies covered with silver ice. Their hair and dresses have been soaked through with water and they huddle together in the shadow of tall rocks like broken fingers.

The unicorns smell of brimstone and blood. Their horns are cracked and their manes have gone white. They feed on these women, these souls without mates.

She is alone now, no longer needed. He reaches for her, and for a moment see sees him, and she wants to reach back.

Her mind returns to the creeping shadows over the fields of war. Her memories bleed to recollections of the glade, her small paradise filled with silver haze and the girls with white skin.

She falls up. Even as the unicorns come for her, all she can think of is how the worst days are behind her. She falls into air filled with tears and leaves.

The sky freezes as she ascends into its embrace, and she remains there, held in gray stasis, forever frozen at the edge of death.

SIX

DESCENT

The black walls rumbled. Cross tried not to think about the fact there was 1000 feet of open air under the wood beneath his feet. At the nadir of that drop was the Wormwood, likely the last place he'd ever wanted to go in his entire life, or the first place he'd always planned to avoid.

Either way, I don't really want to go there. Too late.

"Two minutes!"

They were perched on benches running parallel to one other on opposite sides of the airship, a tight space barely eight feet across and twice that long. A tiny ladder at one end led up to the command deck, while the descending ladder at the other end dropped to the landing platform.

"For as big as these ships are, you think they'd have more elbow room," Graves shouted. They had to shout to be heard over the turbines and rattling walls.

"They're over sixty percent armor," Stone said. "I think they figured you'd rather be safe than comfortable."

Graves just laughed. None of them were safe, and they all knew it.

They were packed six deep: Morgan, Stone, Kray, Graves, Winter, and Cross, all strapped tight to their bench seats. Each of them wore black combat fatigues and a heavy armored coat. Bandoliers and thick belts packed with equipment ranging from scopes and knives to grenades and canteens weighed them down. The armor coats went just past the waist, cut tight so as not to snag on their surroundings and impede movement. Each coat was set with flexible Kevlar strips that helped minimize injury from glancing blows, though there was little they'd do against direct bullet wounds or blades. The regular soldiers wore additional armor under the coats, sections of steel and tightened

Kevlar which protected vital areas. It was all designed to allow mobility and speed. The best soldier, they were taught, was the one fast enough to avoid getting shot or stabbed in the first place.

Snow was upstairs with the flight crew, in part to help the pilots navigate through use of her spirit, but also, Cross knew, because she wasn't comfortable being pent up in tight quarters with a bunch of soldiers. She'd have to get used to that pretty quick.

We all did, Cross thought.

The rickety airship descended through a pocket of turbulence. Cross was convinced he heard the wooden planks pull apart behind him, which was all but impossible since they were held in place by an inch of magnetically reinforced steel plate. The craft shook violently, then fell ten feet in two seconds before it leveled out again. The contents of Cross's stomach clawed at the bottom of his throat.

"This is awesome," he muttered.

"This is the life!" Kray was normally a quiet man, but he acted like a jubilant kid whenever they got to fly to a mission. Cross wasn't sure how anyone could get used to being on airship at all, let alone enjoy it. He had been on plenty of missions, but he wasn't sure if there was some magical number of aerial drops he'd have to take part in before all of the sickness and strained nerves became easier to cope with. He hoped he'd live long enough to find out.

"Hang in there," Graves said. "The real fun starts when we touch down."

"You have a twisted idea of fun, my friend," Cross said with a smile.

"Come on, Cross," Kray bellowed. "Stop being such a woman." Kray was strangely quiet whenever they were on the ground – it was only in the air that he turned obnoxious.

"What would you know about women, Kray?" Winter smiled. The mage was calm and self assured, just like always. Winter, the "old man", was a foot shorter than Kray and twice his age. He was also the senior mage on the team and an experienced warlock, so they all knew better than to mess with him. Winter actually deferred most of the team's arcane matters to the much younger Cross, but Cross was always sure Winter knew how comfortable he was having the older mage in the group.

There are two other mages, he corrected himself. *Snow isn't your sister today. She's your tracker.* As if his nerves weren't already shot because of how important the mission was, Cross also worried about keeping his only living family member alive. *Damn it, Snow. Why did you have to go and be a hero?*

"I know plenty about women," Kray smiled.

"Really?" Stone said with a grin. "What women do you know, Kray? Beside your Mom?"

"I know *your* Mom," Kray said with as straight of a face as he could muster.

They all laughed, save Morgan. "Morg" wore his game face. He stared straight ahead and smiled politely to encourage his troops, but it was clear his mind was already on what lay ahead.

The Wormwood. Perhaps the worst place to go on a world which had redefined the notion of "bad places". It was over a hundred square miles of twisted trees and dank marsh occupied by Chul, Gorgoloth and other things Cross didn't know about and didn't *want* to know about. And in that mire of witched wood and poison swamp they had to find a woman. A traitor.

And we have to find her before the vampires do, Cross thought. *Wonderful.*

Cross knew he needed to stop worrying. He had skills and talents to contribute to the Alliance, and that was just what he'd do. This was what he was *meant* to do...or so he'd been told. Some days he wasn't so sure.

I'm drifting, he realized. *Growing numb, and complacent. Unhappy. Every time I slow down to think about what's going on I freak out. So just get on with it.*

"Gear up!" Morg called. "Check your equipment! One minute! Let's try to make a respectable exit this time!" Morg walked to the back of the airship, using an iron pole running the length of the ceiling as a handhold. "Our deployments have looked like a comedy routine lately. Let's clean that up before you make me unhappy."

Morg was a big man, tall and lean but well muscled, and he had a deep and resonant voice that was loud even when he whispered. He wasn't as big as Kray, but if Cross had to pick which of the two men got to beat the hell out of him, he'd pick Kray in a heartbeat. At least he'd have a chance of surviving.

Cross's HK45 automatic was at his side, and he made sure both the pyrojack gauntlet he'd purchased from Warfield and his spare pair of standard gauntlets were in his pack, which he tied up tight. The pack was laced with armor and clamped to his coat. Emergency release triggers under his armpits allowed for a quick getaway from his pack in case he had to ditch his gear for speed, or if any of his equipment was compromised and turned unstable. The small battery pack for his arcane gauntlets was on his belt. The copper wiring reaching between the pack and his wrists tensed and hummed as he checked the connection.

His spirit tensed, and the air stiffened around him. He felt her cool touch against his skin, a reassuring pressure reminding him of her presence.

Snow came down from the pilot's area as Viper Squad prepared to disembark. Her hair was pulled back from her face, and Cross heard the whispers of her spirit as she prepped for the descent. Her spirit would soon extend and form a wide perimeter so it could better detect distant anomalies and arcane patterns, which would help track their quarry. Cross and Winter would hold their spirits in tighter rein and only allow them to roam short distances for close proximity readings.

Weapons were checked and rechecked. Blades slid into sheaths. Straps of leather and plates of steel armor were cinched tight. Cross checked his pistol again. There was nothing left to do but worry. Those last sixty seconds seemed to stretch on for an hour.

Finally the chemical lamps in the cramped cabin turned red, and moments later turned green. The bay door fell open and crashed onto the dirt.

Black trees loomed before them in a grim wall. Cross smelled moss, brine, mold and sap. The Wormwood was directly ahead. Blood fell from dead branches. Shadows bent and twisted unnaturally, lending the darkness a dizzying depth.

The airship – a bare sailing vessel about ten meters long – hovered in the air behind them just for a moment. Muted turbine engines blew out air and dust in and formed a swirling funnel of dead leaves. Exhausts pushed against them where they crouched down, and they remained that way until the airship lifted up and turned away. It would circle the area until they returned.

Morg signaled, and they silently entered the haunted forest.

SEVEN

WORMWOOD

There was something in the trees.

Cross stepped back. His bone-banded handheld telescope was freezing to the touch. A few years of experience had done little to get him used to the feel of some of his arcane implements, most of which were all as cold as death.

"Well?" Graves asked.

They stood at the edge of the Wormwood, a grim forest of grotesquely misshapen trees and ravenous bogs. The area was populated with refugee warlocks, soul miners, black poison clouds and lost relics of the world before The Black, which had twisted everything with the taint of madness and magic and killed millions of people in the process. The Wormwood was just one of many mutations left behind in the wake of that apocalypse. Thick branches blocked out the sky, and hordes of psychotically carnivorous animals roamed its depths. Arteries of black blood ran through the roots of the trees and into the dark soil.

"There's something there, but I can't quite make it out. Not clearly, anyways." Cross handed Graves the telescope. Up close Cross could clearly see the scars on Graves's cheek and neck, which he'd acquired after the campaign in Blackmarsh when he'd been held prisoner in the Ebon City of Krul, a place where the vampires tortured prisoners and took their time turning them to undead. It was a technique which assured total obedience while still retaining a converted human's original skill set, which otherwise wasn't possible – most vampires held no trace of their former selves.

Cross was no beauty, either. A scar from a vampire attack ran down his left cheek to the lower left side of his mouth and jaw, but nothing as grievous as Graves's wounds. If not for quite a bit of luck and some inside hlp, Graves never would have made it out of Krul at all.

Cross's spirit brushed against him. He quietly breathed in her cold vapors and let her ethereal form swim into his lungs.

"Are you okay?" Winter asked him. The older mage was a few yards behind him, busy adjusting his elaborate thaumaturgy harness. Winter's heavy implement was strapped to his torso like a parachute, weighed a good twenty pounds and was as bulky as a tombstone. Cross didn't need such an excessive pack, at least not yet – his was just a battery, four inches across and barely a pound, strapped to his belt and hooked to his gauntlets with thin copper wires. Unlike Winter, he also only needed his implement when he manifested magic. Winter had to wear his just to stay alive.

Just like I'll have to, eventually.

"I'm fine," he said. "Jitters, is all. I'm worried about Snow."

"She'll be fine," Winter said after he hesitated a moment.

"Damn," Graves breathed. "I see them."

Cross and Winter knelt down behind Graves. They gazed deep into the dank innards of the forest. The bone-pale tree they hid behind was ancient and gnarled and as hard as concrete. Long dried fruit dangled from the withered branches, solid white and covered in gooey webs.

Cross took the scope back from Graves, but Winter put a hand on it.

"No," he said. "Save your strength for what matters. I'll do this."

Cross's fingers ached as they peeled away from the icy steel. Winter took what was seen in the scope and projected it into the minds of all three men. The image wasn't physical, but light bent and twisted into a paradox of ethereal intellect, shifted and sent to their corneas so they could all see the same image when any one of them looked through the scope. Winter aimed the device into the heart of the trees.

The cloaked silhouettes of three men stood past the twisted trees and black marsh, nearly invisible in the clouds of gas and bones dangling from the trees. All three had weapons strapped across their backs. Dark air clung to them like a swarm of icy bees. They were small even in the scope, which meant they were a considerable distance away.

"Sentries?" Cross asked.

"A Creed," Graves said. "Shadowclaws. The vampire version of us. They're looking for Red, too. And they're ahead of us." He spat a dark wad of corrosive chewing tobacco onto the ground. "Again, I say 'Damn'."

"How do you know they're Shadowclaws?" Cross asked.

"Well, for starters, there's three of them," Graves said matter-of-factly. He may have come across as a backwater hick most of the time, but Graves was an expert Hunter. "They wouldn't send a regular unit out this far from Rath. Shadowclaw Creeds move faster, and they're elite."

"But there can be more than one Creed out there, right? Working together?" Cross expected the nod Graves gave him. "Damn it. Have you faced them before?"

"It's been a while."

"Have *I*?" he asked.

"Not with Viper Squad. We fought at least one Creed in Blackmarsh."

Cross suppressed a shudder. He didn't want to even think about Blackmarsh. Sometimes he had still had nightmares about that campaign, his first.

"We'd better get the others," Winter said. He started back towards their base camp, just outside the boundaries of the woods. Viper Squad couldn't actually camp inside the forest, as people had died from prolonged exposure to the fumes the black blood arteries pushed up from the ground and into the Wormwood. Winter told Cross they'd be fine so long as they kept moving and didn't stay in any one spot for too long. For some reason, that didn't make him feel any better.

"Where are Morg and Stone?" Cross asked. Graves held up his hand for silence. He gripped a black chunk of rune carved stone; Stone, somewhere out there in the forest, had another just like it. Shadows leaked from the meteoric rock. With two of the stones, anyone could send simple messages across impossible distances without actually having to utter a single word.

"They're on their way," Graves said.

"Where are they?"

"Dug into a rock bed two klicks east of here. They're watching the path by the river."

Graves stood up. He was only about five-and-a-half-feet tall, all muscle and grit, with a scraggly beard, unkempt blonde hair and black and red fatigues laced with stakes, knives, pistols, a pair of carpenter bombs and a wide-bladed machete strapped across his back. Cross was a good six inches taller than Graves, but Graves was easily the more intimidating figure, especially since Cross was so thin and pale. Cross's fatigues were light and loose – a warlock had to be able to move and to allow his skin to breathe lest their arcane spirits boil or freeze their flesh.

"Did they see anything?" Cross asked.

"We'd have known by now if they had."

The outer ring of the forest was an unstable saltwater marsh. Brackish water littered with floating deposits of calcium and rust turned the flow to a half-frozen sludge settled around beds of thick weeds, thorny brambles and drifts of dark silt. Ancient and gnarled trees, some a hundred feet high, twisted and bent together in an obscene dance. A semi-translucent fog surrounded the forest. Bits of dead organic matter flitted in the breeze like flies.

The Wormwood stretched for miles, and the land around the Wormwood was nearly as lifeless as the forest itself, though not nearly so cursed. There were cold plains, empty riverbeds and steep bluffs overlooking oceans of red and grey sand. They were right at the southern tip of the Bone March, an amply named waste filled with drifts of white dust, ancient bones and other monuments to the destruction wrought by The Black. The air tasted cold and dead.

The camp was in a dry streambed just out of sight from the plains. Winter was already there, and he, Snow and Kray had disassembled the camp and looked ready for trouble. Cross's stomach churned. No matter how many battles he'd lived through the thought of willingly walking into a situation where he could die still seemed idiotic. He'd taken part in over a dozen missions with Viper Squad and had seen more than his share of action when he was still a part of Wolf Company, defending Thornn from blood wolves and Gorgoloth. He'd faced vampires and the animated shadows of their victims in

Blackmarsh. He'd seen people die and he'd been covered in his friend's remains.

Does this ever get any easier?

Most of his anxiety stemmed from Snow's presence. She was the only member of the Squad with less experience than himself, and whether or not anyone liked it one of Cross's constant duties had become taking care of her. And he could only imagine what was going through *her* mind. He had to give her credit: if she had any fear, she didn't show it. The teenage girl who used to be his baby sister looked like a warrior now. There were draconic tattoos on her neck and arms, and she wore a thick armored coat covering the knives she kept strapped to her wrists. She calmly adjusted her leather gauntlets. Her eyes were calm.

I still see the younger Snow. I still see you with that floppy elephant doll, reading books all day in your room. You'll always be that young to me.

Kray and Winter, the old veterans, looked at ease. When Kray yielded that mini-gun Cross was sure there were fewer living beings more frightening to behold. Graves hinted Kray might have been half-Doj, but no one in the squad dared ask.

Cross and Winter hurriedly packed the rest of the gear into their packs. Graves checked and loaded his shotgun, and after a quick check of the camp they silently trekked back up the hill and into the trees.

They came back to where they'd seen the Creed. The vampires hadn't moved.

"They know we're here," Graves said quietly. "Spread out. Morg and Stone are going to meet us in the forest."

The air turned sour as they fanned out in a broken line. They moved with near silence in spite of the marsh water and dismal forest sludge eating their feet. The canopy of trees was so thick it was as if they'd walked into a perpetual midnight. Mud sucked at their boots and spindly tree limbs grabbed their clothing. Viscous gases and gouts of gray slime erupted from the ankle-deep water.

Cross held his HK in his non-shooting hand; his right was clenched around arcane energy. His spirit twisted and crawled across his skin like a rippling liquid tide.

They closed in on the clearing. Graves and Cross moved down the middle of their formation, Kray on the left flank and Winter on the right. Snow floated just above the ground. Her spirit held her aloft as she attuned her senses to the folds between the material world, the shadows and the creases through which arcane energies flowed. Her eyes were dead white as she hovered, her hands trailed behind her. She was their tracker, and she would find what they searched for.

They went deeper. The air was thick with buzzing insects, and the taste of rot in the air was as thick as porridge. White effluvia floated in the water, and Cross glimpsed shadows all around them in the trees. His arm grew numb from holding his spirit ready for so long, but he didn't dare let her go. It was so hard to keep her in check, so physically draining to keep her harnessed and complacent that he feared if he relaxed it might take too long to make her ready her again if trouble arose, and by then it would be too late.

The clearing where the vampires had stood – a dry island amidst the ankle-deep mire – was directly ahead. Twisted trees with half-white roots where the Wormwood had sucked their life away stood at odd angles on the mound, tangled together like strings. Only Graves fully stepped onto the island while the rest gave it far berth, their eyes on the trees.

Cross couldn't see more than a few feet into the thick of the Wormwood. It was like black silk had been strung across the path in every direction. Light simply refused to penetrate those deeper folds of the dense and gnarled forest.

Graves stood on the mound of land with his Remington 870 sawed-off shotgun at the ready. Cross watched Graves and tried to read the air, but the arcane energies were so dense it was like trying to look straight into the sun.

Cross looked up at Snow. She quietly nodded towards the trees. He sensed nothing waiting there for them, but they both knew that could have been interference from the black energies of the forest, which proved adept at confounding their magical senses.

A sharp crack cut through the air. Cross heard a sick splash. Moments later Winter fell to the ground, blood pouring from an open cavity in his skull.

Razor projectiles came at them. Cross crafted a shield of air in front and barely deflected bone needles intended for he and Snow. They both dropped to the ground.

Graves was down. Cross saw a nine-inch bone nail lodged in his friend's left arm, glistening with blood. Shots rang through the trees. Cross fired into the darkness, a distraction while he held the shield and pulled in more of his spirit, focusing her raw form in his fist and holding her there, a dissolving ball of corrosive cold dripping like oil between his fingers.

"Graves?!" Cross called out.

"I'm okay."

"I think Winter is dead," Cross said after a moment.

He felt Snow's spirit as she scanned the trees for the vampires, reaching out with keen senses and probing the clearings in the dense thicket, searching for what wasn't there. Vampires gave off an entirely different energy signature than a living being: they bore no souls, but they could be located through that absence, by the void silhouette they left behind as they moved through the world. It was doubly difficult for her to find them right then, of course, thanks to the barrage of bone needles being launched at them from out of the darkness.

Cross focused his thoughts and breathed icy vapors into his sweaty palm. "Down!" he shouted. He lobbed the cold grenade into the trees, guiding it as best he could with the aid of his spirit. A wave of deathly ice licked against them even from a hundred yards ouot.

The shooting stopped. Cross looked up. Dozens of bone needles protruded from the trees like quills, dripping cold white fluid from the tips of their spines.

"Damn," Graves said. Cross moved over to him, staying low. He clamped his gauntlet around Graves's arm and channeled raw magic into his skin, hoping to burn out whatever poison or narcotic the needles had been coated with before anything spread through the bloodstream. A nervous sensation crept along the back of Cross's neck, like something was about to reach out and grab him from behind.

A rifle shot and a dull explosion sounded in the distance. Moments later they saw a cloud of white and yellow smoke deep in the shadowy murk.

"There they are," Graves said. His breaths were shallow, but Cross hoped that was because of the sudden flux of arcane energies rather than a reaction to the poison.

Cross remembered getting stung by a pair of wasps, one right after the other, when he'd been a boy; those wasps had been tainted by the energies of the Bone March. Drogan, an old warlock shaman, had spent days healing him. Cross remembered Drogan's grim and hollow eyes and the smell of ghosts on his breath.

That was the day I learned I was a warlock.

"Snow, are you okay?" Cross called out. He felt the touch of her mind, the will of the spirit circling around her like a controlled whirlwind. Snow lay on her chest, her head tucked under her arms, as if waiting for something to fall on her. She still focused on scanning the area ahead. "Snow!?"

"I'm fine," she replied.

"Kray?"

"Yeah." The big man lumbered into view. Kray hadn't had time to pull out the mini-gun so he'd drawn his sword, a heavy black-bladed saber with a cord set in the hilt and white gashes carved into the blade to display Kray's number of kills. Cross never understood that practice: he thought keeping tally of how many things you destroyed was just asking for trouble. "I thought there was something moving in the trees, but it never got closer than fifty yards." With Kray being such an enormous man, it was easy to assume he was also stupid. Far from it, Kray probably possessed the best tactical mind in the Squad besides Morg.

"Can you check Winter?" Cross asked him.

"Am I going to live, or what?" Graves snapped at him. Cross felt how clammy Graves's arm was even through the leather and cloth. "Morg and Stone are out there alone, for fuck's sake, and we need to get to them."

"Winter's gone," Kray said from the trees. "Not sure what hit him. Some kind of projectile took him in the head."

"Shit," Cross sighed. His stomach went sour. He'd known Winter a good long time. They weren't close friends, by any means, but serving with someone, being used to seeing them every day, depending on them, learning from them, talking about things that others couldn't understand, for him to suddenly be gone...

Not now, he told himself. *You don't have time for this.*

Snow sat up.

"I'm sorry," she said. She'd known Winter a long time, as well, but not as long as Cross.

"Kray," Cross said, "can you get his gear?"

"Cross?" Graves demanded. "Am I dying or not?"

"You should be fine," Cross said, and he unhanded Graves's arm and drew his spirit back into an orbit about himself. She circled uneasily, a murder of ethereal crows.

"Then let's go," Graves said, and without another word he rose, reloaded the shotgun, and set off into the trees. Kray dropped Winter's belt pouch in front of Cross and followed Graves, hacking noxious branches from his path with his oversized blade.

Cross felt a shudder in the air, and his spirit bristled. Winter's spirit had moved on, no longer tied to the physical world now that its mortal tether had been removed.

Snow came and stood next to him.

"I found Morg and Stone, and I think I found the vampires," she said. Cross looked at her. She was only barely holding herself together. Her lip trembled, and only the thick shadows and grime on her face hid the tears in her eyes. Cross wondered if he looked as scared as she did.

"Let's go, then," he said. He took the pouch, stuffed it into his coat and stood up. "They may be in trouble."

"Are you all right?" she asked, moving in his way as he made to go. Cross watched her for a moment.

What the hell are you doing here? he wondered. *What am I doing here?* He still couldn't look at Snow without seeing a little girl. He couldn't look at her without seeing his baby sister, and all he wanted to do was get her out of there, away from that vile place ...but no. No. *This is where we are. This is where we need to be.*

"I'm fine," he said, knowing she could see the lie on his face. *You have to lie*, he wanted to tell her. *You have to lie to yourself, tell yourself everything is fine, tell yourself you don't care. If you don't, you won't last a day, and that's why I have to lie to you now, even though you know I'm doing* it. "Let's go," was all he said aloud. They went deeper into the trees, towards the black noise waiting for them.

I'm not afraid, he told himself, hoping if he repeated it enough he'd eventually believe it. *I'm not afraid.*

EIGHT

CRYPT

It didn't take them long to find Morg and Stone.

Cross's frost grenade left behind a flat and icy clearing. The marsh water was covered in a film of frost, and most of the dangling tree limbs had fallen away like oversized icicles. Chunks of partially frozen meat and bits of red armor and cloth lay on the ground around the gore-spattered remains of a pale-skinned vampire torso.

"Nice shot," Graves said quietly.

"*Lucky* shot," Cross corrected.

"Yes, lucky shot," Morg said out of nowhere. His voice made both Cross and Snow jump. Morg held a M4A2, as did Stone. Stone was the second-in-command of the squad. He was just as tall as Morg but much skinnier, with thick hair and a short beard. Both of their black fatigues and armor jackets were stained with forest slime, their boots were covered in mud, and Cross noticed Stone's left hand had gashes on the knuckles.

"Are you all right?" he asked, and Stone nodded.

"Yeah. Did we sneak up on you?"

"You snuck up on *them*," Graves said with a nod toward the mages.

"Winter?" Morg asked quietly. Graves shook his head, and Morg nodded. "Any other trouble?"

"Just the Shadowclaws. Snow is tracking them now."

"Don't bother, we know where they are," Morg said. "There's a structure half a klick to the west. The Suckheads went that way."

"How many?" Graves asked. Kray helped him bandage his wound now that Cross had leeched away the poison. Graves didn't seem too bothered by the fact that a needle had pushed all of the way through his arm.

"Two Creeds," Stone said.

"Wow," Graves said with a shake of his head. Cross smelled Graves's strange and sharp-flavored organic chewing tobacco. He wished he had a cigarillo.

"We may not be properly equipped to deal with that many vampires," Cross said, and while Kray nodded and Snow's eyes grew wide he got the response he expected from the others.

"Are you scared?" Stone smiled. Morgan and Graves just laughed and started towards the structure.

The Wormwood was a graveyard. Long-moldered tree limbs sank in the black churn. Piles of bones lay in the dark silt and creamy mud. The squad saw corner-block foundations to old buildings covered with moss, weeds and slime. Vines crept up from the dismal waters. Statues, street signs and mailboxes stood half-out of the mud. Cross saw the remains of a car covered with fungus and overgrowth and bits of a street that had been swallowed up by the forest. The entire Wormwood smelled like an old garbage can or the inside of a stomach.

The silence was unnerving. Cross didn't hear so much as a mosquito. There was nothing alive in the Wormwood – nothing natural, at least – and all they heard as they slowly trudged through the murk was the sound of their own boots sinking and pulling out of the briny black sewage.

Snow floated just above the ground. Morg, Stone, Graves and Kray walked a defensive perimeter around she and Cross. Cross initially objected, but Morg insisted both mages stay protected, especially since Cross was now the lone warlock in the party. Guns and alchemy bombs would carry them for a while, but without arcane spirits on their side humans wouldn't have lasted more than a few years against the vampires, and less than that against more powerful enemies like the Sorn.

Cross's stomach was going haywire. He'd been in areas and situations like this before – the worst had been the catacombs beneath Glaive – but the stakes had never been this high.

And you've never had to worry about whether or not your sister was going to make it out alive.

Cross had once met the woman they now hunted face to face. Red, they called her, but her real name was Margrave Azazeth. She'd been a hero, one of the most powerful witches who ever lived, and after she'd achieved a role of leadership she'd helped lead humankind into a new age, an era of survival. She'd been the voice of the White Mother, the champion of Thornn.

And now she's turned on us. She's stolen something, something vital, and we have to stop her from giving it to the Old One.

And so there they were, ankle-deep in sludge, their senior member dead, all of them intent on killing a woman who not long before had been considered one of the best and brightest of the Southern Claw. Cross thought back to his youth – he'd been doing that a lot lately, in spite of himself – and he remembered chasing his mother after she'd run away, when she'd been unable to deal with the reality that her son had supernatural powers. Snow had been an infant then, not old enough to understand why Mommy had lost her mind, or how she and her big brother would be treated like dangerous animals for the rest of their lives.

"There," Stone said. He was soft spoken for such a tall man. The squad was fast and quiet and carried themselves with the precision of hunter cats.

I'm not one of them, Cross thought. *I'm not a soldier. I'm just a weapon. All of us are, me and Snow and Winter and Chalmers and Cala. They're afraid of us.* I'm *afraid of us.*

Stone nodded at a well camouflaged stone structure Cross would have looked right past if it hadn't been pointed out to him. The stone building was covered with so much moss it looked like a massive tree stump. Cross thought it might have once stood taller and been some sort of obelisk or pillar, but the upper sections had long since toppled into the swamp. The ruin stood on the shore of a small island maybe forty feet across out in the center of a shallow and murky lake. Twisted branches and bubbles of oil and grease floated along the surface.

Bits of the stone were visible through the moss, sections of a fallen monolith covered with images of angels and eyes. A twisted metal gate had been ripped from the main door, and as they drew close Cross realized the structure was the partially crushed remains of a mausoleum. A film of dark slime rendered the crypt nearly invisible, and the roof had partially collapsed. There was no sign of what might have crushed the structure, but Cross got the eerie impression something massive had stepped on it.

"Yes," Snow confirmed quietly. Her voice took on a hollow quality. It wasn't really her, but her spirit speaking through her, using her as a medium, even though Snow was the one really in control. She used her spirit to analyze the dweomer lines and read between the reality folds as she searched for the absence, the void that would tell them if undead were there. She pointed at the building.

"The Suckheads are there?" Kray asked grimly.

"We saw them heading toward it," Stone said. He slung his rifle over his back and drew a 9mm Beretta with dragons carved into the hilt.

"What about *her*?" Cross asked. He and Stone both looked back at Snow.

"What about Red?" Graves repeated.

Snow hovered in place. Cross found the effect of his sister levitating just inches over the face of the marsh unnerving. Only witches could do it. She floated there, her head held back, her back arched, her eyes blank and staring not at the physical world but at some striated arcane patterns and whorls only she could see. In that state, grasped in the cold embrace of her spirit, she only saw what he showed her, or chose to show her. The notion that a spirit might actually be in control, and that a witch or a warlock was at their mercy, was very frightening to apprentice mages.

Snow was lost in concentration. Everyone rechecked their weapons and looked ready to move on, regardless of what Snow had to say, when at last she spoke.

"Yes. Oh my God, I can sense her – she's inside!"

"Move," Morg said. They converged on the mausoleum.

The squad was forced to move slowly through the murky water, and soon they were waist deep in warm slime. A broken staircase made of ancient and crumbling stone was barely visible through the gaps in the collapsing outer shell of the structure. Cross's blood went cold at the thought of where those stairs might lead.

"How did something like that even get here?" Graves asked quietly.

"It was here before the forest was, genius," Kray growled, his sword at the ready. He was the soldier closest to Snow, and Cross knew he'd protect her with his life. Truth be told Cross figured Kray was a better choice to protect her than he himself was. "The forest came later. It buried whatever was here first. Everyone knows that."

"Wow, Kray knew something I didn't," Graves smiled. "That officially makes me the dumbest man on the planet…"

"Yes, it does," Morg growled, with a tone that made his mood clear. "Keep talking and we're *all* dead." Morg glowered at them all for a moment, then took up his spear and carried on.

"Kray's wrong," Cross whispered as he drew close to Graves. "It came later."

"What?"

"'What' what?"

"'What what', as in 'What the hell are you talking about'?" Graves hissed.

"The crypt, moron," Cross laughed. "Things shifted when The Black came. This crypt was probably somewhere else, and it transported here when everything went crazy."

"Why? Just…randomly?"

"Maybe. Sometimes it was random. Sometimes it wasn't. The Black was sentient…it had reasons for some of the things it did. It had a purpose."

They were almost to the crypt. Cross fell back to survey the area ahead with his readied spirit. Edged whispers and static moans echoed through the back of his mind, and the skin on his arms and neck bristled at the touch of an electric cold. Snow was the one capable of tracking their prey, but Cross would be the first to know if anything magical waited for them in their immediate surrounding area, whether a weapon or some sort of trap. He walked on edge through dank waters which had soaked his heavy boots. Cross didn't want to think about what sort of filth floated in the warm and briny fluids.

Snow floated behind Cross and Kray took up the rear, where he watched for any sign of trouble coming from behind. Morg and Stone entered the crypt up ahead, confident Cross would warn them of danger, while Graves stayed at the middle and kept everyone in sight. Cross's skin was icy with anticipation.

He finally came to the small island, which was soft and thick with mud and collapsing soil. The earth was black and seemed to have once been part of a larger mass that had been swallowed up by the swamp. A lair of smooth black stones was just under the surface of the soil. Ancient bones, cracked with age, lay nestled between the rocks. The land sloped steeply upwards, and the ground grew more solid as it rose towards the apex of the hill where the mausoleum waited, slumped and sinking. Shadows oozed and leaked from the stone like dark steam.

Cross felt something pull at his thoughts, a hint of danger swirling around his mind like a nagging fly. He looked around – everything was spinning, like he'd been thrown to the center of an out-of-control merry-go-round – and the whispers filled his head with such force they clouded his eyes and made his gums ache.

He glanced back at Snow. Her eyes were solid white because she was using her magic, but they suddenly went wide with shock. Kray seemed to notice something was wrong, and he spun and looked at the line of trees and the waters of the murky lake, which seemed suddenly bigger and deeper than it had just moments before.

"Ambush!" Cross yelled, but not in time. Shadows erupted from the water and trees.

Horrid figures came at them, ebon flesh and wild hair, leathery bodies covered in pores and cracks. Stark white eyes and claws shone in the dim light. Long serpentine tongues lapped against razor fangs. White veins bulged from dark skin.

They weren't vampires but Chul, denizens of the Wormwood, corrupted souls trapped in the bodies of shadowy and murderous zombies.

Smoking claws lashed out at Snow, but Kray leapt in the way and pushed her floating body onto the isle. He decapitated a Chul with a single stroke of his blade, splattering black blood everywhere.

Cries cut through the trees in a unified squelch of skin and sound, a high-pitched animal call like a chorus of metal. Cross saw at least a dozen Chul emerge from the darkness. His spirit coalesced into a mass of electric liquid across his arms and fingertips. He released her in a fluid motion. Daggers of ice-blue light exploded from his hands like chill meteors. Tendrils of frost laced his fingers and burned the flesh beneath his smoking gauntlets. Orbs of electric cold burrowed perforated zombie bodies with razor shards of ice and gouts of cold blue flame. Black torsos exploded into chunks of dripping matter.

Snow screamed, fell on her back and crawled away from the carnage. Cross could barely catch his breath. His spirit still held him as if impassioned, stuck to his skin like lover's sweat. Cross had hit nearly every Chul in sight, but some of them still pushed forward, their bodies dissolving from the inside out as icy energy spread through their unnatural forms. The smell of entrails was thick. Kray hacked falling creatures apart as he backed onto the shore. Gunfire blasted an uninjured Chul, spattering its misshapen skull.

Cross grabbed Snow by the arm and helped her to her feet. Graves, Stone and Morg mowed ebon bodies down beneath a ruthless barrage of gunfire. Smoke and ear-shattering noise filled the air. Cross kept his spirit at hand and held onto Snow's arms.

The shooting stopped at last, and the Wormwood was silent once more. Oozing bodies sagged and deflated in the water and on the edge of the shore, and black ichors poured out of punctured meat sacks. Fumes rose from the dead and mingled with the other poisons of the forest.

"So much for surprising anyone," Graves said as he reloaded his Remington.

Cross quickly checked Kray, and after he confirmed that the big man was uninjured both Morg and Stone returned to the mausoleum, their eyes on the stairs.

"There's no way they didn't hear that," Stone said quietly.

"They already know we're here, anyhow," Morg said softly. He took a cloth out of his pocket and cleaned off the tip of his spear, a serrated silver blade with runic carvings of elfin maidens armed with swords. Morg stripped down to a flak vest, which left his arms bare and displayed the intricate serpent tattoos on his dark rippled muscles. He wore an iron band on his right wrist and a strip of Kevlar and steel armor around his left elbow. Cross knew he lived for this, the fighting, the struggle. He'd been a gladiator once, they said, forced to fight for the amusement of the vampire aristocracy in the city-state of Krul. "Are you ready?"

It took Cross a moment to realize Morg was talking to he and Snow. Cross hesitated. He was shaken from keeping his spirit on edge for so long (she was still there, poised, hovering around him like a deadly and erotic pet). The stress of having just detonated explosive ice bombs inside a dozen zombies had both he and his spirit coiled and tense. Snow's eyes, in the meantime, were wide with shock, and Cross sensed the anxious emanations of her spirit, confused by what it saw and felt. The spirit was bonded to the soul – one reflected the other. What one felt, the other felt. If one suffered, the other suffered.

You're too young, Cross wanted to tell her. *You have to leave. You don't belong here.*

"I'm ready," Snow said with a stoic nod. Cross glanced sideways at her for a moment, but she wouldn't meet his eyes. She hadn't wiped away the black blood that landed on her from the exploding Chul bodies. The tattoos on her neck dully pulsed with power, the foci for her harnessed spirit.

No one else seemed to notice the depth of her apprehension, and if they did no one chose to say anything about it.

They moved down the steep steps and into the moldy darkness of the crypt. Dank weeds and twisted roots covered with black soil hung across the narrow hole of an entrance, which descended into near darkness. The steps were smooth and shallow, wide but unstable. The air smelled of mildew and age, and they had to light Kray's lamp to see.

Stone was the first to descend, his M4 in hand, followed tightly by others in single file. Kray brought up the rear; the big man was barely able to squeeze down the cramped opening. Dirt and soil fell in occasional drifts from between solid blocks of aged and crumbling stone. The cramped quarters reminded Cross again of his childhood, of crawling around in the air ducts of old buildings, dodging vampires and waiting for help.

Why do I keep thinking about my childhood? Keep your head straight, Eric, or it's going to get torn off.

Cross wasn't sure how far they'd gone until they hit the bottom, when his feet awkwardly found solid ground. Kray's lamp illuminated the area ahead, and it all but negated any chance of their gaining surprise.

Still, I guess it beats falling down the shaft.

He turned and helped Snow down the last step by taking her waif-like waist in his hands. (She gave him a look. He scowled at her, in the way that brothers do.)

They'd descended into a round and empty room with a floor covered in white dust and shattered old pots. Strange emblems adorned the curved walls of the dome-shaped chamber – lightning bolts and bats, eyes and mouths, jackals and teeth.

"What the Hell is this?" Stone said under his breath.

"I hear you," Morg whispered.

"Okay," Graves said as he did a quick turn. "When did we arrive in ancient Egypt? Or is this some of that trans-locative substantiation, or whatever the hell you call it?"

"Tran-substantive locationism," Cross corrected. "And the answer is 'no'."

"Gosh, thanks," Graves said.

"What is this place?" Morg asked him, but it was Snow who answered.

"A crypt, just like it looks. The vampires worship very old deities." She spoke with confidence and poise. Cross knew she was faking it, but he was glad she'd decided to make her presence known.

"Can you still track down here?" Morg asked pointedly.

"Of course." Snow didn't falter a moment.

"Then get to it."

There were three small alcoves in the room, each with a curved door that had to be opened by pressing a stone trigger on the wall next to it. The triggers were cleverly hidden, and it took Snow some time to get a good reading due to the interference created by the stone, which had been built with trans-substantive dampening properties to prevent anyone from using magic to gain access to the inside of the crypt. The only way in was to use the physical entrance.

Talk about being overprotective, Cross thought. *Humans have never been able to teleport. I wonder if this place was safeguarded against other vampires. But who would build a crypt to guard against other vampires?*

Cross looked at the walls, and up the hole.

Better yet...

"I wonder who's buried here," he said quietly.

"What?" Stone asked.

"This is a crypt, right?" Cross said. "Who's buried here? Or what?"

"Who cares?" Stone said. Stone was an intimidating man, not so much from his impressive physical demeanor – his chiseled and dark skin had its share of scars and tattoos, he had an angular face, big eyes and a lean, quick frame – but because of his manner. Stone was generally quiet, and he chose his words carefully. He preferred to kill quickly and from a distance, and he rarely fraternized for any reason.

"*You* should," Cross said. "We all should. It might be useful to know why Red came down here."

"I think it's a bit late to worry about that now," Stone said.

"Which way?" Morg asked Snow.

"That way." She indicated the middle door. Her blank eyes stared ahead. "Margrave...Red...went that way."

Stone took the point, and when he pulled open the door Cross felt a charnel presence, a corrupted arcane energy signature he recognized from his experience in the field.

"There's Crujian technology in there," he said, aware that his own eyes were glowing now, set alight by his spirit. "It's probably coming from suits of hexed combat armor." He focused. "There are at least four vampires waiting for us there. Maybe more."

"This door has been opened recently," Graves said. "It used to be sealed up tight."

"All right, then," Morg said. "Look sharp."

Stone took a breath, and stepped through the door.

NINE

HOLE

The squad stepped into a wide dark corridor. They were under the shallow lake, in an open catacomb of rust-colored rock, broken iron machines and dank sarcophagi covered with mold and mildew. Thick green fluid dripped from the ceiling. The air was cloying and rich. Shallow streams of stagnant water flowed between rows of open stone coffins. Narrow planks of rusted steel bridged the symmetrical isles of the dead.

The water reflected the orange-yellow glow of Kray's lamp and turned the air hazy. Crumbling pillars of steel and mortar and clusters of rotted pipe supported the high-vaulted ceiling.

"Wow," Graves muttered. "Big place."

"Thank you for that, Detective," Kray smiled.

"Zip it," Morg said. Their voices echoed and faded into the distance. There were no easily discernible borders to the chamber – Cross saw a dozen or so stone islands and their resident coffins, but no walls were visible except for the one behind them. The room might have stretched on for miles. "Anything?" Morg asked the mages.

Cross paused and caught his breath. Snow was practically a statue beside him.

Just hang in there. We'll be ok. I don't know how we're not damn it I can't I'm going to lose her down here and I'll be all alone but we're going to be ok.

"Damn," he muttered. "Nothing."

"Nothing?" Graves asked, his tone considerably more exasperated than what Cross was used to. "How the hell...?"

"They're *here*," Snow said quietly. "But there's a lot of old magic here, too. It's interfering with our sight. Our spirits can't find them."

"And there's not much we can do about it," Cross added.

"Spread out," Morg said. "Stone, Cross and Graves take the right side; Snow and Kray with me. Everyone keep your eyes open."

Cross looked at Snow worriedly. He chanced a glance at Morg, who gave him a stern nod.

You can't stay with her. If the groups need to split, the mages have to be separated. If anything happens to one group and both mages fall, the whole squad is screwed.

But still...regardless of logic, or circumstance, or anything else, Cross didn't like the thought of being separated from Snow. Not down there. It felt like throwing her to the wolves.

No. She'll be with Morg and Kray. She'll be safer than you'll be.

He took her aside.

"Are you okay?" he asked her. Cross wasn't sure if the two groups would even be out of sight of one another, but that place seemed vast, and it would be easy to get lost in the murk.

"I can take care of myself, Eric," she said. "Thank you," she added after a moment.

Cross looked at her. It was hard for him to believe she was grown up. He could lose her here. He took in the sight of her, and he saw her face fade, a mask concealing her younger self, wide-eyed and curious, pretty and insightful whatever her age, he watched her grow, watched the years pass, saw her spirit swirl in and cover her in a shroud as she left that old world, that old self, the young girl who liked to drag hand-made dolls and throw stones into the sea and who used to just stand next to him, close against his warmth for hours without speaking, and she was replaced by this older girl, this beautiful, powerful, dazzling stranger he'd distanced himself from without ever even meaning to.

I don't know you like I used to, he wanted to tell her. *And I'm sorry for that. I'm so sorry.*

"All right," was all he said, and he nodded. "Be careful."

You're all I have left.

She hugged him, and he hugged her back.

"I love you," she said.

The groups separated.

Stone had a flare to light their way, and he led Cross and Graves along the eastern wall. They walked through waterfalls of soot. Shadows twisted like writhing worms in the cracks and crevices.

The room went on and on, unnaturally dark and vast. The layout remained the same no matter how deep they went – open sarcophagi stood on grid-like stone islands spaced apart by streams of stagnant water. The general state of disrepair was more apparent the deeper they went, just as the walkways, which were only wide enough for them to move single-file, became more cracked and less stable.

No one spoke. Stone led the way. Cross was right behind him and Graves brought up the rear, all with weapons drawn. Cross's HK45 felt heavy in his hand, but when he allowed his spirit to crawl across his skin it grew lighter, as her arcane energy infused the firing mechanism and shrouded the loaded bullets with deadly ballistic energies.

Cross's senses were on fire. Every sound seemed to stretch out and last longer than it should have. Drops of dead water fell from the black ceiling. His stomach was knotted so tight it was a wonder he hadn't folded in on himself. Despite how wide and spacious the chamber was Cross was seized by a sharp claustrophobic terror, like he was covered in grit, like he'd fallen into the bottom of a deep hole.

Get a hold of yourself. If you lose it down here, you're done.

Cross looked back. He could only barely make out the silhouettes of the other team, about a hundred yards away. Kray's lantern was as dim as a dying firefly.

"Look," Stone said quietly.

They came to the end of the main room and stood before an open doorway leading into a round and dirty chamber built from thick stone blocks. The inside of the room looked like an igloo of black ice. Glacial rock let off subtle tendrils of steam. Cross saw his breath in the air.

There was a hole in the middle of the floor, pitch black and barely big enough around for a child to squeeze through. Something emanated from the hole, a presence, something vast and old. The moldered essence of centuries oozed from that pit. As he looked into the hole, Cross felt the pull of death. It pulled not only on him but on his spirit, and it tried to tease her away, to lull her, seduce her.

"What the Hell is that?" Graves whispered.

"Don't go near it," Cross said. His own voice sounded cracked. He tried to coax his spirit to investigate the hole, to reach into the invisible lines of fey consciousness to catch a glimpse of what lay beneath, but she wouldn't. She knew as well as he that if they went in, they wouldn't come out.

"It's a trap," Cross managed. "It's a trap for spirits. It's guarding something, but its defense is to seduce your spirit into the hole." Cross felt grave dust in his lungs.

"I don't have a spirit," Graves said. "Would it affect a non-mage the same as you?"

"I'm not sure. I don't think so."

"I'll contact Morg," Stone said. He took the signal stone from the leather cord wrapped around his wrist. "Let him know we found something."

Gunfire erupted far away. Kray yelled out. Cross saw flashes of light. The darkness separating the teams was suddenly a pitch black ocean. There were more shot. They heard the insanely fast fire of the mini-gun. Growls and the sound of blades. Snow screamed.

"Go!" Stone shouted. He and Graves ran onto the walkway and traversed the unstable channels, moving past streams and around open coffins.

Cross heard something behind him – more importantly, he *felt* something, and his spirit did, too. Their focus fused and honed in on the darkness. Cross turned around.

Something crawled out of the hole. It had small and thin human hands, a woman's hands, Cross thought. A head poked out, white-eyed and dismal, covered in dirt and black clay. Long nails painted black dug into the soil and pulled up a body caked with mud. It was a female form, full-figured, grotesque because of the effluvia and blood and corrupted earth clinging to it. She looked like a doll shaped from idiot hands. The figure emerged from the hole and rose to her feet before Cross could react. Her eyes stuck on him, and her mouth opened to breathe out a cloud of crimson steam.

Red.

Cross's spirit attacked. Eldritch sparks erupted from his fingers. His spirit took the form of a spear made of ice and flame. Cross fired glowing arrow-heads at the fugitive, Red, the Traitor of Thornn. The witch was alarmed for a moment, but then calmly, as if time slowed for her, she put her palms together and split Cross's arcane fire into harmless wisps of steam. Her eyes were pale red, like glowing blood coals.

His spirit screamed, and Cross screamed with her, taken in by her rage and fear. Black smoke curled off his skin as his spirit flared into a maelstrom around his body. Eldritch armor of living shadow surrounded him. Black lightning crackled from his hands, smoldered his flesh and darkened his eyes like burning bulbs.

Rage overtook him. His spirit screamed like hollow thunder. Red met him in kind. Howls of male pain screamed away from her outstretched hands, and the air between the two mages exploded in a storm of red fire and white noise.

Cross pulled shaped earth into a lance, and he tried to impale Red but her spirit split the attack while Red sent razors of sound. Cross's spirit burned the projectiles away with ghostly fire.

Red raced across the room like she glided on ice. She made for the entrance, towards the sounds of gunfire and pain. Cross ran after her. His spirit's emotions made his blood boil. In the heat of battle it was easy to forget which of them was in control.

Cross kept Red in sight, but his eyes hovered to the fighting. He hesitated.

The vampires were Shadowclaws, just as Graves had guessed – Ebon Cities' elite. They wore blood-red armor made of leather and chain, thick capes and dark masks hiding pale faces. Pitch black hair was tied or slicked back, and they were all male, tall and thin and agile and quick. Their weapons and claws were as black as the room. They seemed to melt into the murk and shadow.

Bodies flailed and clawed at one another. Gunfire flared white in the darkness and blades ground through bodies. Cross made little of it out clearly – the melee was chaotic and fast, swords and bones and guns and shouts.

Snow floated out of the thick of the fray with razors of light balanced around her outstretched hands. Her body was covered in a glowing corona of white flame. One of the vampires grabbed her by the ankle, and although the contact scorched the beast it held on and violently pulled her to the ground.

"No!" Cross shouted. He ran over the walkways and jumped over the streams, through the maze of coffins and pillars. Cross's spirit tore chunks of granite away from the walls and hurled them at the vampire. The undead brute still didn't let go.

Another vampire dropped down on top of Cross from the ceiling. They collapsed in a heap. Cross landed on his back, and only his spirit's shield saved his life. His legs were in the water, and he quickly felt himself sinking, held up by his attacker's claws where they gripped his coat. The vampire loomed over him. Its mask was gone, so its oversized mouth and massive fangs hovered inches away from Cross's face. White spittle and grave breath washed over him.

Cross instinctively threw his gauntlets out in front of his body and sent waves of black heat into the vampire's body. It pulled back, if only in surprise. A bullet tore the vampire's skull in two as it rose, throwing its body sideways. Cross pulled out of the freezing black water.

Morg dropped the Ruger Alaskan he'd used to save Cross, spun around and deflect a vampire's blade with his spear. The sounds of fighting echoed loud through the dark.

Cross struggled to his feet and found Snow. The burning vampire still gripped her ankle and held on in spite of the fire covering most of its body. Cross's spirit transformed to a wedge of razor-sharp ice, which he launched like a spear and watched as it took off the vampire's arm at the elbow; the hand clung to Snow a moment longer before it burned away like scorched paper.

His eyes felt heavy. The act of channeling and holding his spirit for so long had drained his strength. Fatigue rushed over him in a wave. He nearly slipped in the pools of blood and dark water.

The burning vampire came at him. Cross thought it had been destroyed, but even though the immolated undead smoldered with white fire it ran right at him, its one arm outstretched and its oversized reptilian mouth wide with hunger. Claws the size of knives raked across the stone. Cross tripped on something and fell onto his back.

He sent a pillar of fire and stone into the brute's body, but it just shoved its way through. It was easily the largest vampire he'd ever seen, seven-feet at the shoulder and as broad as an ape. Its knotted undead muscles pulsed with grave ooze, and cracked sinew tensed with incredible strength. It drew close, eyes drawn tight and grotesque maw open and hungry.

Graves threw himself into the brute with an armored shoulder and swiped at it with his machete. Cross seized the opportunity and sprang to his feet. The vampire backhanded Graves and sent him flying. Cross cried out and released a three-foot-wide blast of fire into the vampire's chest that pushed straight through its rotted skin.

Something struck Cross from behind. He heard something crack. The flames stopped as he tumbled forward. His spirit absorbed the force of what should have been a killing blow, but in so doing she nearly destroyed herself.

Cross lay there, barely able to move. Blood and sweat ran into his eyes.

Morg dodged a blow from the vampire giant, and in the same fluid motion swung his spear in a wide arc and cleaved open another vampire's skull. Chunks of white bone and flesh flew through the air. The giant took Morg in its grip and locked his arms back. As big as Morg was, the vampire was bigger, but Morg kicked backward and down and snapped the giant's knee-bone backwards, buckling its weight and forcing it to the ground. Still it fought, its giant mouth wide, its arms out. Morg had been disarmed.

A blade of red light took the vampire giant in the back of the head. The brute looked up and stupidly regarded the weapon that had pushed through its forehead from the back of its skull. Its arms went slack, and it fell forward in a thunderous heap.

Snow stood with a blade of purple and white energy fixed to her gauntlet. The force of her spirit swirled around her like a cloud of crystalline dust. Her eyes were fixed and blank.

Cross heard and then saw Stone, but he didn't see Kray or Graves. He slowly and painfully sat up. Blood streamed down the side of his head and the back of his neck, cold as it ran down under the back of his armored coat. His left arm was numb. If not for his spirit he knew he'd be dead. He felt her there, lingering, weakened from having saved him from a pair of blows that should have ended his life.

Stone and a vampire fought near a mound of bodies and splayed limbs. The floor was littered with blades and shattered claws and heaps of humanoid remains. Graves lay on the ground in a crumpled heap.

"Sam..." Cross said. Morg ignored him, his eyes locked on something. Cross followed his gaze.

Red was still there. She'd been blocked off from the exit by another Shadowclaw Creed, pale-skinned and red-armored vampires armed with saw blades and automatic weapons. She'd already dealt with them: their bodies hung from the wall, stuck there by arcane bolts of black force, spikes made of grey ice and blades wrought of translucent amber. The sheer force of Red's spirit cascaded around her, a chaotic cloak, a shroud of male arcane fumes burning like an explosive rainbow.

Morg didn't hesitate. Surprisingly, neither did Snow. The bloodlust was on both she and her spirit.

Cross struggled to rise. He felt a sharp pain in his side, maybe a cracked rib. He reached out with his mind and breathed, tried to lasso in his spirit. She was there, barely, a fade of her normal self.

Snow shouted as her spirit launched at Red in a cyclone of shrapnel. Morg followed Snow's attack like a charioteer behind his steeds. He held a serrated broadsword in his hands and moved like a human train, tearing across the rubble-and-blood spattered ground.

Cross wasn't able to call up his ailing spirit, but suddenly he remembered his HK45, which had somehow found its way back into his unsteady hand.

Snow's attack dissipated before it reached Red. The Witch's spirit met the assault with a shimmering wall of prismatic rain and chewed through Snow's magic like acid through paper.

Morg barreled his way through the chaos, howling with fury. Cross fired his pistol. The shot took Red in the meat of her shoulder and pushed her back.

Red was a blur of motion. She spun with the shot, turned full circle, and lashed out with a violet wave of liquid fan. Cross called up every last shred of his spirit's power. He felt her scream, felt her energy fail, but he willed Snow to do the same. Static explosions of sound filled his mind. His stomach tightened as he was torn inside out.

He sees his spirit at the edge of a cold black mountain, a young girl seated near a stream. She hides in mists of silver silk. He sees bodies fall from the pale sky. Black unicorns covered in grime and gore hunt her across the nightmare landscape, ready to rend her to pieces.

Cross tried to focus, tried to pull himself away from the sight of his dying spirit, but pain and blackness overcame him.

TEN
LOST

Cross woke some time later.

Morg was dead. His body was so covered with wounds it was almost impossible to identify him. He was a bloody road map.

Kray was dead, too, impaled on a vampire's spiked spear.

Cross felt little. He should have felt more, and he knew it. They'd been like brothers without being friends. He'd known both of them long enough that the notion of them being dead somehow seemed unreal. He tried to call up memories of them, specific events or conversations, but he couldn't. They were dead and gone, and part of him had already excised them from his mind.

Stone and Graves, on the other hand, were alive. Graves was injured, but thankfully his wounds were superficial. He was battered and bruised from being thrown across the room by the giant vampire, but aside from some sore bones and numerous cuts and scrapes he'd gotten off lucky. Graves took Morg's armored elbow brace and wore it on his right arm to secure where he felt he'd bruised the bone, but all he really needed was rest and medical attention. Rest would have to wait, but once they got back to the airship they'd have access to more supplies.

Cross wasn't much better off himself. He was fairly certain his ribs had been bruised – one or two might have even been cracked – and his head felt like glass had been shoved into his brain. He was dizzy and weak, but only part of that was from his wounds.

Where are you? Why can't I feel you?

He tried to focus on something else.

The vampires, thankfully, had been vanquished, but Red was gone. And so was Snow.

Cross didn't want to imagine what Red was doing to his sister. He tried to shut it out, to dispel any thought of it, but he couldn't. He shook with rage and fear.

They pulled Morg's and Kray's bodies aside. Stone decapitated the bodies to prevent reanimation, and they'd leave the corpses there in the catacombs. Graves, Stone and Cross huddled together around a makeshift campfire they built from shattered wood and old rags they lit with holy oils. The fact that they rested at the charnel scene of a battle, with the gory remains of butchered vampires all around them, didn't seem to bother them, and Cross tried to figure out when he'd become like that.

"So what happens now?" Graves asked.

Cross wouldn't consider the possibility his sister might be dead. He tried not to think about it all, just as he tried not to call up memories of her, to dwell on what a horrible brother he'd been the past few years. If he thought about anything aside from just getting her back, he knew he'd fall apart.

Tears welled in his eyes. Cross did everything he could to focus them into intent.

Just go and get her.

"We continue the mission," Cross said.

"Say what?" Stone said. "Our tracker is gone. Can *you* track them?"

Cross hesitated.

"No. I'm...not even sure I can use magic." He looked at them. "I think my spirit might be gone."

Graves and Stone looked at each other. Cross knew neither of them really understood what that meant. It was difficult for anyone who wasn't a witch or a warlock to fully comprehend. A spirit was tied to the soul – it was an inexorable part of a mage, intangible and distant, but at the same time as close as one's own skin, as intimate as the most personal thought. Only human warlocks and witches could willingly contact and bond with their spirits. When they did, the result was magic.

"How...how is that possible?" Graves asked.

"I'm not sure if she's really gone," Cross said, his head low. "I can't feel her. She's been at the edge of my thoughts for most of my life, and

for the first time for as long as I can remember she's just...not there."
He shuddered. "I think it happened when she saved me from that head
wound."

"*Morg* saved you," Stone said, and he stood up. "And now he's dead,
and not only can you not track that bitch, but you're useless to us."

"Hey, back off," Graves said to Stone. He stood a full head shorter
than the other man, but it was clear he didn't care. "Cross knows more
about magic than you and me combined. He's far from useless."
Graves looked down. "Besides, his sister..."

"Is just fine," Cross said quietly. His chest ached, and his breaths
were ragged and dry. "And we're going to go get her." He looked at
Graves, then at Stone. "Let me rephrase that. *I'm* going to go get her.
It would be nice to have some help."

Stone hesitated, but after a moment he shrugged.

"Fine," he said. "But if we can't track them, then what the hell are
we supposed to do? We were sent to find and kill Red before she makes
it to the Old One. If we can't do that, we're *all* screwed."

Graves looked down. The longer they sat there, the worse the stink
in the room became. Cross stared at the floor and recalled the grave soil
stench, the measureless sense of age, the sheer dismal draw he'd felt
when Red had first emerged from the pit.

What were you doing down there?

"The hole," he said aloud. He stumbled to his feet.

The room with the hole was silent and still. Cross felt nothing,
further proof his spirit was gone, maybe permanently. The realization
made him shake where he stood...but it also meant he could approach
the hole now that he didn't have a spirit who was vulnerable to its
attacks.

He heard nothing, felt nothing. Whatever horror protected the pit, it
had little interest in him now.

Graves and Stone were right behind him.

"I'm not sure how Red managed it," Cross said. "Maybe some of
those algorithms we found on the map back in Thornn, the parts I
couldn't piece together, were part of some arcane shield she used to
protect her spirit or something."

"Are you nuts?" Graves asked. "You told us not to go in there."

"Cross," Stone added. "This is *not* a good idea."

Cross calmly came to the lip of the hole. It looked like the heart of midnight. The perimeter was smooth black mud crawling with worms. Ancient and knotted roots twisted up from the rim of the pit like gnarled arms. He smelled decay and cold heat. Even without his spirit to guide him, Cross sensed something wrong, something ancient and deep.

"You can't be serious..." Graves said, but Cross removed his pack and put it down, pulled off his gauntlets and set all of his gear aside. Then he removed his coat – his ribcage winced from the effort – so he was down to just his shirt, pants and his boots.

"Cross," Stone said sternly. He was in command now. It was easy to forget Morg was gone. "What in the hell do you think you're doing?"

"Going down there," he said. "We don't know who or what was buried here. We don't know what this place is...not really. Red came here for a reason. Maybe there's some clue as to what she's up to." He looked back at the pit. "Down there."

"We know what she's up to," Stone said. He moved as if to stop Cross. "She's going to give the Old One vital information and royally fuck the human race."

"Which is exactly why I need to go down there," Cross said. Stone watched him. He knew as well as Cross no one knew how to find Koth, the Old One's city. That necropolis of outcasts had managed to stay hidden from both the Southern Claw and the Ebon Cities for over a decade.

"We don't have much else we can do," Cross said. "My sister is gone. We have no way of tracking Red without her, and I'll be damned if I'm not going after her. We have to find out where she's going. I don't know if the answer is down there or not, but I have to try *something*." He heard his own voice crack with desperation.

"Stone," Graves said. "He's right. We have to carry on. If you have any better ideas...I sure don't. Maybe we need to let Eric do this."

"Damn it," Stone said after a long pause. "Do you know what you're doing?"

"No," Cross said matter-of-factly. "Not really."

They secured a rope around his waist and made sure it was tight. Cross rubbed hexed salt and blood milk ointments on his face, hands and arms in order to protect his skin from any poisonous maladies or arcane diseases in the blood-stained soil.

Finally, reluctantly, they lowered him down.

Descending into the hole felt like passing through a fleshy membrane. Rank and moist earth swallowed Cross and collapsed in on him the moment he sank beneath the level of the floor. Grime spilled all over his face, into his nostrils, hair and eyes. He breathed rot and effluvia, and felt his blood run cold. Just like before, when he'd first glimpsed at the hole, he was drawn down. He felt himself wanting to sink deeper, to melt into the folds of the earth, never to pull back, down, safe, forever in that grave...

But without his spirit, the pull was weaker than it had been before. It wasn't meant for him, or for humans at all, but for their spirits, and whatever malign intelligence had created the hole had intended to trap those arcane intelligences, not their human companions. Again he wondered how Red had managed it.

Cross held his breath and let his body sink into the rotting fold.

He sees the maidens beneath the shadow of the mountain. Four women wait in the silver shadows of a vast black precipice. Thick rain and leaves blow through the glade.

The unicorns stalk them through the smoldering trees. Horns glisten with acid and oil. Eyes are dark pits of malicious intent.

He sees the city beyond the hills, a metropolis of black steel and vast furnaces, arcane towers and reflective metal rivers. Soldiers march from it, bound for a dismal end on a dismal field. Dark rain falls as they leave a city caught in the tall shadows of grim monuments.

He sees the battle, the war against pale things from the dark. He sees a prison without walls. He sees the church, and the sacrifice.

Cross fell into a perfectly round and smooth sphere of a room carved from black rock. It was barely large enough for him to kneel in. The air was warm and smelled surprisingly sweet. Cross was covered in filth, and he wiped grime and bits of bone from his eyes. Faint glistening smoke filled the air, which smelled vaguely of hashish.

He looked around and realized he'd found some sort of meditation chamber, a sage's retreat. Hundreds upon hundreds of runes had been written with white chalk on the dark walls of the small egg-shaped space. The runic graffiti took a myriad of shapes: lines and spirals, ellipses and arcane calculations, inverted algorithms and cross-cut runic geometries, all of it nonsensical yet undeniably possessed by a pattern. It was a madman's code.

It was similar to the map they'd found in Thornn, but not identical. That map had been made using the language and code set here. This was older. Ancient.

Cross sat and stared at it all, took it all in, stored bits in his mind and compared them to one another. His brain arranged, stored, rearranged.

He remembered his studies. His mind went back to the grim academy in Seraph, through the hovels of ancient books and age-yellowed parchments, where hunched scholars turned leathery with age and angry and trapped spirits drifted through the texts. When it came to the arcane, Cross was a machine: he had a natural gift for magic, for recalling vagaries and geometries and diagrams, for storing them in his mind, organizing them, recalling details with much greater clarity and precision than he could with anything else in his life. It was work, sometimes, for Cross to remember even his sister's birthday, but he could recall the dynamics of variant hex fields or the schematics for a pyramid vortex bomb with ease.

Cross looked, read, stored, and recalled. He had no idea how much time passed, for it blurred while diagrams and lines and encrypted layers of meaning spun through his mind.

Finally, he saw an answer.

It was a map.

This isn't a crypt at all, he thought. *It's a message. She came here to learn something. That map in Thornn had told her how to get here, to find the second map. She came to gather information the Old One had left when he wanted someone to find him.*

Red had come to learn the location of Koth, the Necropolis. A place of legend and whispered terror. A city that even the mighty vampires of the Ebon Cities feared and despised. It was bane to humans and vampires alike, a black city of outcasts and evil forces controlled by the Old One, who plotted and schemed to further his own nefarious agenda.

That was where Red was going, and after another half-hour Cross knew how to find it.

PART THREE
SHADOWS

He walks in the cold shadow of the mountain.

He wears the same clothes as he had back in the physical world, but instead of being filthy with blood they are filthy with brine. He sinks ankle deep into thick pools of salty bog made grey with sediment.

He makes his way to an island of dry ground. The boundary between land and water is marked by a thin vein of silver mist. The air is cold and still, and every splash of his boots echoes like thunder. Trees like walls hedge the clearing. Leaves heavy with moisture drift down from indeterminate heights.

The mountain looms overhead like a giant, replacing the sky.

Ice shards float past his feet. The riverbed is uneven, alternating between deep pools and shallow runs of sediment and silt. He hears something faint in the distance, a mournful song. There are eyes on him, watching from somewhere in the darkness of the trees.

A white spider scuttles across the back of his hand.

He knows she's there, trapped in a prison of smoke and rain. The demonic whinnies of black steeds echo through the trees, and the brimstone stench of their tainted sweat carries on the hard wind. He walks through clouds of forest steam and arcane frost.

Black leaves gang together in flight like flocks of ravens. He hears her screams in the wind, feels her pain press against his body like a shower of glass shards.

I'll find you, he promises, even as the world bleeds away. I'll find you.

ELEVEN

WOUNDS

They walked under a bruise-black sky. The air felt like rain, but they all knew it wouldn't. It hadn't rained much after The Black.

The three of them crossed drifts of hard red clay and fine white dust. The air was cold and dry and tasted of salt. They rested only sparingly, made cold camps and feasted exclusively on MREs that tasted like wet paper.

Cross slept as he walked, or at least he came close. His entire body was sore, but thankfully even with their continued march his ribs had healed considerably, and the dizziness that had before plagued his every step had started to fade. He had a minor concussion, at worst.

But the pain of his loss was greater, and it hurt deeper than any physical wound he could ever sustain. Cross's nerves were on edge, and he felt anxious to the point of nausea. On top of that his temperature was high and he suffered bouts of extreme chill, so he'd probably contracted a fever.

He didn't know which loss was worse. Thinking about Snow sent chills through his stomach. He tried to push memories of her young face from his mind. Every time he thought of her he saw Red standing next to her, drowning her with dark magic and pain.

The loss of his spirit was more physically painful, and in its own right just as bad. He suffered withdrawal at her loss, plain and simple. His spirit was gone, and he'd never before been without her, not that he could remember. It was like losing a part of his self. He felt incomplete, and hollow, like there was a void at his core.

He, Graves and Stone marched towards Dirge, a borderland outpost and armistice town controlled by the Ebon Cities. It was directly en route to Red's destination, at least so far as Cross's crudely translated map indicated. Cross had determined she was bound for the Carrion Rift, a vast canyon filled with the remains of the tens of thousands slaughtered by the Grim Father's vampire legions in the early days after The Black. It was Cross's guess that Koth, the necropolis ruled by the vampire outcast called the Old One, was there. It was the Old One Red intended to give her information to. He was the one she planned to hand the key to destroying what was left of humankind.

It was midmorning, but they'd only been walking for a couple of hours. The three of them had originally been air-dropped northeast of the Wormwood, and they'd entered the haunted forest on foot, since it was far too hazardous for them to use mounts in. Even pack animals were out of the question.

The airship, unfortunately, was not an option for getting to Dirge.

They'd come across its smoking remains just outside the trees. The pilot's bodies had been flayed and their bones burned. Nothing was left of the vessel but timber. Eventually someone would ask questions back in Thornn when the ship didn't return, but that would take several days at the very least, and it wasn't like the remnants of Viper Squad could expect any backup. Squads had been deployed far and wide to search for Red, and many of the Southern Claw's most elite hunters and soldiers had perished during searches in the vampire-controlled wilds of the Wolfland, the Bone March, the Razortooth Hills and the barbaric winter lands called the Reach. Cross had known members from many of those doomed Squads. Others, like Renaad, he'd learned of later.

There was quite literally no one left to be deployed without leaving the major cities of the Southern Claw almost entirely unguarded, a potentially lethal option to all of the cities, but especially to Thornn, since hordes of Gorgoloth waited perched to strike at it from the Reach. And the Gorgoloth weren't even the biggest threat – the vampire battalion staged at the Bonespire west of Thornn constantly waited for the city's defenses to falter, and the dark tower housed a formidable array of Shadowclaws, blood wings, razor golems and bone-blade shock troops, a force that could do serious damage. The Southern Claw Alliance would live on, but the loss of Thornn would be difficult to recover from.

"Are you up for this?" Graves asked him. Cross got the impression Graves had already asked and he just hadn't heard him. He drifted in and out of awareness. When he was alert, he felt pain.

"Yeah," Cross said after a considerable pause. "I just...I feel..."

"You look like Hell," Graves said when Cross didn't finish his sentence. "I can only imagine how you *feel*."

"No," Cross said, aware of how weak his voice sounded. "You can't."

"Let's pick up the pace," Stone said from ahead. "I want to make Dirge before nightfall. The last thing we need is to spend another night outdoors. Pick up your feet and move, Cross."

"You're all heart, Stone," Graves said. Stone gave him a look. Morg would have laid Graves out for that. Cross was glad Stone wasn't quite so aggressive with his command tactics. In fact, Stone was actually relatively quiet, though when he did say something it was usually unfriendly.

Low and jagged hills seemed to circle them like predators. The deep red sun fell fast behind a flotilla of iron clouds. The temperature continued to drop, but they kept walking. Cross wasn't sure how he managed to maintain the pace.

"She's gone," he said after a time.

"What?"

"She's gone, Sam. Snow...my spirit. Both of them. I didn't think it could happen."

A wolf's howl echoed with bloodcurdling resonance through the menstrual sky.

"How..." Graves didn't seem to know what to ask.

"Is it...is it always like this, for you?" Cross asked. "This...quiet?"

"I don't understand."

"I'm used to hearing her. My spirit, I mean. I'm used to hearing her voice, her whispers. The spirits, they...they don't really say anything, but they're *there*. Always. And I feel her...felt her, I mean...wrapped around me, like a shroud. I'm cold now. And it's so quiet."

Graves didn't say anything.

Cross had no way of knowing if he would ever get her back. He'd never heard of a warlock or witch who'd lost their spirit in the first place. The two were supposed to be inextricably linked, a joining of souls, tied together by an invisible and unbreakable bond. Killing one meant killing the other, or so Cross had always believed.

I was wrong. That, or I'm actually dead. I feel dead.

It bothered him that he was focused more on the loss of his spirit than that of Snow. Maybe it was easier that way...after all, losing his spirit seemed like *his* pain. For all he knew Snow was suffering horribly at that very moment.

Stop thinking that. It doesn't help.

He knew Graves was keeping an eye on him, probably to make sure he didn't pass out. Cross walked in a zombie state. His mind didn't process the act of moving, nor was he really aware of what was around him. He was used to being able to send his spirit out, to feel his surroundings, to search for what was there and what wasn't, and that act was as natural to him as breathing. He felt blind now. Empty and alone.

Near sunset they stopped at a cave in the side of a hill; the cave was filled with heaps of animal bones. Mounds of dry red dust stood to either side of a crudely dug path leading through the dead plains to the small city of Dirge.

Dirge was a squat and ugly town, a shell of haphazard buildings made of brick, clay, steel and timber. It was surrounded by a fifty-foot-tall wall of corrugated black iron held together with rivets cast from hexed steel. The parapets of the city were manned by masked sentries armed with crossbows and assault rifles. Thick streams of black smoke churned from Dirge's smithies and factories, and near the center of the city stood an eighty-foot black stone tower with an apex ringed by black barbs of steel. The sounds of industry churned beyond Dirge's unforgiving walls, and defensive lines of sandbags and caltrops blocked easy access to the city gates.

"God I hate this place," Graves muttered.

"I haven't had the pleasure," Cross said. Even looking at Dirge filled him with a sick sense of foreboding.

"OK, let's lay some ground rules," Stone said quietly. "This is an armistice town, so vampires are in charge here. Humans are only allowed if they aren't associated with the Southern Claw."

"Okay," Cross said. "So how do we explain where our equipment came from?"

"Mercs and hunters use Southern Claw equipment all the time," Graves shrugged. "It's the best stuff on the black market."

"So we bought it, we stole it, or we traded for it," Stone added. "But we need to keep the specialty items hidden. Hex grenades, arcane salts, those gauntlets of yours...anything on us fancier than a gun is going to raise eyebrows."

Luckily their dark fatigues and armor didn't bear any insignias of the Southern Claw, and the design was standard enough it would be easy to pass the three of them off as mercenaries. They stowed Cross's more unusual gear – the grenades and salts, the alchemy tubes, the entropy stones, all of his gauntlets, the wires and battery packs, the arcane fuses – and hid it in thick blankets, coats and other bulky items. They decided to keep Winter's oversized battery pack on hand, which they'd claim they scavenged in the wilderness if they were asked. With even a decent trade for the battery they'd be able to restock their ammunition and acquire extra supplies for the arduous trek north, because in order to pursue Red they'd drive straight through the heart of the Bone March.

"It feels wrong to get rid of this," Cross said as he looked over the rest of Winter's gear.

"We don't have much choice," Stone said. They marched side-by-side down the steep hill. Graves was at the point, carefully approaching the city with his shotgun in plain sight. Cross didn't need his lost supernatural senses to notice the Dirgian flame-cannon mounted high on the wall over the gate. The massive weapon turned in their direction as they drew close. "Don't go soft on us now, Crossie."

"Don't call me 'Crossie'. 'Stonie'."

Stone laughed.

"How you holdin' up?"

"I'm fine," Cross said. "I'm worried as hell about Snow, but if we can get to Red and stop her, I'll feel better."

"We will," Stone said. "Thanks for going down into that mud hole. I thought we were done."

"We may *still* be done," Cross said quietly.

It had taken hours to translate the map, and he was far from certain he'd done it correctly. The calculations, codes and references had been difficult to figure out, and he'd been forced to do it all from memory since he hadn't been able to use magic, but he'd spent years learning everything he could about the arcane. Once Cross had discovered the truth about himself he'd obsessively dedicated his life to understanding magic, especially when it became clear Snow was similarly cursed. He'd decided long ago he'd never be at a loss because he didn't understand something...which was another reason why the loss of his spirit had been so hard for him to take.

This is what I am. All I am.

"We should get a tracker," Cross said, almost to himself.

"A tracker?" Stone asked. "Are you serious? We don't need some mercenary tagging along." He and Graves stopped. The flame-cannon was aimed right at them. "This is serious, Cross," Stone said. "We don't need a loose cannon on board."

"We need all the help we can get," Cross said. "We need someone with magic, someone who can track, and someone who knows more than we do about traveling through the Bone March. Correct me if I'm wrong, but what we know about that place isn't much."

Stone looked at him for a moment, and then smiled. "Man, we *are* screwed," he said with a grin. "I'm taking the advice of a warlock without magic." He looked back at the city. "I'll do the talking."

"Talk away," Cross said to Stone. "I'm liable to throw up any second now."

"Tough guy," Stone said with a sad shake of his head.

"Guys..." Graves asked from the front. He stared right at the flame-cannon, and it stared back. "Any time you want to move your asses and get up here...you know, that would be great."

The gates lay directly ahead, shaped in the semblance of a fanged skull. Walking into the city had the illusion of stepped inside a wide-open mouth.

"Cheery," Cross said quietly.

The gate guard's masks were battered iron plates set with eye-holes. Their armor was a mismatch of steel shoulder plates, face wraps and tunics, leather pants and steel-toed boots. Kevlar and flak vests were just barely visible under their billowing cloaks, their hard steel gauntlets gripped sharp iron poles, and they wore aged pistols and wickedly curved knives strapped to their belts.

Surprisingly the Dirgian guards didn't detain the three of them at all. They gave the trio a brief interrogation as to the nature of their visit, verified they bore neither alchemy or void bombs and didn't suffer from any arcane diseases, made a quick but fruitless search of their belongings, and ushered them into the city.

TWELVE
DIRGE

Inside the walls, Dirge was much as Cross expected – a dirty, dingy, noise-filled mess.

The streets were filled with grimy citizens, their faces spotted with sickness and fatigue. Charcoal dust stuck in the air, iron wheels ground against the broken street, furnace flames burned high into the sky, and walls of arcane steam billowed from vents. People moved in packs and toted sacks of dried goods and pulled carts of potatoes, grain, coal dust, raw steel and machinery parts. The air tasted like industry and sweat.

Dirge's structures were pushed together like crowded bystanders. Buildings had been built with crooked angles, and every window and door looked too narrow. Dirge wasn't a tall city save for the outer walls, but it was thoroughly congested. All of its structures, even the clay and dirt roads, were grey or black. Walking through Dirge felt like passing into an ink stain.

"Do we want to get some rooms?" Graves asked.

"We might as well," Stone replied. "No sense sleeping outside the city when we can stay at an inn. But let's get moving – we don't want to be out after sundown."

Cross thrilled at the notion of spending the night in a bed. His back was as stiff from sleeping in a thin bedroll on uneven ground for the past several days.

Dirge's sparse population dressed in a variety of clothing as haphazard and diverse as the people themselves. Humans of all races and associations were there: refugees from the rapidly dwindling frontier, miners from the Razortooth logging camps, former citizens of nearby Southern Claw cities like Thornn or Ath. Many of the people looked to be working class, and they dressed in dingy grey and brown work clothes and heavy boots. Others wore a hodgepodge of fashions, from the retro-Medieval attire of Thornn to the heavily cloaked garb worn by the Gol of Meldoar.

Cross saw few of the city's black-garbed sentries on the street, but they were easy to spot higher up on the parapets, where they watched both the roads of Dirge and the surrounding countryside. Flame-cannons propped on swiveling mounts allowed the guards to aim the deadly weapons at targets on either side of the outer wall. In addition to the obvious show of force represented in the cannons there were likely more subtle means Dirge's rulers used to keep the streets clean of undesirables, from incognito warlocks and witches to arcane scopes in the towers.

The dark material of the city's buildings set them in stark contrast to the pale red sky, and Dirge was so dark in some areas its people became walking silhouettes.

The black tower at the center of Dirge loomed over the rest of the city, a giant and dirty blade. The thorny obelisk seemed to hover over them as they walked, poised like a frozen black snake.

Stone directed them to the tavern district, located just a few short blocks from the main city gates so visiting merchants wouldn't have to travel far before they came to the hospitality of an inn. Most of the signs in the district were written in High Jlantrian, an archaic tongue used by the vampires. Many Southern Claw officers could read High Jlantrian, but to Cross it looked like a random series of slashes and cuts. He recognized it for what it was, but he couldn't read it. High Jlantrian had no arcane value at all. Cross had spent his time learning Inverted Malzarian, the text of magic.

It was still daylight when they approached an inn, so there were very few vampires about. Those which Cross did see kept their pale faces carefully wrapped and their bodies concealed beneath bulky crimson cloaks, clothing that symbolized their status. Dirge was an armistice town: its rulers had quietly surrendered to the mercy of the Ebon Cities. The city was allowed to retain its human population, but the local authorities reported to a vampire Viscount, who along with a small contingent of undead honor guards held indirect control of the city.

An unmistakable aura of fear existed in Dirge, so palpable Cross could almost taste it. From what he understood there were only a few vampires to be found in the city at any given time, but more could be summoned in a moment's notice, and they had the freedom and authority to do whatever they pleased.

This is no way to live, Cross thought bitterly. *We'll run you out of here, and out of everywhere else, you bastards.*

The establishment they entered, The Blackfang Inn, was spacious, smoke-filled, deathly quiet and cold. Immaculately clean wood-polished floors and a long and sleek bar showed no signs of ever having been even touched in spite of the dozen or so patrons seated at the bar and the few small tables. Those tavern patrons were stoic and silent, deeply focused on their purple liqueurs and thin black cigarillos. Gray and silver air shone down from the skylight over the bar. Cross smelled whisky and hashish.

Stone nonchalantly walked up to the bar while Graves and Cross took a seat. The other patrons looked much as the three Hunters did – dirty, unkempt, sleep-deprived and in need of a drink – but for some reason Cross felt ridiculous putting down their dirty packs on a floor that looked like it could have doubled as a trauma room. A large metallic fan set high in the ceiling sliced the pale light into swirling ribbons. A square balcony bound by black iron rails stood a dozen feet above the main floor.

Stone bought a round of Dirgian brandy. It was one of the weaker drinks available, he assured them, since they needed to keep their wits about them even though they all agreed a drink was much needed. He also set a room token down on the table.

"One room?" Graves said with a groan.

"Don't even start," Stone said. "We're safer if we stay together. I don't trust this place one bit."

They all were all on edge. If someone figured out they were from Thornn the militia would come gunning for them without a moment's hesitation.

"I may have found a place where we can find a tracker," Stone said after he took drink.

"Really?" Cross asked.

"You were only at the bar for two minutes..." Graves said quietly.

"I have a way with people."

"What way?" Graves laughed quietly. Their conversation was undoubtedly the loudest in the tavern, even though they spoke barely above a whisper. "Your idea of a conversation is usually an insult followed by a rabbit punch."

"That reminds me, I owe you a rabbit punch," Stone said.

"Well?" Cross asked.

"The bartender said we should try a place called The White Spider. It's a gambling hall, brothel...our kind of place. She said we might have some luck finding a certain individual who works off the beaten path."

"Well okay, then," Cross said.

"What?"

"Nothing." Cross couldn't say why, but the mention of The White Spider bothered him...which made no sense, since prior to Stone mentioning it he'd never even heard of the place.

"Good," Stone said. "Let's finish our drinks and get up to the room."

Cross kept his uncertainties to himself, chalking them up to fatigue and paranoia.

Renting the room took nearly all of their pooled local coin, and they hadn't had much to start with, since they couldn't use their Southern Claw currency for fear of being discovered. The room was as plain and as boring as Cross knew it would be, with only a single bed, a vacant wardrobe and a bathroom with no mirror, which was hardly a surprise given the town's stance on vampires. One small window let in filtered grey and white light that somewhat relieved the room's otherwise oppressive atmosphere.

They slept in shifts in spite of their fatigue. Someone was up and on watch while the other two slept back to back on the small bed. Cross, despite the misgivings of the other two, took the first watch – he was wired with anxiety and knew he wouldn't be able to sleep for quite some time, regardless of how tired he felt.

He sat in the room's single chair with his pistol in his hand and Graves' shotgun on his lap. Cross leaned the chair back against the wall and kept his eyes on the locked door and window.

Most of the sounds he heard over the course of that night were perfectly normal, things one could hear in any city: muted conversations, industrial machines at work in the distance, the steam whistles of local trains blaring through the night, laughter, even an occasional bout of drunken song.

But there were other sounds, things he'd expected to hear but hadn't wanted to, that reminded Cross he was in a town controlled by vampires: guttural undead throat songs floating down from the rooftops, razor whispers slicing through the air like rags caught in the wind, the garble of unguarded telepathic refuse intentionally released to intimidate the populace.

Cross also heard the feedings.

The vampires never desired the outright elimination of an armistice town – such would defeat the purpose of having allowed it to surrender in the first place. The blood tax was heavy, and after dark all unguarded humans were fair game. The vampires would, by agreement, never enter a closed or sealed home or business, so if you were smart enough to lock your doors and shut your windows and block off your fireplace at night then you had nothing to fear. But if you didn't, or if you ventured out of doors and were spotted by the undead, you were nothing but a meal.

The stipulation should have been simple for anyone to follow, but Cross had heard tales of those who'd defied the blood tax. There were drunks or other homeless persons caught in the open streets, people driven outside by emergencies but who felt confident they could make it in and out of doors before it was too late, children who doomed their entire families because they managed to force a window open while they were playing, or households wiped out simply because someone forgot to properly close the door. Even when it meant life or death, mistakes happened.

The sound of a feeding was impossible to ignore. Cross heard the smack of teeth, and sucking sounds so loud he swore they came from inside the room. He heard pained moans and animal barks. It amused him to think that once, so very long ago, vampires had been painted as romantics by fiction writers. The truth was they were animals, pure and simple, vicious of heart, evil of spirit, malign in their sole drive to wipe humanity out.

Cross waited, and watched. His heart raced and his skin was flushed with cold sweat. Even though he knew they were safe he still expected a vampire to crash into the room at any moment.

He was only on watch for about two hours. It felt like twelve.

He remembered hiding beneath buildings while he listened to other children squeal in pain as they were slaughtered. Some things he'd never forget, no matter how hard he tried.

Cross's sleep, once it was his turn to do so, was fitful, filled with nightmares of gore-covered black unicorns chasing him through a silver glade at the base of a jagged mountain. There were women trapped there with him, and though they ran, none of them escaped.

I've seen this before.

In the morning, not feeling refreshed at all, Cross checked over Winter's battery pack and chemical engines to make sure they were still in good working order. Graves had the last watch, and he sat in the same spot Cross had, his shotgun in hand. He spun a throwing knife back and forth between his fingers.

"All good?" he asked.

"All good." Cross packed everything away. All of their gear was out of sight, and ready to move. "Stone's been gone for a while, hasn't he?"

"He's grabbing breakfast." Graves looked at him. "What's eating you?"

"The White Spider," Cross said. "Something about the name of that place is familiar. And it's bugging the hell out of me."

"Try not to worry about it," Graves said. "And try not to think about...you know." When Cross didn't answer, Graves leaned close. "Hang in there, man. Things will work out."

"Right," Cross said bitterly. "Let me ask you something, Sam: when was the last time something 'worked out' for us?"

Graves thought for a moment. The early morning light came through their east-facing window and cast half of his scarred face in shadow.

"About three years ago," Graves said, "This was before you joined Wolf Company. I was squad leader for a perimeter patrol. The Sorn had been sending skull drones to scout for refugees or farmers to take back to their mines. Anyways, we were out near the Razortooth, and we saw this broken down caravan. It kind of looked like a wagon train from the Old West, but even at a glance we could tell it hadn't been touched in years. We were going to investigate – not for survivors, just for supplies – but before we could we were called back to drive some Bloodwolves away from one of the research towers. Anyways, we didn't get back to check out the caravan for another couple of days, and lo and behold, when we finally got back to it we found two dead Sorn, blown to bits. It turns out the caravan was a trap: there was an Ebon Cities necrobomb rigged to the wagon, set to explode if anyone poked around at it. The Sorn who set it off were the very same ones we'd been sent to find in the first place. So in the end the raids were stopped, and I didn't lose any men in the process." Graves smiled. "So yeah...that worked out pretty well."

"That was dumb luck," Cross said after a moment.

"How is that different from 'just working out'? Look, I realize that the world is shit, but that doesn't mean good things never happen. Things will work out. You have to believe that sometimes."

Cross shrugged. "Sorry, I have trouble seeing it right now. And I'm extremely suspicious of this place we're going to."

"You haven't even *been* there," Graves said.

"I know, I know," Cross said. His mind was stressed to the point of snapping. He couldn't stop thinking about Snow, wondering what Red had done to her, or would do to her...or was doing to her at that very moment...No. *Stop it. That's not going to help her, and it's not going to do you much good, either.* "Something in my gut just tells me the White Spider is all wrong."

"Come on," Graves said. He looked more worried than Cross would have liked.

You must think I'm going crazy, he thought.

"Grab your gear," Graves said, "Let's go find Stone."

Stone, as expected, was downstairs, seated alone at a table and eating a bowl of steaming soup. There were only a few other patrons in the tavern, mostly grey-eyed workmen dressed in heavy industrial boots and ragged fur coats, probably laborers from the mines or factories. Cross smelled coffee, and his gums watered.

"We have some concerns," Graves said quietly. He and Cross sat, and Graves made it sound like both of them were worried they might have been walking into a trap at the White Spider.

"*You're* being stupid," Stone told Graves, and then he turned to Cross. "And *you're* being paranoid. It was your idea to go and find a tracker in the first place, remember? I thought it was a ridiculous plan. For the record, I still do."

Cross was about to argue, but he couldn't think of anything to say. It was hard to focus. He was having difficulty putting even simple thoughts together. It must have showed, because Stone and Graves both gave him a look like there was something wrong with him.

"Are you out of sorts because you lost your spirit?" Stone asked.

"I think so...sorry. Nothing is really making sense to me right now. My head is all...fuzzy."

"Hey, me too," Graves added with a nervous laugh.

"Yeah, but we're used to it from you," Stone said with a perfectly straight face. "You're naturally stupid."

"Screw you, friend," Graves smiled back.

"Sir."

"Fine. Screw you, Sir."

They ate some hearty soup – it was lamb, Cross thought, with artificially grown vegetables and a surprisingly thick gravy-like broth – and drank strong coffee, all of which invigorated him and made him feel better than he had in days.

"Cross," Stone said after they ate a while, "your senses are pretty dull, huh? And your judgment has been...hot and cold?"

"I'll be all right," Cross said. Stone looked at him doubtfully. "I'll be all right," Cross insisted again.

"Stone..." Graves said quietly.

"You stay out of this," Stone said sternly, then turned back to Cross. "We're not going on a parade. If you're not going to be able to cut it, something needs to be done. As it is..."

"I know," Cross said. "Without magic, I'm useless. Well, Stone, with all due respect...go to hell. I'm fine." He went back to his soup.

Surprisingly, Stone nodded, and he didn't bring it up again.

They ate the rest of their breakfast in silence, and Cross steeled himself for having to hand over his magical duties to a complete stranger.

What the hell good am I now? he wondered. *Maybe Stone is right. Maybe I'd be best staying behind.*

But that wasn't an option. Snow was out there, and Cross wouldn't quit until he found her. He knew there was little hope she was still alive – the Blood Witch was no vampire, but he couldn't think of a reason why she'd keep her captive breathing. All he could so was hope.

What else am I going to do? Besides, like the man said...sometimes things just work out.

THIRTEEN
SPIDER

They needed new gear for the trek north, but they all agreed a trip to the market needed to wait until they were on their way out of Dirge, as they needed a guide with knowledge of the Bone March to help determine what equipment they really needed. That being said, Stone's contact at the Blackfang informed them the witch they sought to hire at the White Spider could be found there at almost any hour, at least for the next few days. She was apparently an attraction of sorts, though what that meant exactly was anyone's guess.

The White Spider didn't have much going for it, at least not from the outside. The marble structure looked like it had been clawed by an army of tigers, and the thick columns at the top of the wide stone steps looked to be on the verge of collapse. Refuse and questionable stains covered the establishment. The façade of an elegant spider hung over the doorway, mostly faded. Steady and rhythmic drums pounded up at them as they descended a steep set of stairs located behind some scorched double doors in the side of the building. The blended smells of hashish, alcohol, tobacco and exotic southern perfume made the air thick.

A pair of rough-looking bouncers renovated them of their weapons at the foot of the stairs. While no one was happy about being disarmed, they knew they had little choice if they wanted to find a guide. In any case they'd already left all but a handful of small arms and blades stashed back in their room at the Blackfang Inn, carefully concealed beneath some loosened floorboards. Cross figured Graves would still manage to sneak a blade inside, and both Sam and Stone were capable hand-to-hand combatants. Under normal circumstances, Cross wouldn't have worried about himself, either, given his status as a warlock. As it was he'd have to rely on the small bags of alchemist's powders he's smuggled under his shirt, which he was fortunate the bouncers missed when they patted him down.

Ever since he'd lost his spirit Cross felt more and more exposed with each and every step. He hated to admit it but he felt the pain of his spirit's loss even more deeply than the loss of his sister...and he hated himself for it. Snow and his spirit were beginning to blur in his mind, becoming one and the same. He thought of his spirit, and he saw Snow's face. He was starting to remember them as a single woman he'd lost, that he'd die trying to rescue.

Stop. Clear your head. Focus.

Cross didn't need his spirit to recognize the obvious displays of arcane security in The White Spider. Hex wires had been strung like netting across every doorway, plates of cured cold iron were laid out like doormats at every threshold, and vents were positioned to launch hypergolic fluids across the entry hall. The main room of The White Spider was a long and high-vaulted chamber lit with lamps billowing grey-green smoke into a noxious electric haze. Cigarillos danced like fireflies in the dim light, and people moved and swayed and drank and laughed like ghosts in a fog.

Invisible icy fingers raced down Cross's spine as he moved through the room. He stayed close to Graves and Stone.

The tobacco made Cross's eyes sting, and his nostrils filled with exotic spices, clove and malted liqueurs. Barely-clad women slithered their ways through the throng of working-class and mercenary patrons; their smooth bodies clad in skirts slit up the sides, tall desert sandals and dark leather bras. The sound of rattling dice and coins echoed over the voices and music, a vibrating staccato beat of drums, pipes and harpsichord generated by some hexed acoustic device, since there was neither band nor musician in sight. Money and drugs changed hands openly and without hesitation, and the bump and grind and purchased sex lent vocals to The White Spider's song.

"There," Stone said, and they made for a separate chamber at the back of the room.

That larger room smelled of blood, sweat and money. A sunken pit stood at the center of the chamber, and the pit's metal walls bore dark stains of blood, bile and vomit. Primitive benches sat bolted to the floor around the opening to the pit, protected by loose wire mesh. The room was packed with rowdy workers and sultry women, mercenaries and thieves. Brutal howls issued from the pit, and Cross stepped into the room just in time to hear a blood-curdling scream. A spray of blood and steaming human meat flew against the mesh from below, spattering the first row of spectators who cheered and hollered even as they recoiled in horror.

"Where the hell is she?" Graves asked as the three of them huddled together. "And how will we know her?"

Stone was about to answer when a new challenger was announced. The commentator's voice was unnaturally loud and sharp and seemed to issue from everywhere.

"Let's hear it for...THE WITCH!"

The Southern Claw men inched forward through the wall of excited bodies to get a better view. The corpse of the former losing gladiator – a stout and black-skinned Gorgoloth whose white hair and fanged face had been torn clean away from its muscular body – was being cleared away. The winner, a fierce-looking Vuul, still stood in the pit. He was tall and broad of shoulder, with pale grey flesh covered in dozens of scars so entwined they looked almost like tattoo art. Anemic muscles tensed with thick black blood running through near-translucent skin, and pale eyes bore a subtle glow which cast his hairless head and torso in smoky light. The Vuul wielded a maul with a hilt laced with leather straps and fetishes of bone and teeth, while its tip was set with a sharp black spike still dripped with the Gorgoloth's syrupy blood. The Vuul wore leather pants only slightly darker than his grey and white flesh. He stood stoic and silent, typical of his grim and humorless race. He closed his eyes as the door behind him slid open to reveal his challenger.

'The Witch', they called her.

Oh, God, Cross thought. *You're kidding me.*

The woman was a lithe and pale. Her dark hair wasn't quite shoulder length, and her face was as lean as her athletic body. A dark crimson cloak was cast aside to reveal tight blood-red leather armor set with black steel elbow guards and banded iron gauntlets. She wielded a pair of rune-carved scimitars, and even Cross sensed the swirl of an angry male spirit around her.

"Is that...?" Graves said.

"The woman from Thornn," Cross said. "Cristena."

She's failed to find her husband, so now she's looking for death.

Even though Cross recognized her she seemed an entirely different woman than the one he'd met for breakfast in Krugen's. For starters, Cross hadn't realized just how long she really was. She had to be almost six feet tall, even wearing flat-footed moccasins and after she'd shed her bulky cloak. She'd pulled her hair back tight into a pony-tail, which revealed an angular and beautiful face lined with rage. Her faint scar was only barely visible in the dull spotlights, a trace down her cheek and the left side of her neck. Her eyes were cold and hollow and her movements were sinuous and graceful and entirely inhuman, like a feline predator with blades in lieu of claws.

This woman was nothing like the vulnerable, friendly, sad witch Cross had met just the week before. She licked her teeth and lips in violent anticipation while the Vuul held his fists in the air, much to the delight of the crowd.

"She won't be much good to us dead," Graves said. Cross could barely hear him, as the crowd had worked into frenzy. Noise collapsed against his ears. Cash and coins and notes passed hands with such speed Cross couldn't fathom how anyone even communicated their bets. Maybe that wasn't the point.

"There's not much we can do," Stone said angrily.

Cross watched her. The space behind her cold dead eyes was the deepest point of the room, a center of gravity drawing everything in. An invisible darkness seemed to dwell there, an inky whirlpool Cross felt himself drawn towards, and he realized he wasn't the only one: every spectator was held entranced, gripped by some terrifying fascination like moths to a flame. Even the Vuul gladiator seemed to feel it, and it was only the race's natural resistance to magic that prevented him from being entirely lulled under her spell.

That's not something you can do all of the time, Cross thought. *Or by choice.* Her spirit must have been wholly enraged and left unrestrained to exercise that much power. It fed off of the emotions in the room, which was as dangerous for everyone else as it was for Cristena herself. If she was unable to contain her spirit if it decided to strike out the arcane backlash would be like a warehouse of gasoline lit by a powder bomb.

If Cross still retained his own spirit, he could have helped her. Even as dangerous as it was to mingle spirits – especially spirits of the opposite gender – he could have used his magic to curtail Cristena's raw power and possibly minimize any damage. As things stood, Cross was just a well-informed spectator.

Lucky me, I'm the only one in the room who realizes how much trouble we're all in.

Cristena moved like a violent shadow. Her blades swept across the Vuul's chest and he went to his knees. The Vuul was fast, and before Cristena could strike again he caught her with a backhanded blow in the sternum that sent her crashing against the blood-stained wall. The crowd gasped, howled, and cheered. Cross could almost taste the bloodlust in the air. He watched Cristena and wondered if she'd be able to get back up.

Though injured, the Vuul's supernatural metabolism had already begun to stitch his wounds. Bones tensed and cracked under his sickly flesh. His heavy feet stamped on the muck-stained floor as he strode over to Cristena.

"She's done," Stone muttered.

There was nothing they could do.

Cross decided to do something, anyway.

The sweat and stain of the crowd hung like a miasma. Cross's fingers glistened with grime and sweat. Blood pounded in his ears. He drew a deep and steadying breath and grabbed the bag of alchemical phosphorous. Warlocks often carried explosive powders, sometimes as backup to their own magic and sometimes just for kicks. Cross hated the stuff, but there were times when it proved handy to be able to provide a big flash and bang at the drop of a hat. The powders he carried were so innocuous in their smell and appearance they often escaped notice, which was exactly what Cross had been betting on when he'd smuggled them into The White Spider.

Cross tasted electric dew and salt on his tongue. He pinched some of the powder between his index finger and thumb and dropped it onto the floor. The air around his feet grew instantly cold. Spectral tongues licked his skin. It almost – almost – felt like he'd found his spirit again, but it wasn't her, for the energies he conjured with the arcane hex powder were just trapped ectoplasmic essence, like a recorded voice or a rapidly fading memory. Vapor crept along the floor like a freezing tide. White smoke rose.

Cross glanced into the pit. Cristena had managed to pull herself to her feet. She and the Vuul circled one another. Cristena was bloodied and bruised but her eyes were as sharp as the scimitars in her hands and she still moved with cunning speed. The Vuul barely even looked winded, as his rapid healing had sealed nearly every trace of his wounds.

In moments the sweaty air was replaced with the heady smell of magic, and the first row of spectators was neck deep in a hazy white fog. Ghostly faces shifted and melted in the smoke, aberrant spectral clouds which leered and growled. Cross, Stone and Graves pulled themselves off to the side of the room where they could avoid being trampled by panicked spectators.

The room was suddenly with fear, and what had moments before been a chorus of cheers and angry shouts turned to screams. Bodies pushed together in their frenzy.

"What the hell?" Graves shouted. "Did *you* do that?" he asked Cross.

"Maybe," Cross said.

"Idiot," Stone growled.

Cross kept his body pressed against the wall. Once the crowd thinned and the throng pushed and elbowed its way closer to the double doors leading from the chamber Cross was able to make his way down the rows of seats to the arena. The ground was slick from the touch of arcane powder, even though the effect had already begun its rapid dissipation process.

By the time Cross came to the edge of the pit the fight had already been stopped by White Spider bouncers, tall and heavily armored men with jagged swords and revolvers. The Vuul warrior looked as if he'd calmly accepted that the match was over, but Cristena looked angry.

The pair of guards sent to retrieve her looked like they'd been sent to wrestle a wild tiger.

"Cristena!" Cross shouted. She looked up, and their eyes locked. He saw the same desolate woman he'd spoken to back at Krugen's.

She doesn't want to be saved, he realized, but at the moment there were needs beyond hers to consider.

"Cross!" Stone shouted. He and Graves had fought their way through the crowd and caught up with him. "What the hell are you doing?"

"Good question," one of the sentries asked. "You got business with our merchandise?"

"Merchandise?" Graves asked angrily. "You'd better be joking, you ass."

Stone shot Graves a look, but it was already too late. The departing crowd was massed around the entrance to the arena, which thankfully meant the three of them had some time before any more of the White Spider's thugs could respond to the situation. Cross had his bare fingers dipped in another pouch of powder, a fine crimson dust which sent a burning chill straight up the nerves of his arm and back down into his gut.

"What's it to you, Shorty?" the guard sneered at Graves. The guard's head was arched up so he could see, and one hand was on the hilt of his large-caliber hunting revolver.

There were four sentries down in the pit with Cristena and the Vuul, while Cross, Graves and Stone, in spite of possessing the higher ground, had no actual weapons and were on the other side of a protective wire-mesh fence.

The hell with it, Cross thought. Stone stepped up to the edge, where he'd likely do something intelligent like negotiate a peaceful resolution. *Well*, Cross thought, surprising himself, *I guess I'll put a stop to that.*

"She's coming with us," Cross said. He sounded much more confident than he felt.

"Are you here to rescue me?" Cristena asked him. Her voice was distant and cold. "What makes you think I need your help?"

The guards laughed. Cross nodded at Cristena, motioning for her to duck. She looked confused, but she nodded.

"You just had that 'Damsel in Distress' look about you, I guess," he said. He felt Stone and Graves's befuddled looks without needing to actually look at them. The sound of the frantic crowd had faded. Everything had turned quiet down in the arena.

"I don't need you," she said. Her eyes went to the floor. The guards laughed again, but their hands hovered close to their pistols. Cross's chest felt so tight he thought he might implode.

"Maybe not," he said. "But I need *you*."

His hand flashed forward. Cristena went to her knees and pulled her hands over her head. Necrotic red powder fell onto the guards' exposed faces. Their flesh went black and bloody as the poison dust entered their eyes and lungs. Their screams erupted as liquid spurts.

The other two guards left the Vuul and charged at Cristena with their blades. Cristena stepped back, sideswiped the first guard and sent him careening into the wall with a roundhouse kick. Her spirit moved with her, around her. It was invisible to Cross but he recognized the pattern of movement, and he sensed the bitter cloud of acrid magic and swirls of black dust the spirit left in its wake. The second sentry brought his blade up but Cristena swept his blow aside, used her momentum to keep him off balance and in a quick series of thrusts used her scimitars to take both his arms off at the elbows.

Stone and Graves kicked their way through the mesh fence and leapt down into the pit. Graves landed on the guard Cristena had kicked against the wall, took hold of the guard's head and pummeled the man's skull against the stone until he stopped moving.

"What the hell?!" Cristena yelled at them. "Why did you come here?!"

"Wait, do we know you?" Stone asked. Stone *didn't* know her, Cross realized, but Graves apparently remembered her from The Black Hag.

Cross was the only one still on the main floor. The crowd was gone, and more White Spider sentries were on the way. Cross moved to leap down, but his eyes caught on the Vuul, still down in the pit, silent and still.

"Guys..." Cross said.

The Vuul stared back at him. Its muscles tensed, and its anvil-like fists clenched. Even with the chaos in the background Cross heard those steel-like bones tighten. The Vuul's blank expression didn't change and his solid white eyes didn't blink. Cross had no doubt the Vuul could kill all four of them, but after a moment the Vuul stepped back and nodded towards the open door leading to the tunnels beneath the arena.

"Let's go," Cristena said.

"Wait..." Graves began, but Cristena was quick to cut him off.

"You can stay here if you want," she snapped. "I don't care one way or another."

Cross leapt down into the pit. He landed with less grace than usual, righted himself, and followed Cristena. Graves and Stone were right behind them.

She led them into a dark and narrow network of subterranean passages, the underbelly of The White Spider. The air below was cloying and tight and smelled of sweat, urine and fear. They heard the growl of the Spider's sentries in the distance behind them.

Cristena guided them through a veritable labyrinth of short and claustrophobic tunnels. Side passages led to torch-lit rooms filled with weapons, chemicals and bodies, and Cross guessed that serving narcotic drinks and staging violent pit brawls weren't the only shady activities the proprietors of The White Spider were involved with. Cross's heart pounded as they raced through the tunnels, and after a few minutes he didn't hear any sounds of pursuit. There was no telling how deep or how far they'd gone.

Finally, when the smell of sewage had grown so strong Cross had to use smelling salts to keep from getting sick, Cristena stopped.

They stood at a four-way intersection of greasy and slime-coated passages. Vents released gouts of superheated steam into the dank underground air, and a narrow stream of mucus, grime and muck slithered down the tunnel in a nauseating flow. Dank brown water oozed down from the ceiling like gritty rain. Thick sewer grates stood in the diagonal walls of the intersection, and an ancient and rusted iron ladder led straight up, where it vanished into darkness.

"The ladder will lead you to the surface," Cristena said. "So do me a favor and get out. You've done enough damage."

"Damage?" Graves said. "Honey, we just saved your life."

"Thanks for nothing, then," she snapped. "I didn't ask for your help."

"No you didn't," Stone said. "But we're asking for *yours*."

Cristena laughed. She was exasperated, Cross thought, maybe surprised and undoubtedly angry. With all of that, he was glad that all she did was laugh.

"You have a pretty funny way of asking for my help," she said with a mean-spirited smile. "Of *course* I'll help you! You busted in on my fight, started a mass panic, and made it so there's no chance I'll ever be able to talk my way back into the Spider again. I owe you SO much!" The smile faded. She pointed up the ladder. "I hope there's something horrible waiting up there for you. I really do."

Cristena stalked past them, back the way they'd came.

"Why did you help us escape?" Cross asked her. He saw the spider in his mind, the white spider from the field that day he and Snow had visited their mother's grave. The same spider he'd seen in Krugen's, when he'd learned Cristena's husband was among those lost in the search for Red. The same spider that was the name of the place they'd found Cristena.

I'm supposed to be here, he thought. *That's the deal with the spider, it has to be.*

Cristena hesitated. "Because I know why you're here," she said. Her back was to them. "And I want you to succeed."

"Then come with us," Cross said. "We need your help."

Cristena turned around slowly, her boots sloshing in the muck.

"I already told you," she said quietly. "I'm not interested."

"Yeah," Cross said. "I can see that. You're busy trying to get yourself killed."

"Go to hell," Cristena answered.

"Look," Cross said. He stepped closer, leaving Stone and Graves so he could speak with her alone. "I get it. I really do. I've lost...everything...in the past few days. My spirit. My sister. My hope. But this *has* to be done. I'm not even sure if I'll live through this or not." Cristena regarded him stoically. She was strong, but he could see the strings holding her together coming unraveled. She was almost ready to die. Almost. "If we have to die," Cross said, "I want our deaths to mean something."

Cristena smiled bitterly. "You're such a romantic. I think I pity you."

"Look, enough, all right?!" Cross said. "Just cut the shit. We need your help. I've *needed* your help. Remember when I asked you to be our tracker back in Thornn? Well my *sister* became our tracker instead, and now she's gone. We have no chance of finding Red unless someone helps us, and right now that someone is *you*. Maybe you've given up on living, but there are a lot of people who haven't. If you're too selfish to see that..." Cross took a breath. "Then I don't know what to tell you."

They stood silent.

"Nice speech," Cristena said after a moment. "You do that a lot?"

"No," Cross smiled sadly. "I'm actually pretty impressed with myself right now."

They waited. Stone and Graves looked on silently. Cristena's eyes focused on something only she could see.

"Cross?" she said after a moment.

"Yeah?"

"Why did you try to save me? I would've been all right in that fight, you know. I could've taken him."

Cross thought for a moment. "I know," he said.

"Then why?"

Cross hesitated. "A spider told me to."

"I'm sorry?"

"Don't worry about it."

"So is she with us?" Stone asked.

"*She* is capable of answering for herself," Cristena said coldly. "Thanks."

"This is our Squad leader, Abraham Stone," Cross said. "That gnarly looking blonde fellow is Sam Graves. Gentlemen, this is Cristena..."

"Da'avros," she said.

"Cristena Da'avros."

"Your new tracker," she added.

"Pleased to meet you," Stone said. "And now we need to move. With what Captain Impulsive here just pulled," Stone said with an eye on Cross, "we'll need to exercise a bit more caution from here on out."

"A bit *more* caution?" Cristena said dryly. "Why don't we start with *any* caution. Period."

"We're cautious," Graves said defensively.

"No offense, but if what happened up there is your idea of being cautious...well..."

"You can say it," Stone smiled. "We're screwed."

"Yeah."

FOURTEEN
PALE

Cristena quickly took control, in part because she knew Dirge better than the rest of them, but also because she simply had a very forceful personality. Besides having been competently trained in the arts of tracking and combat Cristena was also a powerful witch. Unlike Cross, she'd never had any institutionalized magical training, but had instead received tutelage from a shaman. Cristena was also highly opinionated and very sure of her own abilities, also unlike Cross.

While common sense dictated they should remove themselves from Dirge as quickly as possible, Stone pointed out they still needed basic supplies and ammunition, as there would be little to be found in the way of civilization once they left Dirge and entered the Bone March.

"If only you could've been a bit more...subtle...when you decided to 'help' me," Cristena pushed. She'd grown noticeably colder towards Cross since she'd agreed to go with them.

She's still not happy about her decision, and she's going to blame me for everything from this point on. Terrific.

The market was a busy place. It was located inside a series of hollowed-out buildings made of cracked sandstone and supported by steel girders that had turned red from rust and age. Vast tarps made of red and grey cloth were hung over the roofs of the open buildings, forming a makeshift tent linking the ruined structures together. The vendors, traders and smugglers populating the market set up their wares in tents, on open tables, or on rugs spread on the ground. The market was filled with dust and haze.

Cross had the uneasy feeling they were being watched. Stone more or less handled the negotiations while they shopped, with Cristena's occasional support. Cross and Graves had to step up from time to time to provide assessments of desired equipment, much of which was in less than passable condition.

The local militia, who were as interested in satiating the vampire authority as they were with actually maintaining peace, were notoriously crafty at rooting out insurgents and malcontents, and Cross knew that under close scrutiny they'd ultimately be detected for who they really were. The fact that an active search for them had likely been initiated didn't calm his nerves any, but thus far no major alarm had been raised, surprising considering how much damage they'd done at The White Spider.

They got less than the desired trade value for Winter's equipment, but it was still enough for them to acquire a good deal of fresh ammunition, rations and blankets and coats for the cold northern weather. They also purchased a durable camel to carry everything they'd purchased. The pack brutes were accustomed to survival in the inhospitable Bone March, so the camel would greatly reduce the wear and tear on the horses they planned to acquire next. Cross thought the brown-furred camel was about the ugliest thing he'd ever seen.

After they wandered the bazaar for a while Cross knew without any doubt they were being followed. He'd been more than willing to write off his suspicions as paranoia until the third time he saw the same pale woman watching them there in the bazaar. She had alabaster skin but was otherwise difficult to get a good look at, like the air bent around her and the shadows crowded her space. She dressed in an over-sized black and a blue cloak that smothered what appeared to be a tiny frame.

Cross first saw her in the crowd when they purchased fresh blankets from a diminutive Gol trader. He saw her again when they haggled over the price of dried rations with a local dealer whose half-Doj bodyguard stood nearby, intimidating shoppers with his muscle-bound arms. Cross saw her for the third time when he perused what passed for an alchemy dealer, a battered and overcrowded table packed with chemical vials, Bunsen burners and a very small supply of basic powders and salts. With all of the banned substances in Dirge there wasn't much to be had from the alchemist, and everything of any value was buried in piles of discarded clockwork components and spare automaton parts. Cross tried his best to look interested at the wares while he watched the pale woman.

"Graves," he said, not looking up from the copper wiring in his hands. The speckled merchant who ran the table had finally left Cross alone.

"I see her," Graves quietly said beside him. "She's not being very careful."

"Which means?"

"We're meant to see her," Graves said. "She could be a diversion."

"I don't suppose it could mean she actually *is* trying to hide from us, and we're just *that* good."

"Um...no," Graves said.

Stone and Cristena had gone off in search of map paper and compasses, which had a propensity to randomly break down in the magic-soaked wastes of the Bone March. They regrouped in short order, and Graves told them about their tail.

"Damn," Cristena said. "She's Raza."

"Huh?" Stone said. "Never heard of 'em."

"They're new to Dirge. Monks who've sold their services to the Ebon Cities. They're like constables. And they're onto us."

"Monks?" Graves laughed. "Who cares about monks? What are they going to do, serve us champagne, drown us in porridge and 'vow of silence' us to death?"

"Monks with martial arts training, magic, and guns," Cristena said shortly.

"Oh, okay," Graves said with a nod. "Monks."

"Monks that aren't very subtle," Cross added. They pooled their purchased goods together and made for the weapons dealer carts, the last intended stop on their trip through the market bazaar. Cross thought they had more than enough guns and blades, but Graves insisted that wasn't possible.

"The Raza are unsubtle by design," Cristena explained as they walked. The market was busy, but at least people weren't shoulder-to-shoulder. "Do you guys *really* need to shop for more weapons? It might be best if we left before the Raza decides we're worth more than just a casual glance."

Cross agreed, but Stone and Graves reminded him that with Kray gone they lacked anyone with good experience with the mini-gun. And Cross lacking magic meant they were short a heavy hitter. It couldn't hurt, Graves argued, to make a quick perusal of the armaments, regardless of whether they were being followed or not.

The weapons racks of the bazaar were spare – the sale of magic artillery was illegal inside city limits, so the selection was limited to jury-rigged arms and old blades, many of which weren't worth even the modest prices being asked. There were a few grenades (which they purchased) and some arming wire for explosives, but it wasn't until they neared the exit they finally found what they were looking for.

"The grenade launcher is the M203 model," the merchant explained. He was a tall and skeletally thin man with a thick moustache and a long black coat that made him look like a villain out of a Western. "The rifle is an M16A2. Both are well maintained, and I have ammo for sale."

"How much?" Graves asked.

The thick-stocked rifle of the machine-gun was attached to a short tube-like launcher underneath, an intimidating looking weapon with its own trigger and a barrel the size of a baseball.

"And I'm sure you *don't* think using that thing would be overkill," Cross asked Graves.

"Are you kidding?" Graves laughed. "That *thing* is my dream girl."

In spite of Cross and Cristena's misgivings they used most of their remaining coin to purchase the weapon and all of the available ammo, and even then they could only afford it all by exchanging half of the remaining ammunition from the mini-gun. (Cross was of the opinion they should have just traded the mini-gun itself, but he was again outvoted.)

They finished up their business and made for the camel. Cristena urged them to hurry. Based on her mood Cross grew more and more afraid of the Raza by the second.

It was mid-morning when they finished packing the camel out on the crowded lane where they'd left it – Cross thought they'd actually made efficient use of their time, all things considered – and the sky had turned a shade of blood red. Thick and sulfurous clouds massed overhead. Long shadows fell over the streets, lending a dusk-like appearance to the mid-day air. Homunculi delivered messages or missives for their masters, and mules towed heavy carts loaded with copper and iron ore. Cross looked up and saw the bodies impaled on the spikes around the central black tower.

The camel, ugly beast though it was, was highly cooperative, and it didn't balk at all as loads of blankets, food and the weighty mini-gun were all strapped to the cargo boxes affixed tightly to the grotesque creature's back. Cross was handed the duty of handling the brute, by weight of the weak argument warlocks had a natural sense of animal husbandry. Cross told the others what he thought of that theory. It took him a few attempts tugging on the reins and espousing a number of encouraging thoughts to the camel before the beast would be coaxed into following him.

"I can teach you how to ride it," Cristena told him as they started out of town. They'd managed to acquire horses with the aid of Cristena's more trustworthy contacts there in the market. Cross was given a bay that seemed relatively unconcerned by his presence on her back, and her lack of spunk and fallen arches gave him the impression she was far from a young creature.

They rode nonchalantly towards the north gate. Dirge's streets widened at that end of town, and the number of inns, factories and other business noticeably dropped, replaced by shorter residential buildings and the remnants of old parks, greenhouses and statues, all of which stood in a general state of disrepair. Thunder growled on the horizon, a false precursor to rain.

"So how long did you pit-fight there at the White Spider?" Graves asked Cristena while they rode. Cross knew Graves's flirting when he saw it.

"Not long," she answered. "I get around."

"Do you now?" Graves smiled. Cristena gave him a look that could've killed a vampire. It took quite a bit of control on Cross's part not to laugh.

"Are we going to have any issues getting out of Dirge?" Stone asked.

"No," Cristena answered. "They shouldn't even notice us so long as we keep our heads down."

They approached the gates. A crowd had assembled around a street brawl, and they had to take some time to navigate around the throng of people. The lower tip of the iron portcullis hung down over the open portal like onyx teeth. They had to pass through the center of a four-way intersection to get to the gate itself, which stood next to a small wooden guardhouse. The crowd was a hundred yards behind them by the time they reached the crossroads. Most of the buildings near the gatehouse looked deserted, and the entire area was surprisingly dark. There were no gate guards, at least not there on the ground, but Cross saw sentries up on the parapets.

"I think there may be a problem..." he started, but Cristena cut him off.

"Damn it!"

Two pale women, their blue-black hoods thrown back, stood in the center of each of the streets left and right of the gate. A third identical woman appeared out of nowhere and stood just outside the city, blocking their way at the far end of the neck, the walled road leading out of the city and to the portcullis. They could have been triplets, and any one of them could have been the woman Cross and Graves earlier spied in the market. They had bizarre runic markings on their skin, serpents and spirals which twisted around their heads, necks and chests. Their eyes were blank and pale blue like pools. The air felt suddenly static.

Cross dug his heels into the flanks of his horse, and she took off with such speed and force he was almost thrown clear. Gunshots rained into the dirt around them. Cross led his horse through the open gateway, half expecting the iron portcullis to drop down and perforate him and his mount mid-step.

The portcullis didn't move. Neither did the Raza sister standing in his path just outside of the neck. If Cross had been an accomplished rider he would have steered his horse in a wide berth around her...but he wasn't an accomplished rider, and he didn't intend to stop, so he kicked the horse again, lowered his head and held on for dear life.

Cross smelled the magic before it came, a thick and meaty smell laced with fire. Red light flashed around the small woman as she whipped her hand backwards. A spiral of black and red glass cut through the air. The horse reared, and Cross was thrown from the saddle.

The world spun as he fell on his back. The wind was knocked from his lungs, and for a moment everything went black. Sharp pain throbbed in a solid line from the bottom of his skull to the base of his spine. He opened his eyes. The horse and its severed head lay on the ground next to him.

The Raza monk stood glowering at him. A halo of cold fire hung over her head, and it sapped away Cross's strength just to look at it. He was dumbfounded, trapped in place when he tried to rise.

Gunfire erupted close by and whispers swirled through his brain. A cold dead wind enveloped him in its spectral chill. Cross's chest seized up with frost.

The Raza pointed a jagged fingernail and a beam of impossibly ebon light drove into his core. The blackness grew and rushed like soiled water through his veins. He saw a void unfold out of the air like grisly paper. Cross fell into an unending liquid pit, a whirlpool of darkness.

He sees the mountain, and the girls. He feels the presence of the black unicorns. He sees men on a field caked with blood, marching for a place they can never reach to fight an enemy they can't defeat.

She falls into the sky like the leaves, adrift in silver rain, falling and falling without end, forever trapped, unable even to die.

A sharp pistol shot sounded directly over Cross's head. He ducked from the blast and threw his hands over his ears. The vision of falling into the midnight vortex and the slaying glade were violently snatched away.

The monk's head snapped back in an explosion of blood and bone. Graves stood with a smoking SIG Sauer in hand. Stone was behind him, firing the M16 at an onrushing mob of Dirgian pike-guards, while Cristena conjured a wave of liquid wraiths which spiraled out of her clenched fists like an exploding cyclone.

She shielded me, Cross realized. *Cristena saved my life. My God, she's got some serious power.*

Impressive as it was, Cristena's shield rapidly began to deteriorate beneath the hail of bullets. Cross felt her power buckle with each shot, just as he felt the shield shift and rattle like a piece of glass buffeted by heavy winds. He sensed her exhaustion, noted waves of power exuded by her spirit.

How did I feel that? What the hell is happening?

Moments later the sensation was gone. Cross's stomach felt like it had been filled with sewage.

Graves fired into the mob of onrushing soldiers as he re-mounted his horse. Graves and Cristena had made it through the neck and were just outside the open portcullis but still beneath the protective stone outcropping of the barbican towers, which lucky for them made it difficult for the sentries up on the city walls to get a clear shot. Cross didn't see the other Razas, but he remembered the flame cannons up with the gunners.

We are so screwed.

Cristena sent an arc of electric blue energy into the portcullis. The gate rumbled in place and groaned against its own tracks. Stone just managed to get his horse and the camel out of the neck before the thick iron slammed into the ground with a reverberating crash and a cloud of dust. The squad was outside of the city.

"What about the monks?" Cross asked. Graves hauled him up to ride behind him. Cross's ribs stung like fire.

A klaxon sounded inside the city. Shouts and battle cries filled the air as more of Dirge's finest answered the call.

"Stone killed one, and Cristena got the other," Graves said. "She's a badass, man. She looked like you out there."

Cross hoped he'd live to resent his replacement later.

A rifle shot struck the ground in front of them. There was open country ahead, a steep descent into rolling red hills and dusty plains. A dead forest stood in the distant, and beyond the trees was the Bone March.

"The riflemen will kill us the second we make a break for it," Graves said. "Being under the barbican is the only thing keeping us alive, and it won't take those soldiers long to make it out here."

"Ride forward, then," Cross said. He reached into his coat pocket. "Slowly."

"What?"

"Do it."

Graves did, even as Stone and Cristena both shouted at them to stop. The horse moved out from under the barbican, one step at a time, until they were in the open, just far enough for Cross to look up and see the edge of the roof directly over their heads. Cross threw the grenades up and onto the top of the barbican, one and then the other, and he let the pins fall into the dirt.

"Whoa!" Graves shouted. He turned the horse around and raced back under cover.

The blast was deafening. Chunks of metal and dust cascaded to the ground. Fire and bodies fell amidst a wreckage of machinery parts, broken wood and chunks of shattered stone. The squad seized the moment and urged their horses forward, hoping the riflemen positioned further down the wall wouldn't be able to get a clear shot through the haze and smoke.

At least we got rid of the flame cannons, Cross thought with some satisfaction.

He glanced back through the smoke and saw streams of fire spread along the tops of the walls as liquid fuel reserved for the cannons exploded. Black smoke billowed into the air.

The horses thundered down the hill. They raced down steep slopes leading down to the plains. Cross hung on for dear life, his hands locked in a death grip around Graves's waist.

They tore towards the badlands, riding through drifts of fire smoke and dust stirred up by harsh winds. Cross heard nothing behind them to indicate that any sort of pursuit was still underway, and for a moment he thought they'd gotten away clean.

That was when the mortar shells started to fall.

The blasts began slowly, a distant chorus of soft booms. It was difficult to make out the origin points of the mortars, but they heard the bombs tear down through the air with sonic force, a cavalcade of building momentum.

The first blast hit about 300 yards behind them, well off the mark but close enough it rattled the ground and spooked their horses. Graves had to fight their mount to keep it from sending all three of them to the ground. Chunks of earth scattered and fell like dice. The second blast hit a few yards closer.

"Ride!" Stone shouted. "If this smoke clears and they get a clean shot, we're dead!"

They raced down the steep hill, nearly out of control. The mortar blasts drew closer and closer and fell one after the other in quick succession. Cross expected every blast to hit home. His spine tingled, and the hairs on the nape of his neck froze in spite of the sweat. His back tensed, ready for the blast, ready for the shrapnel.

Somehow they made it. Within a few minutes they'd left the crash of mortar shells behind them, and the city of Dirge faded until it was little more than a dark stain.

The land continued sloping to the north. The path widened between the rocky and jagged hills. Past the last line of dying vegetation stood a realm of red dirt, black soil and white trees. The Bone March.

They rode in silence for a time, listening for the sound of pursuit. Surprisingly none came, but they kept their pace for another hour. The air turned metallic and stale. There was no breeze. The land ahead was already an eyesore, a dread panorama.

"So," Cross said at last. His voice was surprisingly loud in the prevailing quiet. There weren't even insects or bird calls.

Stone rode the point, and the others filed in behind him. The camel, who'd shown surprising endurance through the entire ordeal (or perhaps not that surprising...Cross realized he didn't know a great deal about camels), brought up the rear, tethered to Graves's horse.

"So...what?!" Graves asked. "You have a habit of starting a conversation and then falling asleep."

"I was talking to Cristena, you moron."

"Bite me."

"Yes, children?" Cristena said with a sigh.

"What did you do?" Cross asked her.

"What do you mean?" she hesitated.

"I mean, *what did you do?*" Cross asked again. "Back there, at the gates."

"I heard you. That doesn't mean I know what you're talking about."

"Your magic," Cross said. "Something about the way you channeled your spirit, maybe, or..."

"You're not making any sense," Cristena said, and she cut Cross off when he tried to respond. "Listen, Cross, no offense...but I don't want to talk to you about my spirit. I don't want to talk to you about much of *anything*. All that should matter to you is that I'll help you get through the Bone March. That's it. I don't want to get to know you. I don't need you. You need me."

"Yeah," Cross said.

I felt you touch your spirit, he thought. *I felt your magic back in the city, even though my spirit is gone. And I don't know why. I shouldn't be able to do that. How did that happen?*

Was it you that somehow made that possible? Or was it me?

"Is there a problem?" Stone asked from up ahead.

"No," Cross said. He met Cristena's gaze until she finally looked away. "No problem at all."

PART FOUR
SCARS

He stands alone in a wasteland of black sand. A realm of charcoal graveyards. The black mountain stands impossibly tall, a rip in the sky. The forest lies at its feet, subjugated by the peak's brutal size. The stink of crumbled empires and the breath of ghosts drift on the icewind breeze.

They are adrift, an island in a sea of nothing. Black sands run to infinity. He feels the cold of the open desert, gazes up to a bloody red sky filled with swirling steel clouds. Heavy wind kicks up sand into a black storm.

Night spreads like a stain. He senses the women in the glade, trapped in a prison of trees. He feels their heartbeats across the dust, hears tears fall like raindrops.

The lonely dirge of a train cries out. A plume of churning smoke appears in the distance, spat into the sky by a steel goliath tearing across the ground, a train with no tracks, an iron juggernaut bringing clouds of black souls in its wake. He's afraid of this ghost train. He knows he will see it closer, and soon.

He calls out to her, but all he's rewarded with is the sound of his own meaningless voice, a fading echo carried away by the wind. The train draws closer, inevitable, unstoppable.

He has lost her. He is alone.

FIFTEEN

BONES

They rode through a land of dust and ash.

The Bone March was a region of midnight sand. When the sun eventually sucked down into the horizon they knew it would be difficult to discern where the world began and where it stopped. Red dust had been blown into drifts as tall as a man, but the ground beneath the sand was all black: black soil, black water, black stone. It was like everything had been burned and had yet to heal.

That's not far from the truth, Cross thought.

Once beyond the dangers of Dirge they rested and made sure all of their supplies were in order and they had their bearings. Cross compared his translated map with Cristena's knowledge of the area, and they used the compasses and water-globes to align the sun's position with their location to make sure they were in the right place. Once they charted a course, they set off.

After an hour of riding into the Bone March it felt as if they'd traveled to another planet. The world was a black desert, an endless sea of onyx soil and crimson dust and gnarled lifeless trees protruding from the ground like dug-up bones. The air was as dry as paper, but the soil seemed unstable and almost fluid at times, and they rode with an eye out for sinkholes.

The utter stillness of the March was unnerving. There were no insects, no coyote or wolf calls, and no wind. Even the footfalls of the horse's hooves were almost silent. The loudest sound to be heard was the creak of the saddles as they rode.

It was midday, though it was difficult to tell, since the sky had been the same pale shade of red for hours. The color reminded Cross of a bloody steak. He dismounted and led the nameless camel for a time so he could stretch his legs. The air was cold and smelled like something sick. Cross had been constantly thirsty since they'd entered the March, and the horses were, too. Luckily they'd had the foresight to stock up on water, but at the rate at which they had to consume it in order to stay even relatively hydrated, and thanks to the apparent scarcity of potable water there in the March, they knew their supply wouldn't last very long.

I guess it's a good thing we aren't going far.

"This is where it all started," Cross said.

"What?" Graves asked.

"The Black broke through into our world here. Well..." Cross turned around in a circle, taking in the breadth of the Bone March. "*Somewhere* out here. They think."

"They think," Cristena repeated. She rode at the rear of the group. Her palomino looked downright exhausted, and Cristena looked listless and sleepy herself. Cross suspected that raising that shield back in Dirge had taken more out of her than she'd let on. "It's a guess. There's no way to ever prove it."

"Well, they did find arcane residue from The Black out here in the wastes a few years ago," Cross answered. "Not to mention the remains of old Soth. We shouldn't even be too far from some of Soth's ruins, if my map is right."

"Old Soth is just a myth," she said. "El Paso used to be here, not some faerie vampire capital."

"I am *so* lost," Graves said.

There was no way anyone could prove or even understand the truth about The Black. All that could really be agreed on was that there was a time before The Black, and a time after, and that no two worlds could be further removed.

The destructive phenomenon called The Black had arrived completely unheralded, and it had ravaged the world with a single-minded fury the likes of which humankind could barely conceive. Millions had died in the months following The Black. The initial colliding of worlds had caused tidal waves and earthquakes. Entire cities had been swallowed into the earth and lost as the land resealed itself. Fires covered entire coastlines. Seas drained, and deserts sank.

But that was only the beginning. After the initial devastation that had ripped the boundaries between worlds humankind still had to contend with what had come through the cracks. People were hunted through the night by living shadows and haunted by the ghosts of apocalypse cities that had stood for centuries but that no one could remember being there in the first place. Worst of all, earth was besieged by hordes of vampires led by the enigmatic Grim Father, who established a military regime over most of what was left of the northern continent.

Monsters were real. Myths and legends and horror stories were all real, and it was as if they'd *always* been real. Even magic became real shortly after The Black. The ruins and histories of cities that had never existed melted into reality and the collective consciousness of humankind.

At the same time, while many cities were ruined and violently torn apart, it was commonly agreed that other cities had simply faded, like they'd never existed at all. The Black had merged some realities and destroyed others. Worlds had bled together like spilled fluids.

No one even knew what The Black really was, where it had come from, or if it was really gone. All anyone knew for certain was that it had destroyed the known world and rewritten all that had come before as indelibly as it had forever altered what would come after.

"Where else would it have started?" Cross asked. "Can you tell me one other place, besides the Bone March, that fits all of the criteria?"

"The Skull Plains," Cristena answered.

"It's lifeless enough," Cross conceded, "but it bears little to no arcane residue, and least none that's ever been found."

"Rimefang Loch."

"No. Even taking into account the residents of Ghostborne Island, the Loch is relatively unaltered by magic."

"'Relatively'," Cristena laughed. "Listen to you. All right, then...the Bleeding Straits."

"Now who's talking about myths?" Cross laughed.

"I've *been* there, Cross," Cristena said. "Have you? Look, the point is, there are plenty of areas where The Black *might* have come through. It's foolish to assume it's here in the March just because it's the most popular choice. I've been in and out of the Bone March and all those other places, and I've never once seen anything to convince me The Black started in *any* of them, let alone *here*."

"There's a reason the popular theory is the Bone March..."

"Oh who cares?!" Graves said. "What does it matter where it started?"

"It doesn't," Cristena said.

"Then why argue about it?" Cross asked with a bit of sneer.

"I wasn't arguing," Cristena said. "I just don't like to listen to others spout off theories like they're facts."

"Well it must be nice to be right all of the time," Cross said.

"It is," Cristena replied, and she spurred her horse around them and rode ahead to take the point.

"Cross, you are so smooth," Graves said with a laugh. Cross didn't answer.

Time crawled by. They hoped to only be stuck in the Bone March for two or three days at the most, but that first day had already felt like ten. They crossed sluggish streams of greasy grey water and shallow fields filled with black lichen. The temperature grew noticeably colder, and after a time the air was filled with a semi-translucent freezing fog that smelled like rotting food.

They crossed fields of bones yellowed by time and the excess of sulfur in the air and passed skeletal white trees with snaky roots jutting from the ground like frozen serpents. Black husks of prune-like fruit seeping sickly purple juices dangled from the gnarled limbs. The ground around the trees was pitted, like it had been eaten by acid.

Navigating the Bone March took its toll on them. There was no shade or cover, and the absence of any notable landmarks had a disheartening effect on Cross's psyche. The ground remained soft and uneven, and consequently was difficult for the horses to tread, especially on their already weary legs. The group rested their mounts often, noting the thick and foamy sweat on the animal's necks and chests in spite of the incessant chill. The air tasted like salt.

This is taking too long, Cross thought. *We have to hurry, or we'll never stop her in time. We'll never be there in time to save Snow.* But they couldn't go any faster, he knew that, they all knew that. They wouldn't be able to stop Red at all if they pushed themselves too hard.

They passed the hollow remains of a large stone building and a lonely well filled with briny black fluid. There was a long-abandoned motorcade, the skeletons of cars left to rust and fade in the frozen heat. These landmarks were fleeting, momentary distractions from the great black and red waste surrounding them.

This, they knew, was what had become of the old human civilization, and if the vampires won the war then places like the Bone March would be all that was left. The Ebon Cities would lay everything to waste and rule over what was left from the confines of their graveyard cities.

They made camp just before nightfall next to a steep path leading to a rickety wooden bridge which stretched over a deep gorge. The bridge looked less than stable with its splintered posts and rotting rope bindings. They decided it would be better to try and cross in full light, or what passed for full light there in the Bone March.

Cross sat warming his hands by the fire, nursing a flask of water and an open can of beans, when they heard the howls of wolves off in the distance.

"Hooray," Graves said, and he tossed the remainder of his coffee into the flames. The fluid was strangely combustible, which about summed up the quality of their coffee.

"They're still pretty far," Cristena said. She huddled inside a thick green blanket, shivering and holding a steaming cup of the same dangerous coffee. "But we'd better keep our eyes open. There isn't much for them to eat out here except each other."

"And us," Stone said.

"How can they even survive out here at all?" Graves asked. The crackling flames cast them all in flickering shadows.

"Not much lives here," Cristena explained. "The March can trap you. It's unnatural, and it's easy to get lost. Some things wander in from the borderlands and never find their way back."

Their camp swam in a sea of darkness. They might have been in outer space. Cross looked up at the sky. It was frighteningly vast and deep, and he felt like he could fall into it. Between the fathoms of space and the darkness of the March Cross imagined his body plummeting, on and on without end.

He dreams of falling. He sees the woman, the refugee from the mountain glade, but while he falls through a black sky hers is white. He falls down, and she falls up.

Wolves woke him. Cross sat up with a start. His head ached and his heart pounded.

"It's all right," Stone said. He was on watch nearby with the M16A2 in hand. "They're far away. Try to get some sleep."

The next morning, as they drifted along the bleak landscape spurred by the fact that with any luck they'd be out of the Bone March by day's end, they realized they were being followed.

A group of riders trailed them in the distance. It was impossible to glean any details from that distance, save the number. There were six.

"Could they be nomads?" Cross asked. He already knew the answer. He wasn't even sure why he'd even bothered to ask.

"They've been tailing us for a while," Stone noted. "They probably just stayed out of sight until we crossed that gorge. The terrain has been pretty flat since then, nowhere for them to hide."

The squad carried on with an eye behind them. The riders didn't quicken or slow their pace but kept a perfect distance, dangling right at the edge of sight.

"Should we just take care of this?" Graves asked after a while.

"No," Stone said, clearly wishing he had a different answer. "Not yet. There's no way to get any sort of advantage over them right now. All we'd be doing is riding right up to them. I wish there was some cover out here."

"When we get closer to the Rift the ground gets rocky again," Cristena pointed out. "And hilly. We should be able to lose them then."

"Or gain the advantage," Stone said.

They rode on.

Cross felt cold. He sensed whispers in the air, the touch of the spirits tied to the area. The feeling intensified as they rode out of the open desert and into a region of hills and dead trees. The air was thick with dead whispers. Cross felt the breath of ghosts on his skin.

I shouldn't be able to feel this. My spirit is gone, and I can never have another. What's lost can't be regained.

He sees the woman, falling into the sky.

Who are you?

Cross felt like he was losing his mind.

Dusk approached. They rode through a field of sharp stones, some as large as their horses. The rocks were black quartz shot through with red crystal veins, and the seared edges of the stone smoked like glacial ice. The dark soil underfoot was crystalline and coarse.

Bones dangled from dead trees, skeletons of those left to rot. Shreds of ancient clothing fluttered in a dry wind carrying the smell of carrion and rotted flowers.

They were getting close to the Rift.

And after they'd kept their distance for over an hour, the mysterious riders suddenly closed in.

SIXTEEN

WOLVES

They rode fast, but it wasn't fast enough.

The six riders closed the gap between the two groups seemingly without effort. At the rate they approached they'd be face-to-face before nightfall. The howls of the wolves started in again, closer this time. Much closer.

"Let's put some distance between us," Stone said. "Now!"

The terrain had become much more difficult to manage, particularly in the failing light. A scarlet filter was draped over the sky. Thick patches of rubble lay in their path, leading to a high hillside at the edge of a forest of dead trees. The bloody sunlight was rapidly fading. Cross looked into the trees but all he saw were more shadows beyond the thickets.

"Are we going in *there*?" he called back.

Cross rode with Cristena at the head of the party. The riders were right behind them, only a few hundred yards back, their thick red cloaks fluttering in the wind. They wore red armor and bandoliers stocked with knives, hex rods and grenades. The vampires had thick black hair, pale and gnarled flesh, red eyes and ebon fangs. They rode Blood Wolves: massive and horse-sized lupines with mottled dark fur. The wolves' oversized heads bore half-moon eyes and enormous slavering jaws.

Graves fired on them with a SIG Sauer in one hand and a snub-nosed Colt Python in the other. Most of his shots went wide, but one took a vampire in the shoulder and nearly threw it from its wolf mount, but the undead clung to the leather reins and held tight.

The vampires had the momentum of a runaway train. They were suddenly so close it was as if they'd been right up on the squad's heels all along.

Cross and Cristena were nearly to the forest.

"Go!" Stone shouted. He leapt out of his saddle, turned and knelt down with the M16A2 and the grenade launcher in his hands.

Cross pulled his pack off and desperately dug through it for something – anything – that might prove useful. He found vials of anti-toxin, rolls of bandage, chemical batteries...

"Cross..." Cristena said as they rode closer to the forest.

"We're not leaving," he said, and he dismounted. Cristena followed suit. He heard the wolves draw close. Their staccato howls came in unison.

Cross found the pyrojack and quickly pulled it over his shaking left hand. The leather and steel gauntlet fit snugly. There were two open nodes on the outside of the glove between the second and third knuckles. The first node still held a red-black stone whose face swirled with energies humming with arcane potential.

Graves fired his third and last loaded pistol, a banged-up HK45 like Cross's. A shot hit the lead rider square between the eyes, and both he and his wolf came crashing forward in a violent heap of skin and fur.

Stone knelt close by with his rifle at the ready. He was alone on the lower stretch of ground. He aimed at the riders as they thundered towards him. The riders drew to within a hundred yards.

Cross felt a spirit whisper in the air around him. He even felt her against his skin. Something nearby howled with a rancid and bloodcurdling cry.

The vampires were fifty yards away when Stone pulled the trigger of the M203. The grenade tore the ground apart with a violent explosion. Two riders and their mounts exploded in a mess of blood and fur, and two more crashed to the ground behind them.

One wolf had started to rise when arcane bolts of black rock skewered it and its rider. Cross felt Cristena's effort beside him, felt the strain the magical attack placed on her spirit.

Graves and Stone fired at the other wolf and rider. The shotgun took the wolf's head off in a gruesome spray, and Stone moved in to finish the vampire off with his black-bladed machete.

The vampire was quick. It sprang to its feet and leapt up and over Stone with a whirling flip that put it in position behind him, but Stone anticipated the move, turned and took its head off with a clean turnaround swing.

The last vampire-and-wolf pair leapt through the smoke left behind by the grenade blast. Stone's back was turned, and the wolf landed on him and threw him face down to the ground. Graves called out, reached to his back and unsheathed his machete. Cross felt the pyrojack tingle against his cold flesh.

Cristena screamed behind him. A vampire had slithered out of the woods and grabbed her. Its black eyes reflected Cross's face back at him. Cristena's blood splashed across its pale cheeks. Her eyes went white. Her open jugular oozed beneath the caress of black fangs.

Cross heard her spirit screaming. He almost saw gossamer entrails as it poured every last bit of its form into protecting her, into keeping her alive when her body should have already expired.

Stone shouted. Graves cried out. A beast snarled. Cross's heart raced so fast it felt ready to explode from his chest like a cannon shot.

He aimed his HK at the vampire eating Cristena, right between its eyes.

She falls

He closed his eyes.

up

And he is there with her in the glade. The black mountain looms over them, powerful and vast, dripping power so raw it congeals and falls like sick rain. The air is moist and cold. Ice floes drift in the stream. Rain-addled leaves plummet from the trees and land on the forest floor.

She's there. She hasn't fallen, hasn't left him alone, not yet. He only thinks she has. She isn't gone.

"What is this place?" he asks. His voice echoes in silver notes.

"My prison," she says. "The place from where I watch you, guide you, protect you." Her voice is soft, like liquid in the air. Her hair shifts in the cool

wind. The light illuminates her white-silk body and raven hair. She floats in a pale sea.

"How is it I'm here?" he asks.

"You're not, Eric. We're stuck. I'm still weakened from saving you. We two hover at the edge of death. I'm here, where I've always been, but I can't reach you. Not alone."

The wind grows stronger. Wet leaves stir and hard rain splashes in the laggard waters. Dark shapes move in the trees. The mountain seems to creak and groan beneath its own weight.

"Save me," she says. "Save all of us, before it's too late..."

Cristena was dying. He felt his spirit's touch at the edge of his consciousness, like the memory of a sweet kiss.

The vampire howled and spat blood, and at that instant Cross pulled the trigger. The bullet soared into the vampire's mouth and crashed through the back of its skull in a mass of blood, hair and bone.

The vampire hadn't even fallen to the ground before Cross spun round and ignited the pyrojack. Hot white fire streamed around his fist. The last stone on the gauntlet cracked and launched, and a screaming incendiary missile left a trail of rancid black smoke in its wake. The arcane missile soared down the hill, maneuvered past Graves and flew straight into the wolf, where it burned and sizzled its way through fur and skin and into the beast's heart like a vicious volcanic worm. The lupine howled as its insides exploded. Smoke and blood streamed from its mouth.

Graves battled the vampire with his machete. Cross steadied his HK45, took aim, and fired. The shot didn't quite hit the mark – it tore the vampire's ear off in a fine red spray – but it was enough to distract the creature long enough for Graves to behead it with a well-placed swing.

Cross looked at Stone and feared the worst. He knelt down next to Cristena, who'd already lost a great deal of blood. Cross yanked a strip of cloth from his coat pocket and tied it gently around her neck, then pulled a pouch of hexed salt and several vials of seawater from his pack. With one hand pressed against the wound he dropped his other hand into the salt pouch and coated it before dousing it in the seawater. That done, he rubbed the mixture onto the wound, careful not to do any more harm to the damaged tissue, but if he could contain the spread of the shadowy plague her spirit could heal her mangled flesh. The trick was to keep her alive long enough for the weakened spirit to do its work.

"Graves!" he shouted. Cross was fairly certain he'd stemmed the flow of the infection. "How's Stone?"

"Unconscious," Graves shouted back. "And he's banged up pretty bad."

"Was he bit?"

"No. Clawed, not bit."

"Clawed is okay," Cross shouted. "No one ever got turned into a vampire from being clawed."

"It doesn't *look* okay!" Graves shouted.

I'll have to worry about him later.

The flesh on Cristena's face and neck was discolored and dark, like she was drowning. Her eyes were open and blank, and black spittle ran from her between her lips.

"Graves, where's the camel?"

They stabilized Cristena and Stone as best they could. Cross tended to them while Graves went out to search for the stalwart camel, which had wisely fled as soon as the fighting started. Thankfully the ugly brute hadn't gone far. While Graves was gone Cross sat, still aware of his spirit at the edge of his mind, a memory he couldn't quite recapture, a taste he couldn't quite recognize.

He thought he'd figured out how to carry on without her, but now that he felt her presence again he realized how wrong he was. Longing filled him, twisted him, quickened his pulse and pulled at his soul.

If only I could touch you again.

He focused his attention back on the wounded. Stone, as Graves had put it, was indeed banged up – there were claw wounds running deep into his back, and Cross was pretty sure Stone had suffered a broken rib and possibly a concussion, not to mention a twisted ankle. He'd be far from a hundred percent, but he was alive, and so long as the concussion was minor he'd be able to hold his own.

"You always were a tough guy," Cross laughed.

Cristena was the real worry. Cross kept trying to convince himself she *wanted* to die, that maybe she wouldn't even want to be saved, but he knew that was crazy, that he was just trying to take the pressure off of himself and that that was the last thing he needed to do. She'd saved their lives more than once, and, perhaps of greater import, she was *meant* to be there with them. He wholly believed that, and that was what really mattered.

Graves returned with the camel, which had all of the equipment Cross needed strapped to its back. Cross was able to extract the rest of the vampiric poison from Cristena's bloodstream with plastic tubing and a small electric engine; he'd taken to carrying that handy combination of devices ever since his short tour in the Blackmarsh, land of the ear mites and brain worms. The infected blood came out thick and syrupy, almost like oil, and it crawled with tiny black insects that looked like scarab beetles.

"That," Graves declared, "is some nasty shit."

"Now," Cross answered, "we give her blood."

Graves wasn't particularly crazy about the tube apparatus and spider-shaped needles Cross used to perform the transfusion, and he griped constantly about the pain, but in the end the three of them – Graves, Cross and Stone, who certainly couldn't object to being a donor given his unconscious state – were able to give Cristena enough blood to keep her alive.

They made camp right there at the edge of the forest. Graves cleaned their weapons in the flickering campfire light while Cross looked over the maps. Stone and Cristena lay nearby, unconscious and wrapped tightly in woolen blankets. Stone woke once or twice, just long enough to make rude comments regarding the state of the campfire and to consume an MRE before he drifted back to sleep. Cross was pretty sure he'd be okay. The concussion seemed minor, and while a broken rib was nothing to be thrilled about it could have been much worse. Once Cross and Graves cleaned and stitched his wounds and cleared away any possible infections with hexed seaweed and honeysuckle balm they knew he'd pull through.

Cristena, on the other hand, hadn't stirred at all.

"Wow," Cross said after he'd studied the maps for a while. The night air sounded normal now – there were crickets and birds, occasional owl hoots, even the wind. "We're actually close to a town."

"Say what?" Graves asked.

"A town. You know, with people, and stuff? We're close to one."

"How did we manage that?" Graves had cleaned and loaded his pistols, and he set about doing the same with the M16A2 and the M403. "I thought we were in the dreaded Bone March, end of the earth, last chance to get killed for four-hundred-miles, middle of friggin' nowhere."

"Are you ever *not* bitter? In any case, you're right, buuuut..." Cross checked the map he'd made down in the hole in the Wormwood, compared it to Cristena's land maps, and re-took his compass reading. "Yeah. We're close to Rhaine. It's a borderland trading town, I think, half a day's ride to the northeast. It's about as isolated as you can get for a populated area, but they're bound to have supplies."

"I've heard of that place," Graves said. "A bunch of prospectors live there, mountain men, ex-soldiers, stuff like that?"

"That's the one."

Graves stared off for a second, then looked to the north. "You know we don't have time to go there, right? There's no telling how far ahead of us Red is. Hell, she's probably almost to Koth by now. If she gets there before we get to her..."

"She will, Sam," Cross interrupted. "I hate to break it to you, but she's got two people to worry about, just her and Snow, and that's assuming she even took my sister with her." Cross had to let that cold notion settle in. His hands started to shake, but he did his best to ignore it. "We're a whole group, complete with a camel, for fuck's sake. We're not even completely sure we know where she's going. Of *course* she's going to beat us there."

"Wait a minute," Graves said, suddenly angry, and that made Cross nervous. Graves may not have been the most physically imposing man but he had a temper like a wolverine, and he could be just as hard to deal with. "What do you mean 'not completely sure'...you have the map!"

"Translated and decoded from an archaic language. I cracked the code used to write it – I think – and translated it from memory. I told you this already." Cross stared back at the fire. He wasn't going to stand up and argue. "I told you this."

"Then what's the point?" Graves said with a shrug. "I mean, damn it, Cross, why aren't we back in Thornn, waiting for the end in style instead of wandering around out here, watching our friends die one at a time..."

"Because I'm going to find my sister!" Cross just avoided shouting. "If that's alright with you."

Graves shook with anger and frustration, well aware, Cross was sure, there was nothing and no one around to take it out on. After a moment he sat down hard and wiped a hand over his face.

"Sorry."

"It's okay," Cross said.

"I wouldn't leave your sister out here," Graves said. "I'm sorry."

"Listen," Cross said. "It's not like the world is going to end the second Red gets there. The Old One is still trying to buy his way back into the graces of the Ebon Cities, right? She'll give him what she's got, and he'll need to arrange things with the Grim Father. Everything is politics with the vampires. It'll take some time."

Graves looked puzzled. "One thing that's always bugged me, Eric...why doesn't Red go straight to the Suckheads? Why go through the Old One at all?"

"I don't know. Maybe he's giving her something in exchange for her information. Maybe she's his girlfriend. Maybe the vampires just won't talk to her directly. I don't know."

Cross looked up past the heat blur of the campfire and into the night sky. He knew how exposed they were, and how easy it would be to spot them from a distance, but for some reason he didn't think they'd have any more trouble that night. It was almost like he'd regained a sensation of the surrounding areas, a heightened sense of what was where.

It was almost as if he had his spirit back.

"We need to stop in Rhaine," he said after he rechecked the maps again. "If I'm reading Cristena's maps correctly there isn't really a way of actually getting across the Carrion Rift this far west, but there's a bridge and a pass to the east, right within a few klicks of the city."

Graves nodded.

"We'll get supplies," Cross continued. "We can leave Stone or Cristena there if we have to. Maybe we can get a message to Thornn."

"Wow," Graves laughed. "Listen to you, Squad Leader."

"No," Cross said nervously. "I'm pretty sure *you're* in charge, actually. Chain of Command, and all."

"Ah, Hell with that. You're doing great. I'm not much for giving orders." Graves stared out into the night. "Do you think Snow is ok?"

"I don't know," Cross said. "It's been driving me crazy. I keep trying not to think about it, but…"

"But then *I* bring it up."

"No, no…I can't help but worry. I hope she is. I hope she's okay." Cross stared into the loathsome dark. "She's all I have left."

"I know," Graves said.

"I can't imagine losing her."

"Yeah," Graves smiled. "Look, she'll be fine. Red may be a bitch, but she's not stupid. Snow is a hostage, after all. And besides…is Red a tracker?"

"I don't know," Cross said. Not all witches were trackers. In all her years as Thornn's leader and the voice of the White Mother, Red – Margrave – had never displayed any of a tracker's talents. "You know, Sam, I'd never thought of that. Powerful or not, I'm guessing Red must've had the same problems with that translation that I did…I mean, don't get me wrong, my map is pretty good, but having a tracker with us will help when we get closer to the mark. Cristena can navigate the arcane streams and follow the weylines once we're close enough to Koth. She can get us there when the map can't give us any more useful information." His heart lifted at the thought. "Maybe Red will need that kind of help, too."

And maybe, just maybe, that means Snow is still alive.

"She's going to be all right," Graves said.

"You think so?" Cross said. The crackle of the campfire popped loud. "I keep thinking about our childhood, Sam. I keep thinking about all of the things she and I did, all of the…memories. Stupid things, really. Just us, together. And I keep thinking about…about what a terrible brother I've been to her lately."

They sat in silence for a time.

"I felt the same way when my Dad died," Graves said at last. "Like I'd been a horrible son. Like I should have spent more time with him. Trust me, Eric...it doesn't help." He looked at Cross. "What's done is done. Do what you can now to make things right."

Graves finished cleaning the weapons, then he retired to sleep.

Cross stared at the fire for a long time. He couldn't stop shaking.

SEVENTEEN
SPIRIT

Cross sat first watch. He used coffee and warm porridge to stay awake and alert. He jumped at every shadow and felt dwarfed by the shotgun in his hands and the fathomless black of the surrounding night. Cricket song filled the air with an almost ear-grating intensity. Cross wanted to set the forest on fire to shut them up.

He couldn't feel his spirit at all through the long night, so he stayed up alone at the edge of nowhere. He distracted himself with the maps he'd already gone over a dozen times and by checking on Stone and Cristena for any signs of their conditions worsening. Finally, after it felt like years had passed waiting for something to pounce out of the dark, Graves woke for his shift and Cross went to sleep. He didn't dream.

In the morning, Graves woke him with a hard nudge.

"Wake up, pal," he said in a whisper. Cross struggled and moaned for a moment before he saw Graves's face. "Morning! We're screwed."

Cross opened his eyes the rest of the way.

The forest had changed.

They were in the middle of a twisted copse that looked absolutely nothing like the spot they'd camped at the night before. It was like the entire campsite had relocated to the middle of a dead woods webbed with shadows.

"What the hell...?" Cross stammered.

"Yep," Graves said. "I have no idea what happened."

"Did you fall asleep?"

Graves gave him a look. "Bite me. I *never* fall asleep on watch. That's *you*." Graves turned around in a quick circle and scanned the area. "I checked on Stone, I checked on Cristena, I made a fresh pot of coffee, I looked up, and...this."

Something cracked loud deeper in the forest. Cross thought it sounded like a tree being snapped. The grey morning air was heavy with dew and mist, and it was impossible to see anything beyond about fifty yards. The ground shook. Cross smelled hex and toxins.

"We have to get the hell out of here," he said.

"You think?!" Graves snapped.

"Let's get them up and grab what we can."

Graves tried to rouse Stone. Cross, seized by a notion, quickly tossed through their belongings and pulled apart blankets, tore open bags and kicked aside cooking pots.

"What the hell are you doing?" Graves asked him. "Does making a mess help somehow?!"

"You like to take stuff from places we travel through, right?" Cross pulled open a bag filled with dry rations and tossed it aside. "Like souvenirs? Kray used to do it, too."

"Yeah, sometimes," Graves said. "So?"

"Look at these trees," Cross said. "They're different from the trees that were here last night."

"Again....SO?!"

"This is a different forest."

"How is that possible?" Graves asked as he tried to wake Stone. "What, so we were pulled through time and space and dropped in some random forest? I mean...where in the hell are we?"

Cross finally found what he'd been searching for amidst Graves's things, and cursed to himself.

Damn it, Sam, you may have killed us without even realizing it.

Cross held the Wormwood branch up so Graves could see it, a twisted and gnarled piece of wood shaped almost like a claw and smelling of sulfur.

"It's not some random forest," he said. "It's the Wormwood. And we didn't go to it – it came to us."

Graves laughed the kind of laugh one might have when they found out they had cancer, or that their father had just died.

"Are you saying the forest *followed* us?!"

Cross snapped the branch in two and tossed it into the smoking remains of the campfire.

"Part of it did. I've heard of stuff like this happening, but I'd never actually seen it. Most cursed locales possess some intelligence, and sometimes they can be...vengeful."

"The forest is pissed at us because we got away?" Graves asked.

"It's pissed at us because we took some of it with us. It used the branch to follow us."

"Awesome." A loud crash sounded, closer than before. "Let's move!"

Stone was glassy-eyed and disoriented from having slept so long, but Graves quickly explained the situation and the squad leader rose right to his feet, one arm wrapped about his bandaged ribcage.

"I can't leave you two alone for one God-damned minute, can I?" he growled.

Cristena proved more difficult to rouse. After three applications of smelling salts Cross finally woke her. Her eyes were bloodshot and her speech was dreamy and slow. She might have been drunk.

"I need you to get up, Cristena," Cross urged. "Right. Now."

Another crash sounded, closer than the last. Cross saw a shadow in the distance, a mass of something crawling through the forest maze like a school of oily black eels. Trees fell before the advance of the ebon nightmare.

"Just take what we need!" Stone barked. He pulled his armor jacket on as he winced in pain.

"Damn!" Graves cried. "The horses are gone! The friggin' camel, too!"

A bestial roar issued from the forest, a dismal sonic wave like screaming animals and cruel fire.

"Run!" Graves shouted. They took up weapons and scrambled away. Cross pulled Cristena behind by the hand. When she stumbled and fell, still too groggy to move on her own, Cross took hold of her waist and hoisted her onto his shoulder. He ran, surprised by his sudden strength.

They ran through the grey mist and leapt over broken branches and bubbling bogs. They dodged skeletal trees standing like sentries in the mist, their ranks without end. The air turned blacker as their pursuer drew close.

They'd been at the edge of the trees, but now the forest went on forever. They were marooned in a dead wood.

Trees exploded at their backs and showered them with painful splinters. The force of the blast sent Cross and Cristena onto a dead tree root that struck Cross in the sternum. Cristena landed limply across his back, pinning him to the ground and knocking the air out of him.

He heard screams and shouts circling around his head in a spiraling whirlpool of noise. He sank into it, a lost ship, down to darkness so deep he couldn't hear the beast looming over him. Cross was only dimly aware of the smoking shadow's feet behind him, of the unformed black mass of a snout probing his back, of the cold white eyes. Its whole was an impenetrable mass, a midnight solid. He felt breath on him like a hot wind in a butcher's yard.

He's in the glade. The sky is filled with churning black clouds spiralling away from the mountain. A terrible chill crawls across his body. Ice-hard wind blows through the pale clearing and pushes back the trees.

She's there, at the center of the stream. She stands near another. They're nearly identical, and both of them are soaked through to the bone. Her counterpart is an androgynous male, and he so closely resembles the raven-haired beauty they might be brother and sister.

Across the clearing, on the other side of a shallow pool, stands Cristena. She looks dazed, unsure of what she sees. The wind blows stronger. Black lightning rips open the sky.

Their spirits meet in the water and embrace. They kiss passionately.

Warmth flows through his body. A channel of energy like heated milk works its way up from his toes to his fingers, from groin to neck, a heat which nearly paralyzes him even as it heals. More important, he realizes, is that it heals her, his spirit, his soul. He feels fire burn behind his eyes. The blood warms in his heart.

The spirits heal each other. Their erotic embrace somehow revitalizes their ethereal bodies. He feels himself lifted from the ground.

Movement catches his eye. He sees Snow, just beyond the tree line. Her eyes are black and terrified. He tries to call out but he has no voice. He moves to help her, but something in the shadows grabs her from behind and yanks her away with such force it nearly folds her in two. She's sucked into the darkness of the trees.

He sees Cristena, and she sees him. They hear the shadow in the trees, ready to pounce.

Cross opened his eyes. Pain flared across his chest, and Cristena's weight, light though she was, nearly suffocated him. His body pressed painfully against stones and twigs on the forest floor. The air was hot and stank of charnel matter. Something stood over them.

A sharp blast tore through the air. Cross saw Graves and the grenade launcher just a few yards away. The 40mm shot drove into the shadow, and the creature bellowed an utterly inhuman noise, a hurricane melded with a chorus of dying animals. Cross rolled over, pulling Cristena with him.

Their pursuer stood in plain sight. It was an oily morass, a gargantuan caricature of black liquid held together in the vague semblance of a canine beast. Greasy green and black smoke billowed from swollen jaws, which opened to reveal an impossibly deeper darkness within.

Cross leapt to his feet and pushed Cristena away. Graves fired a few rounds from the M16 and launched another grenade. This time the shot vanished into the beast's folds of shadow flesh with nothing but a soft thud, doing no visible damage. The hound reared up, and Cross just managed to jump back as smoky claws ravaged the earth where he'd stood. The ground shook, and he was nearly knocked to his knees.

Something held him aloft. Cold white whispers ran smooth against his skin, wrapped around him like a lover's warm breath.

She was back. His spirit had returned.

Whatever healed must must also have healed Cristena, who used her magic to tear chunks of stone from the ground and launch them at the hound in a tightly contained spiral of rocks bound together by vines, a barbed wire topiary. The strands lashed at the beast but the hound discorporated itself, split the folds of time around its unnatural flesh and pushed its body between moments, collapsed into spatial cracks and escaped the attack unharmed. Its attention turned to Cristena. A thousand bodiless voices screamed in unison from within the monster's dismal core.

"Run!" Stone shouted as he uselessly fired a Beretta at the creature.

It was clear Cristena was still weak, and it was only by the grace of her spirit she even able to stand. Cross's spirit swirled around him, fused to the skin of his soul with a diamond-hard bond. Her power surged around him.

The creature bayed at Cristena. In that moment, that frozen second, Cross surrendered himself to the power of his spirit. His eyes smoked. Black blood oozed from his nose and ears. He sent power through his left hand, which he thrust forward without thinking. He screamed.

He watched the hound unfold, saw it split the seconds, saw it divide time around its body in a razor field and use those shards as protection, a slipstream which it navigated to escape harm. Cross targeted the folds, not the beast – the splits in the shields, the chinks in the moments. He cast thorns of black force captured from the beast's own smoking body back into its dark hide. He assaulted shadow with shadow.

The act of using that necrotic power, of channeling without the aid of an implement, nearly tore him apart.

The beast folded in on itself. Cross saw a vague flash of scenes – screaming, burning, thrashing against the shadows. He held his spirit at bay. He allowed her to lend him strength to fight the necrotic attack on his system, but not to fight it *for* him. Despite the pain and dizziness he managed to hold onto that thought, that command.

I lost you once, and I won't let it happen again. You nearly destroyed yourself protecting me the last time. This time, you have to let me survive on my own.

He dreams of the silver glade. He's the only one there. He screams at the memory of having seen Snow and being unable to rescue her.

Cross floated through seas of pain. He slept on a bed of thorns. Hurt attacked him from all directions and crawled over his skin like spiders.

His blood burned beneath his skin. He felt things inside him, black insects, dark beetles, painful and angry, burrowing straight to his soul.

At least I got to hold you again, he thought, *before we died.*

EIGHTEEN

SMOKE

He dreamed of a white spider.

It was well past dark when he finally came to. Cross couldn't feel his left hand.

He was was relieved when he realized they weren't in the forest any more, but instead camped on a steep overlooking a rocky plain at the edge of the cold desert. Irregular stones and patches of brackish water dotted the landscape. The moon hung low in the sky, cold and dead. A massive shadow lay to the north, a gulf so impossibly deep it seemed to suck in the moonlight: the Carrion Rift.

Cross sat up. His left hand was fitted in the old training gauntlet he'd carried in his pack, a leather and steel glove set with numerous iron nodes which could connect to a portable battery pack. The gauntlet had safeguards and dampening fields much stronger than those Cross was used to, and the device was meant to be used by novices who needed help keeping their spirits contained. Cross carried it only as a spare.

Now it was bound tightly around his damaged hand and made it heavy. He watched the fingers of the glove flex and bend as he willed them to, but he might as well have been watching someone else doing it, as he felt nothing beyond his burning wrist.

Graves was on watch, staring out over the moonlit flats with the M4A2 in hand. Cristena and Stone sat near the campfire eating from bowls of steaming hot soup.

"Can I have some?" Cross croaked out. His voice sounded like he'd been breathing factory fumes.

Cristena slowly walked over to him. Stone gave him a surprisingly friendly nod.

"Good to have you back," he said.

"You crazy bastard," Graves added.

Cristena knelt down beside him. She was still very pale, and the dark lines under her eyes and the creases on her face made her look twenty years older, but still she smiled. She looked at his gauntleted hand.

"How do you feel?" she asked.

"Like hell," he said. "I imagine I *look* great, too."

"Spectacular," she said with a smile. "I'm glad you're back." She paused, as if uncertain of what to say next. "Thank you."

"For what?"

"For saving my life."

"Thank you for saving mine," he said with an awkward nod. He held up the gauntleted hand for inspection. "Is this what I think it is?"

Cristena just nodded.

Well, damn.

Warlocks were forced to rely on arcane implements to properly manifest the power of their spirits. The implements could take the form of gauntlets, rods, rings, even specially modified pistols or blades. Witches, on the other hand, had no use for them. No one had ever really been able to figure out why, just as no one really knew why only women could be trackers. Whatever the reason, a warlock who channeled without an implement to protect him from the touch of his spirit's raw power was just asking for trouble. At best he'd do physical harm to himself; at worse he'd burn himself and his spirit to a crisp.

"I'm not sure what's on your hand, exactly," Cristena said. "Some kind of necrotic bacteria. It was emitting an incredible amount of magic."

"I know," Cross said. "It's what that stupid hound was made of. I took pieces of the hound's body, sort of reshaped them, and used them as a weapon. I killed the hound with...pieces of itself." He smiled weakly. "Cool, huh?"

"Stupid," Graves said. Cross looked in his direction, but didn't feel like answering.

"The gauntlet is holding the necrosis in check, keeping it from spreading," Cristena explained. "I wouldn't recommend taking it off until we get you to a healer, or to a good hospital with thaumaturgic equipment. It would start to eat you again." She swallowed. "And I think it would spread really fast. Even if it wasn't a bacteria, releasing that much pent up magic..."

"Would suck," Cross finished. *It would turn me into jerky is what it would do.*

"Man, what the hell were you thinking?" Graves looked at Cross in anger. "You piss and moan because you've lost your spirit, so as soon as you get her back the first thing you do is try to get yourself killed. What the hell?"

"Graves!" Stone barked.

"Oh, screw you!" Graves shouted back, and Stone leapt to his feet. He did that in spite of a broken rib, which was probably why Graves backed away.

"I didn't have time for anything else." Cross stood up. It took a moment for the dizziness to subside. "I'm sorry, all right? But I wasn't about to let Cristena die," he said. "I killed it, didn't I?" He looked at Graves. "Didn't I?"

Graves shook his head, and turned his eyes back to the plain.

"How close are we to Rhaine?" Cross asked.

"Not far," Cristena said.

"Half a day," Stone added. He brought a bowl of brown soup over from the fire and offered it to Cross. "You did good," he said. "We'll see if we can't get you fixed up in Rhaine." Stone glanced at Graves, who stepped over the ridge and moved a few paces down the hillside. "I don't know what *his* problem is," Stone said.

"He's tired of watching his friends die," Cross said quietly.

"We're *all* tired of watching friends die. It doesn't make him special."

"Well," Cristena said, "it doesn't make it easy, either."

Stone shook his head and went back to the fire. Cristena waited for a moment, made sure Cross was all right, then returned to her place by the fire.

Cross stood alone with his spirit. She brushed against him like a soft blanket, and reassured him with her ethereal touch.

I missed you.

It was awkward for Cross to do anything without sensation in his left hand. He still had full mobility, but he had to concentrate just to make his digits perform even the most mundane task. He could imagine what the skin looked like beneath the gauntlet – black and blistered, covered in puss, maybe crawling with necrotic worms and larvae.

The gauntlet's spirit dampeners used to drive me crazy when I was an apprentice. Now it's the only thing keeping me alive.

Cross experimented with his magic after he ate, both to reacquaint himself with the practice (it had been a few days, after all) and to make sure he could do it in his newfound state. He donned his normal gauntlet on his good hand in order to channel, and he only used his damaged hand for equalization and stabilizing. He conjured palm-sized flames and warped shadows into shields, hardened dust into spheres and summoned daggers made of ice. Every act was awkward, but he got the hang of it soon enough.

It felt good to touch his spirit again. He'd felt so hollow without her, and now he didn't want to let go.

Eventually, when he'd nearly worn them both out, he wandered away from the campfire. Stone and Cristena had both fallen asleep while he'd been practicing.

Graves walked a perimeter around the camp, keeping watch. There was a small shelf of flat land a few feet down from the top of the hill. Cross was surprised to see the camel carefully tethered, down on its haunches and asleep.

"Wow," he said with a laugh.

Graves looked up at Cross. After a moment he looked at the camel and quietly laughed.

"Yeah, the ugly bastard was waiting for us outside the forest. He was the only one with enough brains to run for it when things went to hell." He waited a moment, gathering himself. "You were right about the Wormwood following us. It spread around us to something like a two mile radius. Even Cristena said she'd never seen anything like it." He paused again, out of things to say.

"I'm sorry," Cross said.

"*I'm* sorry. I'm not angry at you. You're a hero, whether you'll admit it or not. If not for you, none of us would be here now. I mean...*I'm* the one who had to pick up a haunted branch. I just..." Graves shook his head. Cross knew he wasn't normally one to talk about his doubts. His emoting was usually done with a glass of whisky in hand and a stripper on his lap. "This shit is getting to me, Cross. I just want to wake up." A cold gust of wind came at them. "Do you remember what things used to be like?"

"What, you mean before The Black?" Cross asked.

"Yeah."

"Not really," Cross said. "I was so young...five, maybe six when it happened." He looked at Graves. "Same with you, right?"

"Yeah." Graves looked out into the dark, his face half lit by the firelight. "But I remember a lot, actually. I remember my dad pushing me on the swing. I remember sunlight that didn't look all bloody." He spat on the ground. "I wish I didn't remember. I wish I had no idea. Maybe then I wouldn't know how shitty this all is, because I'd have nothing to compare it to."

"Sam..."

"Don't worry about it," Graves said. "I'm fine, and I'm going to do my job. We're going to find that bitch Red, and we're going to make her pay for what she's done." He looked at Cross. There was something cold behind his eyes. "We'll do it for Morg, and for Kray, and for Winter. And we'll get your sister, and we'll take her home."

Cross nodded.

"I've got your back, man," he said. He offered Graves his good hand. "Thanks for everything." Graves shook it.

"All right," he said, "enough of this male bonding shit. Get some sleep. You're on watch in four."

Cross sat quietly through his shift. His eyes were alight with white shadows. The gossamer threads of his spirit danced around him in a nimbus of spectral strands. She stayed anchored at the corner of his mind, poised and dangling in the thick gloom of the dead night. Cross watched the stillness of the plains and stretched his arcane senses across the deepness of the wastes.

Something was wrong. There was something broken, something out of place.

That sense of wrongness nagged at him all the next morning as they marched northeast, out of the hills and into the deep northern tundra. They were out of the Bone March now, nearing the most northern areas ever explored by the Southern Claw. Patches of frozen moss and blue-black lichen stood in shallow pools of briny slush and icy reeds. The red sky hung low and oppressive, and the air was bitter and sharp.

The earth seemed to be made of rust. They walked across the tundra, following trails of vaporous red clouds which stained the sky, passing drifts of great spider silk and sinkholes filled with frozen mud. Black pits of congealed tar lay like great footsteps to the southeast. Ahead, still at a good distance off but so massive it was impossible to miss stood the Carrion Rift, a cold black cut in the land. The entire landscape seemed to drift towards the Rift. Mournful brays carried in the dead wind.

The squad spoke sparingly. Graves and Stone had their weapons at the ready. Their eyes were alert, as they expected to be ambushed at any moment. Cross kept his spirit at the edge of his thoughts, tethered to his consciousness by an emotive line, just far enough out she could sense if anything approached. His legs ached, and he felt blisters on his weary feet. Cold sweat dampened the shirt beneath his armor jacket. They hadn't rested for quite some time, and they wouldn't until they found some sort of cover from both the bitter air and from any prying eyes.

The tundra eventually gave way to cracked hills and rocky ridges of sharp stone. The path soon grew steep enough even the camel seemed to complain by its reluctance to carry on.

It was just past noon when they stumbled on the first signs of slaughter. Thin lines of dirty grey smoke spiraled up from the nadir of a low canyon to the north. Cross's eyes followed the winding plumes down to the canyon floor. The amount of debris and carnage thickened closer to the source of the smoke: a smoldering husk of shattered trucks positioned in a crude defensive circle. Black stains marred the ground around the broken perimeter of vehicles, and as the wind shifted in their direction Cross gagged on the charnel musk.

The group investigated, despite their misgivings. Cross's eyes and spirit were alert as they walked into the canyon. The walls were jagged and deep, and every cleft of rock was filled with shadow.

The bodies were at least two days dead, most of them horribly burned. There were too many to count, and Cross didn't care to try. He pulled his spirit in as close as he could to keep her shielded away from the worst of that deathly air.

There were no barriers between arcane spirits and the spirits of the recently dead. To Cross and Cristena's spirits, those dead souls in the canyon were like a pack of rabid wolves, just waiting for an opportunity to maul intruders who dared venture into their territory. Even with his spirit safely hidden behind every safeguard he could muster Cross felt the pain of those lost in the doomed caravan. He heard the haunted cries and felt the stirring of unquiet dead, forever trapped in a nightmare of their own demise.

"Settlers," Stone concluded. "Probably bound for Rhaine."

"Settlers, this far north?" Graves asked. "I'm surprised anyone would want to come this deep into dangerous territory."

"There's still unclaimed land up here," Cristena said, clearly as uncomfortable in that butcher's yard as Cross was. "Not everyone wants to be a part of the Southern Claw, and most of the good land south of here is claimed. Plus there aren't many vampires this close to the Rift."

"Well, there's *something* up here," Cross whispered.

They searched the field of ashen bodies and open vehicles. There was scattered bedding, crockery, open bags of seed, grain and rations, tools broken apart and scatted by the chill valley winds.

While most of the bodies had been burned it didn't take long for the squad to realize fire wasn't what had killed those people. Skulls had been smashed in by hammer and boot, and a number of bodies north of the truck circle had been impaled on oversized barbed spears. Gaping bullet wounds were visible on many of the less burned corpses, and the holes left were far too big to be the handiwork of human weapons.

"Shit," Graves said. "Sorn."

"Yeah," Stone said. He looked at the rest of them. "Only a large group would have been able to tackle a caravan this size. And I guarantee there's no way that a Sorn raiding party would pass up a target as tempting as a remote human city. Not a chance."

"We have to warn them," Cross said. "We have to get to Rhaine and warn them." Everyone looked at him uneasily. He expected Stone to say something about how that wasn't their mission, how it was probably already too late. Instead Stone looked at each of them in turn, finishing with Cross.

"All right. Let's go."

NINETEEN

RHAINE

The remainder of the trek to Rhaine was grim. The air turned greyer the further they walked. Cross's eyes hurt, and he almost fell asleep while they marched. Only his spirit's anxiousness kept him conscious. Dread built deep in his chest.

To a mage, being near death was like walking through a freezing waterfall. There was no mistaking its presence, and Cross had to constantly hold his spirit close and anchor her to his will, or else she might be drawn out and ambushed by free-roaming ghosts, or so distracted by the deadly lull of lost souls she'd never be able to return to him.

The task of keeping her contained grew more difficult the further they went. The squad passed the ruined remains of a remote cabin, once the property of a trapper or a mountain seer, now partially crushed beneath some great concussive force. Bone weary and on edge they passed through a field of dark soil, and while both Cross and Cristena felt the proximity of death they still managed to slosh halfway across the clearing before they noticed a pale arm jutting up from the loamy earth. Their boots sank in thin pools of blood just beneath the surface, and soon they were ankle deep in crimson slush.

They'd stumbled into a mass grave. Bodies addled by bullets and blades had been piled up and crudely buried under the mud. Soggy flesh sagged away from the corpses' bones like melting fat, and everything was covered with worms.

Cross and Cristena were forced to flee the scene. Cross was sick. He felt like someone had pulled his insides out through his mouth.

He heard the screams of lost souls. He felt his spirit suffer as she was battered with clouds of pain still surrounding the recently dead like a grim shroud. Everything Cross had ever seen and heard led him to believe a person's soul continued to exist long after the body had gone. They stayed, trapped in their last moments, forever locked in the eternal final seconds of life.

The squad made haste to move away from the field of carnage, only to discover more bodies, this time off of a wide trade road Cristena thought led directly to Rhaine. The naked corpses had been burned and hung at unnatural angles, held up by strands of razor wire affixed to metal poles in the ground. Dead eyes stared at the squad, almost accusingly. Cross did all he could to keep their voices at bay.

"We're too late," Graves said after they passed the bodies. They came around a bend in the hills. The sky was full with sickly bulbous clouds. "These people were either bound for Rhaine, or else they came from it."

"We'll check it out," Stone said. No one questioned the decision.

They had to see Rhaine, but they already knew what they'd find. The Sorn didn't take prisoners. If Rhaine's residents were lucky they'd been killed quickly.

They rested for a short time, drank some water, and calculated their position on the maps. No one ate, and they barely spoke. No one really wanted to move on, but they had to, and they all knew it.

They caught their first glimpse of Rhaine over the next ridge. It was a large settlement, spaced across a massive hillside and built right up against the edge of the Carrion Rift. The walls protecting the city were low but solid, set with battlements and a large number of crude towers. The city rolled and curved with the hill, and its districts had been separated by short intervening walls, visible even from outside the city.

Smoke drifted over much of Rhaine and filled the sky with red and grey war pollutants. Even from a distance the smell of burning fuel was strong. Cross saw large grey-skinned figures moving around in the city even at the squad's distance, and through his scope he confirmed their identity by their bladed armor, black iron weapons, heavy steam-powered firearms and the single central eyes on their smooth heads.

Sorn.

"The easiest way to cross the Rift," Cristena said, trying like the rest to ignore that the city was likely filled with hundreds of dead people, "is to cross that bridge. We have to go through Rhaine to get to it."

"Of course," Graves said bitterly.

"There may be survivors," Cross said quietly.

"Doubtful." Stone took the scope and surveyed Rhaine's smoking husk, starting at the gates and inspecting all of the way to the bridge at the far northern edge of the city. The bridge had been built into a tower set in Rhaine's north wall and stretched across to a second tower on the far side of the Rift. From what Cross could tell, Rhaine's north wall was flush with the canyon wall, which meant there was no other means of accessing that particular bridge from their side of the canyon.

Cross tasted hex in the air, as thick and as pungent as the pollution. It was known the Sorn made use of powerful military technology, steam and gear-driven devices powered by arcane fuel and machines which relied as much on magic as they did gears or engines.

He heard dead whispers in the air, but fewer than he expected. The Sorn must have cleared away the bodies of their victims, maybe even dumped them into the Rift. They were nothing if not efficient.

"The Sorn may be setting this place up to use as an outpost," Stone said. He still held the scope to his eye. "They're a big raiding party, but they're conducting a very systematic search for survivors." He lowered the scope. "This wasn't a random attack. They're making sure they've cleared the place out. They're hunting survivors."

"How many Sorn are there?" Cross asked.

"I only saw seven, but a full raiding party is usually ten strong. The others might be invisible to us right now because of the smoke, or they might be out on patrol. We need to stay sharp."

"The other three Sorn could be dead," Cristena said, dubious by her tone. "Maybe they were killed during the attack?"

"I doubt we're that lucky," Stone said.

"We're *not*," Graves groaned. "Trust me. We're not." He looked down at the Rift. "But even if Cristena is right, there are still seven of them. Seven Sorn commandos," he laughed. "Shit."

"Are they as bad as I've heard?" Cross asked.

"Worse," Stone said, and Cross was officially sorry he'd asked.

They decided to approach using the foothills southeast of Rhaine for cover. Gunshots and bodiless cries issued from deep inside the city. The setting sun bathed the world red. They decided it would be best to enter the city under cover of darkness so as to capitalize on the Sorn's poor night vision.

The foothills came to an end just a few hundred yards short of the city walls, which meant the squad had to cross the last stretch across exposed ground. Lucky for them the city gates had been left wide open, and there were no sentries in sight anywhere on or near the walls. Just to be sure, Cross and Cristena loosened their holds on their spirits and conducted an arcane reconnoiter. Cross breathed in ghostly steam and tasted bitter eldritch power. They sensed a tremendous amount of residual magical energy inside the walls – most likely stemming from the Sorn's weaponry – but none of it was located near the gates. There were also very few whisperings from the dead, all of them scattered and weak, and that was more alarming than anything else, as there should have been more dead whispers if the city had been wiped out.

Maybe they're not dead. Maybe the Sorn took the city hostage. Based on what they'd seen on the road leading into Rhaine, Cross doubted that. *We'll have to figure it out later.*

The sun had almost completely set by the time the squad made their run. Rhaine's bulky shadow loomed before them. They had to leave the camel behind, since the load it carried jingled and clanged so loudly it was a surprise the Sorn hadn't already heard them coming from a league away. They raced across brittle ground and passed through Rhaine's gates. Not alarm was raised, and no shots were fired.

A good start.

Stone directed them with Southern Claw hand signals, the same system used by the old U.S. Army Rangers. Stone was at point, Cross and Cristena and their anxious spirits roamed in the center, and Graves brought up the rear. They moved quickly but quietly, checking every corner, careful not to trip in the thick shadows.

The level of debris and wreckage blocking the way increased as the squad moved deeper into the city, and swift navigation soon became very difficult. The darkness didn't help. An array of sounds echoed through the streets – gunshots, bomb blasts, shouts, working machinery

– but it was all so distant it was hard to gauge its direction, especially with the echoing effect of the nearby Rift.

They passed buildings that had been hollowed by mortar blasts and grenades. Entire streets had been cracked apart by gunfire. The red flames of burning buildings grew more intense as they neared Rhaine's epicenter, and the fires cast everything in a bloody glow. Most of the flames were clustered near Rhaine's heart, and those blazes lit the squad's way through the ugly night.

Fountains were cracked and dry, entire houses had been leveled, statues had been toppled and the fronts of buildings had been torn away. The streets were so littered with wreckage the ground was barely visible beneath it.

They saw only a few bodies, and detected no lost spirits to accompany them. If Rhaine's citizens were dead their spirits were no longer in the city. Both Cross and Cristena should have been deaf from the cries generated by that many lost souls.

Maybe that mass grave was filled with the people from Rhaine, Cross thought. *It would explain why it's so quiet here now.*

But that wasn't it. There should have been something more, some whispers of a lingering soul, some background spiritual static, a general unquiet in the nether region between worlds. There was nothing. Everything was empty, and utterly abandoned.

The squad passed through the open shell of a building, and for the first time the four of them were able to look into Rhaine's central city square. Roaring fires burned in the shells of destroyed vehicles. Bright smoke billowed into the sky and showers of sparks fell to the bloodied pavement. A large crater rested at the exact center of Rhaine, and an imperfect orb of black iron hovered over the hole. The lopsided sphere hummed and turned in place. Subtle lines of black lightning raced up and down the surface of the metal ball, and tendrils of energy danced between the orb and the ground in a ghastly web. The area surrounding the crater was occupied by smoking buildings, their ruins illuminated by red flames. The ground was torn granite rent asunder by explosive blasts.

The wrecked plaza was paved with the dead. Scores of bodies lay heaped in orderly piles ten or fifteen feet high, neatly arranged columns of dead husks. The smell in the air was ghastly. The bodies had been left to decay for some time, and their proximity to so much heat and flame had sped the rate of deterioration. Cross gagged on the taste of overcooked meat.

"Holy shit," Graves whispered.

"That's an Egg, isn't it?" Stone asked with a nod towards the floating black ball.

"Yeah," Cross coughed. "That's why we couldn't sense any roaming spirits," he said. "Because there *aren't* any. There are no souls left to detect."

"What do you mean?" Graves asked quietly. They all crouched down and did their best to stay out of sight.

"Sometimes the Sorn feed the souls of people they kill to the Black Eggs. No one has seen an Egg in over a decade. We thought they were all gone."

The squad kept quiet and clung to the shadow of the building. From their vantage they spied a half-dozen Sorn carefully navigating the urban graveyard with silent stoicism. The nearest was just a few blocks away.

The Sorn were essentially humanoid, save that their skin had the hue and texture of worked stone, and they stood nearly twelve feet tall. Their hairless heads were decorated with runic markings and ritualistic scars, and each bore a short row of onyx horns on his forehead. Each Sorn had but a single large eye in the center of its face, so large there was barely any room left for its tiny mouth. Sorn armor was coal black steel set with iron plates and jagged spikes, and their weapons looked like industrial machines, heavy, functional, covered in gears and knobs, ugly but efficient.

Cross didn't feel a single spirit aside from his and Cristena's. There wasn't a human soul left in Rhaine which didn't belong to the squad. He didn't exactly know how the Sorn fed souls to the living artifacts they worshipped, but he tasted the vile stench of black magic. All of the Black Eggs were thought to have been destroyed during the Southern Claw's last major engagement with the Sorn, back at the Battle at Horn's Peak in A.B. 13. The spheres were malignant and intelligent orbs made of arcane iron reputedly taken from the core of an ancient meteorite. They possessed their own magic, and demanded unquestioned loyalty from their Sorn followers. This one had been well fed.

"We can go around it..." Cristena said.

"No," Stone replied. "We can't." His tone made clear he'd broker no argument.

"You don't have to do this," she said.

"I'm sorry, Cristena," Stone said, "but we do. There's no getting around this." He quietly removed his extra equipment, keeping just his armor and weapons. Graves did the same.

And so did Cross, without even realizing it until he was almost done. *Am I insane?*

"You can't help these people," Cristena said. "Do you hear me, you stupid, macho assholes? They're dead, and their souls are dead. You should be worrying about the people you *can* help. I don't believe this...why am I the only thinking about your mission? Eric, what about Snow? If you get yourself killed..."

"He won't," Stone said.

"God damn it, what will this prove?" Cristena said, loud enough Cross was sure the Sorn overheard them, but the giants just tended to their business, organizing bodies and patrolling the field of dead.

Nothing, Cross thought. *This will prove nothing. And yet we have to do it.*

He stands in the glade. She's there, lovely and snow white pale, her hair blown in the gentle breeze blowing down from the black mountain.

He thought of Snow. He hoped she'd understand.

Cristena conceded without further argument: after a minute or two of silence she too readied herself for battle. Cross wasn't surprised. He knew she still wanted to die, even if she seemed to have forgotten for a while.

He didn't think they were going to die. He wondered if she'd be disappointed.

It took a few minutes to set up the mini-gun, which they mounted on a low wall near a hollow building overlooking the crater. Stone, still slowed from his cracked rib in spite of plenty of arcane first aid, decided to man the mini-gun, while Graves took the M16A2 with the M203. Cross and Cristena loaded up with most of the handguns. For some reason Cross wondered about the camel, and hoped the creature had the good sense to stay out of danger.

They fanned out across the nearby section of town. There was debris everywhere – shattered stone, broken pieces of furniture, collapsed ceilings and cracked walls – so there was plenty of cover. Cross found himself alone in the blasted remains of an old house.

This is insane. But it's too late now.

A stream of white light burst from the rotating barrels of the mini-gun just a few houses away. Stone had waited until a pair of Sorn walked directly into his field of fire before he'd opened up on them.

Deafening blasts filled the air. Heavy chunks of Sorn armor collapsed beneath the thunderous barrage of the mini-gun, and while the creatures managed to draw their massive blades Stone eventually put them both down.

More Sorn appeared all over the square. The eye-numbing light made it so many of them were difficult to see in spite of their size. Weapon blasts tore through the night. The Black Egg shifted and turned in place.

The mini-gun strafed the area. Small explosions boomed. Black dust drifted across Cross's field of vision. He let his spirit swim out and over his body and through his fingers like water, molded her form, squeezed his fingers together, shaped her essence into a chain of eldritch blades which he cast out into the dark. The edged blasts punched through concrete and embedded themselves in Sorn targets with audible force.

Moments later a Sorn crashed through the walls of the building Cross hid in. It had suffered a gaping blade wound in its stomach but still yielded an enormous axe made of black steel. Its single eye glared at Cross, who saw his battered and bruised reflection staring back at him.

Cross leapt back. His spirit exploded away in a battery of razor sharp stones which curled up and shredded the Sorn's face, ruining its massive eye. Even blinded the Sorn was relentless, and its axe-blade sank into the ground less than a foot from where Cross stood. Cross moved his hands in a slicing motion. His spirit curled like a moonlit razor and cut clean through the Sorn's throat, spilling purple blood. One wall of the building collapsed, and what was left of the roof came down like oversized chunks of hail.

Cross ran for the square. A Sorn stormed after him with a wide-muzzled cannon-like weapon connected to its pack with tubes and wires. The weapon growled like a locomotive as it fired nails the size of railroad spikes. Chunks of wood and stone flew everywhere. Cross fled, trailed by a barrage of projectiles.

He ran through the field of bodies. His spirit was shrouded around him. Dead eyes stared from mattress-like piles of corpses. He brushed against cold hands and rotting feet. Cross heard the chaos of the battle: the mini-gun's rapport, heavy mortar shots, the crackle of evil magic.

He was suddenly lost. He kept his spirit at hand, felt her excitement and fear burn against his skin. Cross tried to get his bearings.

He rounded a corner in the maze of the dead and found himself thirty yards away and face-to-face with another Sorn. The stoic brute was armed with a broadsword in one hand and a pipe bomb the size of a watermelon in the other. Cross heard the dull hum of a metallic dirigible in the air behind him.

The Black Egg.

Its shadow loomed over him. He saw the great orb reflected in the Sorn's hateful stare. Cross pushed his spirit away in an eldritch wave. She melted in a tidal flare, a jet of molten fuel. Pyromancy leapt from the ground and into the Sorn, setting its body ablaze. Even dying the creature remained silent. It threw the bomb.

Cross ran. The heavy roar of the Egg's chain guns and chemical charges filled his ears. The air tasted hot as exhaust from the Egg's turbines washed over the ground like a blast of desert wind.

The pipe bomb soared over his head. Cross heard it bounce against the Egg's outer hull with a thud.

The force of the explosion threw him forward. He hung weightless for a moment, flying through air filled with shattered steel. Sharp pain drove through his body as he landed.

He was on his back. The air had been knocked from his lungs. He felt deflated. The bomb had detonated behind him. He felt shrapnel in his back.

Still struggling for breath, Cross tried to rise, but didn't have the strength. His ears rang. Gory chunks of exploded corpse bits were everywhere.

The Egg was damaged, but not destroyed. Thick black smoke churned from a visible rent near the top of the machine, and a few metal plates burned and dangled from the sphere. Cross saw ancient gear works and broken tubes dripping dark fluid through the damaged hull. The Egg listed to its left, incapable of properly maneuvering or lifting as high as it had before.

Damaged or no, the Egg bore down on him. It was as big as a wagon, and it drew within a few yards before Cross got his exhausted legs under him and ran. The Egg strafed the earth with small rotating guns built into its underbelly. Fist-sized bullets shredded the ground.

Cross moved as fast as he could. His chest pounded. He ran without any idea of where he was going. He heard the Egg closing in.

He saw Cristena at the end of the row. Her leg was injured, and she hobbled along. She didn't see him, just as she didn't see the Sorn rushing at her from behind. Its great blade was held high to deliver a killing blow.

"Cristena!" Cross shouted.

She looked up, surprised. Cross dove forward and sent his spirit ahead as a missile of pure force. He landed hard to the ground. The arcane bolt took the Sorn's legs off at the knees in a splatter of purple blood, and the giant fell soundlessly.

The Egg kept firing. Massive rounds soared over Cross and found Cristena. Blood exploded out of her back. She fell in a crumpled heap.

Cross turned, screaming. He held his fists in the air, and with a breath his spirit exploded from his hands in a white maelstrom. The blast scorched his eyes and boiled his blood. Cross felt himself smolder. His soul burned and smoked.

A phalanx of hot razors converged on the damaged Egg and struck through the rent in the weakened hull. White fire flashed in a destructive corona. Cross was thrown backwards as shards of flaming metal flew from the explosion. The wind smelled of molten steel. The shriek of blasted metal deafened him.

Cross lay on his back for a long time, barely conscious. There was no more gunfire, no more sounds of fighting. He looked up at the blackened sky, which seemed impossibly vast and deep. He could have fallen into it.

Cross rose slowly. His body was wracked with pain. He'd been burned and badly bruised, but he was alive. He felt his spirit, soft and weak, clinging to him, but she was *there*. They were both there.

Easy, he thought. *Easy*.

Cristena.

He looked to where she fell, and slowly moved towards her. She'd warned them of the futility of their revenge. After wanting so much not to come with them, not wanting to be involved...not wanting, even, to die a meaningful death, but instead to waste herself in the pits as just another anonymous gladiator in the lurid history of Dirge's criminal sports...

She didn't have to die. This isn't what was supposed to happen. She was supposed to be here, I know it.

None of that mattered now. Cross's legs burned with every step. He only made it a few feet when an injured Sorn appeared from around the bend. One hand clung to a gaping wound in its chest while the other gripped a wide-bored pistol with rotating barrels the size of pipes. The Sorn blinked its one eye, and its expressionless face regarded Cross as it took aim. Cross braced himself, knowing he was about to die.

I'm sorry.

"Hey tough guy!"

The giant turned to face the voice. Graves came out of the shadows. The M203 belched a grenade with a hollow thud. The shot took the Sorn in the chest and tore straight through its armor with a noisy explosion.

The Sorn fell backwards and fired its weapon as it died. The bullet slammed into Graves and snapped his body backwards.

Cross screamed so loud his throat nearly tore.

He left the Sorn and Cristena behind him and ran as fast as his failing legs would carry him. He nearly passed out.

"SAAAAAM!!!"

The enormous bullet had blasted most of Graves's face away. Bits of jawbone and ruined tongue were just visible in the bloody mess. Cross put a hand on his friend's arm and doubled over, sick.

He didn't move for a long time. If there were more Sorn there in Rhaine, he hoped they'd just find him and finish him off.

Later, sometime near dawn, Cross left Graves and Cristena and went and found Stone, who was also dead, having been cut down by Sorn gunfire. Stone hadn't left without giving them the proverbial fight. No fewer than four dead Sorn were near his body, each torn to ribbons by mini-gun fire, small explosions or sliced open by Stone's black-bladed kukri. It was remarkable he'd lived long enough to do such damage. Cross only barely recognized the body.

Cross stood at the edge of the Rift and stared out over the long and rickety bridge. Thick grey fumes floated in the depths of the canyon, a rich and poison fog. Strange shadows hovered like drowning birds. Dismal calls echoed from the depths. The walls of the Rift were jagged and impossibly tall.

Across the canyon waited a dismal wasteland of cold steam and black hills. That bridge might as well have led to another world. No reliable data of what lay on the other side of the Carrion Rift had ever been gathered.

Movement from behind caught Cross's eye. A pale spider crawled across the ground, separated, it seemed, from the destruction all around it. It scuttled off into the shadows.

The camel found him some time later. It had wandered through the city, carefully avoiding the flames. Now it stood nearby, waiting. It knew they weren't done.

But I am, Cross thought. *I'm done.*

No, she says, a voice from the edge of the glade. *Will you let it end like this? Will they die in vain?*

We all do, he replied. *Each and every one of us.*

And yet...

And yet there he was.

He wouldn't leave this unfinished. He felt hollow inside, broken, exhausted beyond measure, but he was alive, and their mission was now his burden alone to carry.

He decided, right then and there, that he would carry it.

PART FIVE
SOULS

TWENTY

WITCH

Cross and his last remaining companion crossed the bridge and entered a dead land. Blue-gray fog enshrouded everything. The land on the other side of the Rift was thick black mud interrupted by occasional islands of dry earth. Deep saltwater marsh and bubbling pools of acrid slime made walking a chore, and before Cross and the camel had marched for even a few minutes they were both covered up to their knees with sludge. The air was bitterly cold and icy, and their breath hung heavy in the air.

There were spirit voices in the fog on the other side of the Carrion Rift, more than Cross had ever heard in any one place before, but they were surprisingly passive. They moaned like lost children, confused and frightened.

The camel trudged on behind him, slow but stable. Cross spoke to the pack animal in a reassuring manner from time to time, his voice alien in the silence. He was just happy to have someone to talk to.

"We're doing well," he told it. "We're doing just fine."

Cross wasn't exactly sure where they were headed. The map he'd translated put Koth's location somewhere just north of the Carrion Rift, but that was as specific as it got. They'd come to where the map had told them to go.

Now he felt as if he were nowhere. They seemed to have reached the end of the earth.

Cross saw signs of lost civilization in the form of baskets set out on the ground at irregular intervals. The baskets had been filled with bones. Cross decided not to investigate them.

They rested often. Something about that place seemed to drain his strength, and Cross sensed the same in the camel. The squad had kept most of their supplies on the pack beast, which meant Cross now had little need to worry about rations or fresh water. He wanted desperately to start a camp fire, but for some reason he doubted that was a wise idea.

The air was sullen and grey. Cross heard insects buzz through the air, and the occasional call of a distant bird. There was no breeze. It felt like the world had paused, frozen.

They continued north, or so he hoped. It was difficult to tell in that endless fog, and he'd lost his compass somewhere back in Rhaine. Cross quickly lost track of time. It was difficult to measure the hours, or even the day, when the dull grey light never changed.

Trenches appeared in the landscape, deep and wide enough for Cross and the camel to fit down inside them. Cross decided against using them at first. After a while, however, there were so many trenches it became challenging to navigate around them. The higher ground became a maze of preposterously thin earthen paths. Cross succumbed and led the camel down a gentle slope. The earth down in the trenches was even muddier than the higher ground, and soon they sloshed through ankle-deep water turned brown from sediment and rust.

All the while spirits passed around them at a distance, curious, watching. Cross kept his own spirit close for fear she'd be drawn away by these others.

"I'm not going to name you," he told the camel some time later.

Cross's body had grown bone weary. He was wet and cold, and the wrist of his left hand itched terribly inside the gauntlet. The air felt sick, and he was constantly fatigued no matter how much or how little they rested. Still, he refused to stop for any extended period, sensing it was dangerous to do so in a place which already robbed them of their strength. He was afraid to sleep in that undead land.

"I've never named my spirit, either. Things I name tend not to last very long."

He wondered how Cristena's spirit had endured her death. He'd heard its pain and rage when she'd died. Cross had half expected the spirit to follow him, if it was able. For all he knew its voice was mingled with the others now, just a part of the ghostly choir drifting through the mist.

They walked on through the mud, endlessly. He knew they had to stop eventually. They'd have to sleep.

Where is he? Cross wondered. *Where is the Old One? Where is Koth? Where's Red?*

"Here."

He stopped.

They were no longer in the trenches. And it was no longer *they*, but *he*.

Cross stood alone in the fog, ankle deep in brackish water. A tall red-headed woman stood before him, her body wrapped in a tattered black cloak and a dark riding skirt. Her eyes were large and expressive and as blue as sapphires. Long hair hung loose, and a braid dyed coal black dangled down one side of her face. She wore leather gauntlets set with metal studs, and her feet were bound in tall black boots covered with mud. Her beautiful face bore a perfect and happy smile, like she greeted an old friend.

"Bitch!" he shouted.

Cross didn't hesitate. He called his spirit up to form an eldritch shield, and breathed her into a lance of ice...

Nothing happened. His spirit was gone. Again.

Oh, no...how?...

"She's fine," Red said. She made a sweeping gesture, and the fog burned away. A flowing stream of water ran cold against Cross's booted feet. Ice-laden leaves fell from the wet canopy of trees. The dark mountain loomed over them, an edifice of the past.

"I'm dead," Cross said aloud. Red laughed. "Or not." He thought about it. "Asleep."

"Unconscious," she said with a smile. "But I like that you immediately assumed the worst."

"Go to hell."

"Drop the tough guy act," she said patiently. "You're not Graves, and you're not Stone. You're not even Cristena. *She* had more balls than you."

"What do you want?" he asked. Dream or not, his flesh felt frozen as he stood there in the stream. His gut churned. He knew how powerful Red was in real life. He had no idea what she was capable of there, wherever they were.

"I wanted to meet you," she smiled. "The best way to do that seemed was to approach you when you couldn't do anything foolish."

"So you waited until I fell asleep?"

"I *put* you to sleep. It wasn't hard. Even if you hadn't been completely exhausted – which you were – the Carnivore Mists would have worn you down eventually."

"So what's become of my body?" he asked.

"We'll get to that," she said. Cross could see how men found Red attractive: she had smooth skin and a voluptuous frame, her voice was seductive and she was surrounded by an air of authority. He, personally, found her loathsome, full of false confidence and empty charm. "You know," she said, "I may not be able to read your thoughts, but I can sense your emotions."

"Good for you," Cross said. "So, here we are in a dream. What now?"

"We both know you're not up to this."

Cross didn't bother hiding his emotions. He called up memories of fallen Southern Claw soldiers. He thought of the wreckage and refuse, the coffins and funeral services, the songs of sadness and pain.

"Do you want to know how many have died because of you, 'Red'?"

"Is it so hard to call me by my real name?" she smiled. "Margrave Azazeth. You used to revere it, after all. I authored many of the Southern Claw's laws. I led you through Thornn's darkest hours."

"And then you betrayed us," Cross said quietly. "All that time you were leading us you were setting us up to fail."

"You're an idiot if you believe that," Red said bitterly. "The Southern Claw Alliance was doomed from the start, and you know it. All of us were. Even the warlocks and witches everyone thought were so special, who were supposed to be humankind's last hope in the war against the vampires, never had a chance. No one could accept the simple truth: if we keep on fighting, we're all going to die."

And so she'd taken their sacred codex, the Tome of Scars, the closest thing to a human artifact they had. It stored the assembled knowledge of all humans had accomplished in the new dark world – what they knew of magic, how they used thaumaturgy and science to pull life and resources from a poisoned earth which didn't want to give them anything, how they'd cheated their own evolutionary demise and had kept civilization going long after it should have failed. It was a handbook for survival in a world turned insane.

There were many who thought it foolish to store so much vital knowledge all in one place. As it turned out, they were right to be skeptical. It was discovered too late that creating the Tome of Scars had been Red's idea all along. Even at the beginning, when everyone poured their faith and devotion into this woman who seemed to practically be an avatar of the distant and unseen White Mother, Red had planned to steal the Tome, which contained knowledge she could never have amassed on her own. But with the help of scholars, leaders and mages, the Tome had become a living document, a place to record how humanity had endured after The Black. It didn't matter there were copies of the Tome: it was the secrets held within that had been lost.

Margrave – Red – fled with the Tome so she could give its information to an ancient and decrepit vampire seer known as the Old One. He, in turn, would provide those secrets to the lords of the Ebon Cities.

"So what do you think they'll do with it?" Cross asked angrily. "Wipe us out?"

"You can't be that naive," Red said sadly. "The Ebon Cities want this war to end as badly as we do. They'll use the information in the Tome to force us to stop fighting. My story is not one of genocide, Cross. This is the tale of a surrender."

"Bullshit."

"Fine," she breathed. "Bullshit. Either way, the Tome is in the Old One's hands now. You're too late." She stepped closer. "Give it up. The rest of your group died foolishly. You don't have to."

"Why did you do it?" he asked quietly. His words were sharp and clear in the brittle air.

She smiled a surprisingly vulnerable smile.

"I'm naturally evil, I guess."

"We're in a dream," Cross said. "There's nothing I can do to you here. Even if this were real, you're much more powerful than I am." Their eyes locked. "What could it hurt to tell me the truth?"

"I was tired of all of the death," she said after a long silence. "This way, it ends. No more suffering. No more living in fear."

"But we *want* to live," Cross said. "Life in the Southern Claw sucks...but it's *life*. People want to keep on living. We want to survive. If we didn't, we wouldn't be doing this."

"You haven't seen half of what I've seen," she said, her anger rising.

"Lady, I've seen plenty," he spat back. "This decision isn't yours to make."

"I was the only one of you the White Mother would even talk to," she said. "Of *course* it was my decision. I was your leader."

"You lost that title and the right to represent us the moment you stopped thinking about the Southern Claw..."

"I was ALWAYS thinking of the Southern Claw!" she shouted, her voice strained with desperation and defiance. "I'll end the war. I..." She regained her composure in a heartbeat. "It doesn't matter what you think. It's already too late."

The imaginary wind picked up, a reflection of Cross's anger. He heard the neigh of dark horses. The bloody ebon unicorns from his visions crashed through the trees.

"You're afraid I'll stop you," he said. "That's the only reason you'd even bother appearing here to me now."

"I'm not afraid of a pathetic warlock who can't even muster up the skill to protect his own sister." Red laughed.

"Where is she?"

Red nodded towards the trees. Cross saw Snow just inside the canopy. She was bloody and bruised, soaked and terrified.

His spirit was there with her. The cadre of black unicorns surrounded them, prodding the women with their jagged horns.

"She's waiting for you," Red said. "You're almost there, Cross."

Cross took a deep breath.

"You know I have to kill you," he said.

She nodded, almost sadly.

"Yes," she said. "Yes I do. But to do that you'll have to come and get me."

The sky pulled apart like tissue in water. Everything faded and cracked. Patches of red light punched through the sky. The world became a breaking mirror.

"I'll see you soon," she said, and the sky melted.

Cross's body shattered like glass. He was ripped back to the waking world.

TWENTY-ONE
CLAWS

Cross woke on his back, looking up at the sky. Ooze pressed against his sinking body and greasy water filled his eyes like polluted tears. He lay half submerged in a grave of mud. Everything was brown and black. Night stood beyond the ambient mist.

He rose unsteadily, his body soaked to the bone. Silver light danced in the distance, a muted aurora. Mud had caked to his face. It was difficult to even stand up in the sludge.

Cross looked around and found he was alone. The camel had gone, or had been taken, but if that was the case he reasoned he'd have been taken, too. Likely the stalwart creature had finally wandered off on its own, bored of a companion who always seemed to be unconscious.

He listened for the whispers, waited for the silken touch of his spirit, but as he feared she was gone. Again.

Cross wanted to just lie down and be done with it. Angry tears welled in his eyes. He crouched down heel to haunch and put his eyes and ears in his hands.

It quickly grew dark. He was in the middle of nowhere, awash in a sea of inky night, standing in shadows so thick he could taste them. It was just he and the silence, trapped together in a black prison without walls.

Cross walked through near pitch-black darkness. His boots splashed in mud and marsh. The cold air froze his clothes to his skin. He still wore his armor coat and had his weapons and alchemy, but he had no food and, more distressing, no source of light. His eyes might as well have been in his pocket for all the good they did him. He could've been at the edge of the cliff or about to walk into a wall and he wouldn't have known it.

He walked, bolstered by the thought of seeing Snow again, almost believing it would happen.

Time passed. He couldn't say how much. Nothing changed. The world remained black and moist and quiet.

Cross stopped, even though he wasn't sure why. Something felt wrong. He had no spirit to tell him what, and he certainly hadn't actually seen or heard anything. But he felt something, a sense of a presence in the dark…or maybe an absence.

He took some small comfort in the weapons he still carried: Graves's Remington 870 sawed-off shotgun, his own HK45 and Graves' SIG Sauer, a hex grenade, and Stone's kukri machete. But even with all of those armaments he felt largely defenseless without his spirit.

Something moved in the dark. Cross heard it this time, and he smelled something charnel, like grave soil and excrement.

He readied the HK and tried to step quietly. His feet splashed and slurped in the mud in spite of how slow he moved. Cross cursed under his breath and stopped, waiting. Clicking sounds echoed around him, fading in and out of the shadows. He heard little voices and growls closing in.

To hell with this. Cross moved forward in a half run. The mud grabbed at his feet. The noises grew louder, circled him, surrounded him.

Cross fired into the dark. He heard a wet explosion, and the sound of whatever it was scattered. He carefully continued forward with his weapon held before him.

He stepped on the body before he saw it. It was small and grey and covered in mud. Its eyes were glazed open and it bore a hole from Cross's bullet in its chest. The creature was the size of a human child, and might have been mistaken for one if not for its oddly square head, thick and sharp teeth and glistening black claws.

Ghouls, Cross thought, and he started to panic. Ghouls were pack hunters. And those packs were big.

Gnashing sounds converged on him. Leering grey faces loomed from out of the darkness. Black teeth flashed darker than the surrounding night. Cross shouted as razor-sharp claws slashed his face, his chest, and his arms. He felt fingers in his hair. Blood splashed onto his cheek.

Cross lashed out and whipped bodies aside. He smashed melon-sized skulls with his pistol and pried away hands and teeth. The ghouls came at him from all sides in a tide of hungry mouths. Cross found an open maw, shoved the pistol inside and fired. Chunks of bone and flesh splattered everywhere.

He pushed and kicked and kept firing. They held his legs, his torso and his arms even as they beat and tore at him. They grabbed his coat and tried to pin his limbs and drag him to the ground, where they'd be able to finish him off with ease. He was trapped in a tide of angry little bodies.

Cross managed to pull the machete free from the sheath on his back and somehow shoved and kicked his way to his feet. He chopped through child-sized bodies with ease, cut off limbs and cleaved skulls in two. His ears filled with hideous screams.

They're not children, his mind shouted. *Not anymore.*

His muscles were on fire. He felt like he was covered in nothing but wounds. Cross chopped and hacked in every direction. He swam in a field of meat. Claws raked his body, tore at his stomach and legs. Finally, after a savage blow that sent a wide stream of blood across his chest, Cross found an opening in the wall of ghouls. He pushed his way free and fled.

He ran through the dark without direction. He couldn't tell if he moved away from the danger or toward it. The darkness was near absolute, deepened by the steel-hard mist. Black mud made every step uncertain. The chattering and gnashing of teeth was right on him, closing around him like a cage.

Something took hold of his legs. Cross painfully tripped and landed face first into the mud. The machete flew from his hands.

Small and spindly hands tipped with wickedly sharp talons reached up from under the ground. They tore at him, grasped him, pulled him down. Needles of pain tore at his body. Cross breathed wet earth. He would drown in the mud.

The ghouls in pursuit were nearly on top of him. Cross lashed out and pried hands off of him long enough to reach into the pocket of his armor coat. An earth-bound claw slashed at his ear and took off a chunk of skin, and pain flared down the side of his face.

The crowd of ghouls in pursuit had closed to within a few yards. They were ready to pounce. Cross threw the grenade, turned and lay prone in the mud while shielding his head and neck.

The explosion rocked the ground. Cross saw white fire through his clenched fingers, and the flash briefly illuminated the surrounding area, revealing muddy plains populated by dark pits and covered with some two dozen more ghouls, which screamed as the blast took them. Chunks of body and drifts of gore crashed to the earth.

Cross waited for some time after the explosion. No more ghouls attacked – he'd either killed them all or forced them back into hiding. His chest heaved, and every breath was like swallowing chunks of ice.

He recovered his discarded weapons from the ground. The SIG was broken. Cross sheathed the machete, reloaded the HK and the shotgun, and gathered himself. There was still no sign of the camel. Likely the ghouls had gotten their claws on it.

Dawn spread like a milky stain. The sky bled from black to grey, and the fog lifted enough for Cross to realize he was in a mass graveyard. Unmarked mounds lay in every direction, and the holes he'd seen before were in fact half-dug graves. A few shovels and picks lay discarded in piles.

These were no ordinary graves, but ghoul graves. Living children had been cast into specially prepared necromantic soil and buried alive, and over the course of their slow and terrifying deaths they'd been gradually transformed into the undead.

I'm close, he thought. *I'm almost to Koth.*

A whimpering from behind him drew Cross's attention. Some of the ghouls had survived the worst of the grenade blast by using their fellows as shields, but that hadn't saved their limbs from being destroyed. Those ghouls mewled pathetically, their arms and legs smothered like ground meat. They stared up at Cross, as if begging for mercy. He left them there.

The sunrise would be in the direction where the light burned brightest through the fog. Using that information, Cross headed north. He was caked in blood and dried mud. Scars and aching cuts covered his face, arms and chest, but the bleeding had stopped. Layers of filth had stemmed the blood flowing from his wounds.

Cross walked, ignoring his aching knees. His own exhaustion pulled him along, stumbling through mud and mist, nearly devoid of thought.

He looked at the grave mounds and wondered how many of them still contained children's corpses, and what suffering and fear they'd experienced at the hands of black-fanged vampires and their maggot-addled wight servants.

He thought of Snow, alone and afraid, subjugated to unimaginable cruelties at the hands of Red and her soulless patron.

He thought of Graves, his best friend, annoying and taxing at times but like a brother to him, but Graves was just a body now, a blood-spattered corpse no one would even recognize. He thought of Stone and Cristena and Morg and Kray and Winter, of Snow and his mother and father, of the streets and shops and the frightened people he'd left behind in Thornn. He saw random images, meaningless in and of themselves, a candle in his sister's window frame, an open door leading to a pub where he and Graves liked to drink, a boxing match where he lost forty coins, a fortune teller who told him he'd live to a ripe old age, an elephant ride he and his sister took, all the while wondering where such a beast came from, a brothel where he lost his virginity, the only place he ever really enjoyed the company of women, an apple stand where he worked, a steam engine and a railroad his father took him to when he was very small, before The Black, one of the only memories he had of the man, a sunset he watched with Snow, an eclipse, a waterfall and a lake and a bucket of cold white fish, a summer day when Snow was inside, mother was in the kitchen, and he looked up at the sky and wondered, he saw possibilities, he knew he was trapped in one of those small eternal moments when his life had not yet been decided, when there were still choices to make, when nothing was certain, and all of those moments taken together were the chaotic collage of his life, a snapshot of his memory, his soul. There was no one thing, no ill-defined feeling or heart-moving song, but a sea of memories, a soup of emotions. It was life, *his* life, and his home, a place he wouldn't let be destroyed by a woman who'd tried to be a savior but in the end had decided to become a God.

Cross walked on. His eyes were cast forward, and his pace quickened. He was ready to finish it. Even naked as he was without the shield of his spirit he marched towards his end, and he was not afraid.

TWENTY-TWO
NECROPOLIS

The prison of fog came to an end at the edge of a dead city.

The walls of the necropolis were so dark they seemed to suck the light from the air. Sheets of black iron pitted and dented by a history of calamities had been riveted over the spaces between the stone blocks. The fog ended a few hundred feet short of the onyx city, far enough away for Cross to take in the impressive breadth of the utterly silent necropolis on the fields of ice cold mud. He saw a coastal shore at the far end of the city, and though the waters were some distance away he noted the faint odor of salt. Skeletal and jagged towers stood at the corner intersections of the walls, each capped with a belfry of preposterous size and crooked angles. Red flags hung limp in the dead air, and barbed iron spikes surrounded the city like animal spines.

A wide grey path led to the open portcullis granting access. Crowded houses had been packed into the same unseemly angles as the towers, and the stone streets bore not a trace of refuse. Silver mist and dark green chimney smoke rolled over everything. The streets wound out of sight, winding into shadows.

Cross stood frozen. This city bore a citizenry, who even as he stood there in awe moved down the dank and lifeless streets. They went about their business, their eyes gone or their limbs missing or their mouths sewn shut.

This was a city populated by corpses.

They moved in near silence, so stiflingly quiet that Cross's breaths sounded like hurricanes, his footfalls like thunder. The air tensed as if ready to pounce.

The dead carried on as living people did. They were occupied by any number of mundane tasks.

Cross wasn't even aware of the zombies behind him until they passed him by and entered the city, oblivious or unconcerned by his presence. He watched them go. Their flesh was rotten and leathery, and they bore gaping holes in their bodies through which he saw black worms swimming in their veins in place of blood. None of the undead so much as turned their heads in his direction.

Maybe they don't know I'm here, Cross thought. *How? Am I expected? Maybe they're supposed to let me pass.* Cross swallowed. The act of breathing seemed to drag rocks up and down the inside of his chest, and his stomach boiled with worry. *Do it now, or you never will.*

He stepped into the necropolis.

The silence was unnerving. Bound in by walls and towers, walking along clean streets under the shade of tall buildings, passing storefronts and sewer grates, Cross could almost believe he was somewhere else, in some normal city. But where another city would have bustled with activity and the air would have been filled with shouts and whinnies and steam engines and noise there in the necropolis there was only the quiet shuffle of corpse feet on the stone roads, the low and nearly inaudible moans of the undead, the distant toll of some mad church bell sounding utterly alien in that dread landscape.

He read a word on the face of a large building with stone columns: *Koth*. The Old One's city. The vampires who'd defected from the Ebon Cities came to Koth. It was a city of undead outcasts, rebels, traitors in the eyes of the vampire elite. Those undead not tolerated by vampires – lich, ghouls, zombies, utterghasts, kai'thoren, mummies, necrofilch, others – were welcome in the Old One's city. There they hid, hated by both the living and the dead.

But just like Red, the Old One is willing to compromise, Cross thought bitterly. *The Old One is willing to give the Ebon Cities the means to defeat us so he can rejoin their ranks.*

Cross brushed against dead bodies and realized he couldn't look much better than they did. He felt numb. The air in Koth was chill and damp and froze his clothes to his skin. The mud and gore caked to his body itched. He wore a suit of gritty armor.

He wandered the streets, wondering where he'd find Red.

Twisted and narrow lanes led down curved hills and snaked like rivers between the crooked buildings. Piles of bones stood at street intersections, illuminated by fire pits filled with cold blue flames. Tapestries of flayed skin dangled from the rooftops. Cross saw vehicles made of bone and turbines fueled by blood. He saw factory-bred zombies with false skin expertly sewn to their bodies with industrial seams. He saw feeding vats filled with entrails and bloody slime and tanks filled with black necrotic fluid used to embalm and preserve rotting corpses, a privilege of the vain upper echelon of the damned.

Every building was dark and had been carved with rampantly elliptical angles, lending Koth a shadowy and organic feel. Black smoke silently churned from distant processing plants casting industrial shadows over the city. Cross tasted exhaust and rotten nectar in the air, and he smelled turpentine and embalming fluid, sumac and hemlock. Beneath it all was an inescapable fog of decay.

Cross rubbed shoulders with shambling corpses and gaunt wights. Flame spirits floated through the air and cast blazing trails behind them. He gazed into eyeless sockets and mummified heads with mouths frozen in permanent grins. The black sidewalks were coated with white corpse dust.

He went through the city in a quiet panic. It was a struggle every step of the way to maintain his resolve. There was always something undead within arm's reach, and at any moment he expected one to turn and pounce on him.

Nothing happened. He was left alone.

Cross searched for some sign of the Old One's residence. It would be plain, Cross reasoned, for the Old One was not an ostentatious ruler. He'd been a soldier in life, a man who'd earned his reputation doing the impossible and asking for little in return. His lair now would be fortified, but it would by no means draw attention to itself. Quite randomly, Cross took down a steep lane, and he entered a lower section of the city.

He walked down a road paved with faces: flayed skins pulled taut and stretched out in a mockery of caricature screams, a collage of human masks under his boots. He saw pillars of black stone and passed a temple made of saw blades.

Cross came to the edge of a dock over turgid grey waters. Iron mists clung to the surface of the sea, low enough for him to see the outline of a land mass out in the smoky bay, an isle dotted with buildings. Massive ice floes drifted in the water, black glaciers cut through with frozen veins of crimson quartz and bits of stony debris still cleaved to the ice, the refugees from some long forgotten structure.

Cross compiled what he knew of the Old One. In life he'd led an expedition north some months after The Black, before the first warlock or witch sightings. That expedition, evidently, had been to try and rescue some special child, a child which a prophet or fortune teller had determined would give humans the means to survive in their suddenly devastated world.

The Old One – *Knight, that's what his name was, Dane Knight* – had died there along with all of his men, trapped and ambushed in a church by vampire shock troops. The child had died, Knight had been turned into a vampire even though the rest of his men had been slaughtered, and in time he became a separatist and a defector known as the Old One.

I wonder why he left, Cross wondered. *Why did he defect from the Ebon Cities?*

The void where Cross's spirit should have been gnawed at him, left him weak. He felt hollow. He wasn't sure why but he was certain the Old One was on that isle. The misty waters were laggard and sluggish. They'd once been frozen and solid, just like the lands that had surrounded the church where Knight and his Company fell, at least according to the tales.

You're still there, Cross thought. *The church where you died is on that isle, and that's where you are. Trapped in the past.*

Cross walked to the docks. Ancient and rotted wood creaked under his weight. The smell of sea salt was muted by the odor of undead fish, which Cross spied swimming just beneath the smoke-colored surface of the water. Tall smokestacks on iron dreadnaughts moored in the bay belched acrid black smoke. The air was brighter there by the water, pale and empty like a frozen winter. Dead waves splashed against the heavy pylons.

The city carried on behind him, unconcerned by his presence.

Cross descended a wooden staircase and stepped onto the floating walkways leading to the ships. Most of the vessels were large sailing crafts made of iron, bone and black wood, and they bore sails woven from tanned skins. There were also a number of submersibles, one- or two-man submarines equipped with massive viewing portholes and sharp propellers.

He spied a small sailing craft big enough for perhaps a dozen people. A hooded wight stood at the bow, its undead face partially concealed under a grey hood. If the wight found Cross out of place or suspicious it made no sign of it; instead it gestured with a skeletal hand for him to board the ship. Its wide and frozen human eyes seemed to regard Cross carefully as he approached.

I am expected.

He chilled at the thought, but boarded anyways. The vessel shifted and lurched as he stepped on the slick deck. Cross walked to the iron railings securing the passenger pit and looked out at the island.

Somehow Cross wasn't surprised by this turn of events. Maybe he'd even known this was how it would happen.

The wight stepped aboard in silence. It regarded him with its molded skeletal smile.

"You're expecting me," Cross said. He was surprised when the figure nodded. "Where are you to take me?" he asked.

The wight pointed with a bony claw at the misty isle. Cross nodded.

A few minutes later the thaumaturgic turbines sputtered to life and the vessel lurched forward into dark waters, slowly propelled by its noisy motors. Cross held onto the railing as the craft sliced through the oily sea. Black smoke from the city and the docks spread across the sky like an ink spill, painting a path to the black island.

Cross was certain he wouldn't be coming back.

TWENTY-THREE

OBELISK

Buildings took shape in the mist as the boat drew close to the isle, standing like gravestones in the white fog. The shore was rocky and jagged, a fan of blades. White waters heavy with slime crashed against the stones. The air was icy and thick and pressed against Cross's skin like a razor's kiss.

The boat came ashore at one of the few points in the labyrinth of deadly stones where the beach was accessible. Cross disembarked and waded through polluted waters to a beach of pure white sand. He noted something odd about the sand, so he knelt down and took up a handful. Tiny bits of broken bone and tooth, so fine they were almost invisible, drifted between his fingers. The beach was ground bone: he stood on a shore of the dead.

The ship silently cast off, as Cross knew it would. Ghostly calls sounded through the chill of the afternoon.

Cross marched toward the structures. The dark chain of buildings was arranged in a semi-circle near the edge of some craggy foothills, similar in appearance to the dagger-like rocks of the shore. The fog blocked his vision beyond the buildings, which loomed wraithlike in the mist.

The air was shockingly cold. Cross walked through a floating curtain of ice which coated him in a brittle shell of frost. His lips and eyes felt numb. He breathed warmth into his hands and quickened his pace.

Unnaturally dark cobblestone streets ran right up to the bone sand. Cross stepped up carefully, so as to avoid slipping. The buildings were mostly wood, and they, too, were utterly black – the siding, the porches, even the windows were pitch, like they'd been dipped in tar. The rickety wooden shacks were in a general state of disrepair.

The buildings encircled a solid ebon obelisk apparently made of black ice. The monolith stood twice as tall as Cross, and it was covered with silver runes and glyphs he recognized as High Jlantrian script. Similar markings had been set on a disc of dark stone which served as a sunken and inverted platform supporting the obelisk. The disc and the ice pillar looked like a dial, or a clock. A short set of steps descended from the platform to the ground.

Cross felt drawn to the pillar. The obelisk emanated cold so absolute it made the air raw. Bitter steam curled off the stone. He stared and moved closer without at first even realizing it. There was something intimately familiar about the obelisk, like the feeling of coming home, just as there was something terrifying about it, a danger he couldn't put out of his mind. He saw voices in the obelisk, and felt something claw at the stone from the inside. As Cross drew near he realized the obelisk wasn't black at all – it was transparent, and filled with a desolate midnight smoke.

His legs grew weary. Each step was a trial, like his feet had melded to the stone. He felt like he could fall to the ground and never rise again. The obelisk seemed to grow further away and recede in his vision even as he moved close to it. Each step forward took him back.

He saw inside it. He saw the mountain, and the silver mists. He saw the glade.

"I wouldn't recommend touching it."

Red stood behind him. Cross felt like he was stuck in a dream. His movements were sluggish, and the air stretched and twisted like watercolors. Words sloughed toward him as if made from congealed liquid.

Two others stood with Red. One was Snow, beaten and bruised. She wore a grey cloak cast over her like a shroud. Cross's chest seized up at the sight of her. She looked barely alive and her eyes were blank, not willing or capable of meeting his gaze.

The other individual was a tall and lean man with eyes like white pits. His hair was silver and cropped short, and his bone-thin arms were covered with old military tattoos. He wore a purple and black cloak over an infantry uniform, and his rotted flesh had taken on the pallor of the north.

The Old One. Dane Knight.

"It will kill you to touch it," Red said. "But I suspect you gathered that, didn't you, Cross?"

Cross tried to pull himself together. His thoughts were forming slowly, like he'd been drugged. He feared he might pass out at any second.

"So you...tell me," he struggled. Every breath was like a gasp for air. "Why did I come here? You let me get through. Why would you...do that?"

"I'd rather *show* you," Red said with a smile.

The Old One nodded, but remained silent.

Something reached out to Cross. Black smoke poured out of the obelisk, a serpent of vapor which curled around him. Cross looked through the ebon murk and saw through the cracks of time. He fell into liquid clouds and uncertain storms.

The bullet tears the child apart, and her tiny head explodes in a spray of blood. Knight screams, not believing he did this, knowing, as they all did, he had no choice. The girl is dead, and the cursed candles spaced around her on the floor consume her soul. Their fires burn bright.

The ritual, prepared over the course of days, has awaited this final sacrifice.

He doesn't know how this part works, but he knows it should have been done before now. He'd wanted to find an alternative, wanted to find some other way. Before The Black, Knight didn't believe in magic or in vampires. But the world is different now. The world he knows is gone.

The vampires came to stop them from making the sacrifice, because they knew it would change everything.

The air grows dark. The vampires and their grisly weapons force their way into the chamber

and Cross realized he was in the remains of that chamber now, decades later, but the walls were gone, everything was gone but the disc of stone *by crashing through the door and walls. A silver stream of smoke bellows from the child's ruined corpse. A voice is trapped in the fumes, and something forms in the core of the sacrifice. Beams of unlight slice up from the ground and cut the air apart. The candles snuff out and the light solidifies and congeals into something both invisible yet more solid than steel.*

It's a prison. And a weapon.

Black energies tear from the sacrificed soul and fill the air with a whirlwind of shadow. Knight dies at that instant, but he also remains, and he screams in terror as he witnesses the apotheosis. He is flung through the unlight, bathed in a maelstrom of darkness spilling through the breach he created.

He's made a hole, and sealed it up again. He's created a prison of souls – a cage without bars, an endless source of unwilling power. Humankind has searched for it for centuries, but until The Black they never understood what had to be done to acquire it.

The sacrifice is complete. In order to combat hordes of undead invaders, Knight has opened a doorway to an even blacker power.

"Now," he utters from newly undead lips. "We have magic."

Cross fell to his knees.

"Magic..." he coughed. "You...*you* made it possible?"

Yes, the Old One said without speaking. Its voice was a vast echo, a howling wind from the depths of a great pit. *A weapon was needed. When conventional means of survival failed we turned to the supernatural, the very thing destroying us. We consulted religious and so-called arcane texts. There were many failures and lives lost before the answer was finally uncovered.*

"And...this?" Cross looked at the obelisk. His body grew weaker by the second. Life leaked from him.

It is the anchor. The prison. It tethers the souls of the departed to this world so they can't escape to the next. We use them – they are the fuel which powers our magic. Without the exploitation of the dead humankind would have been lost long ago. They are our saviors, and our weapons.

The glade, Cross realized. *The glade is inside the obelisk.* "How are they...tied to warlocks, then...and witches..."

"No one really understands that part," Red said. "You know that. Even the greatest arcane scholars understand just enough about magic to make it work." She smiled. "Until I came along, none of us even knew where it came from."

Cross was on his knees. He struggled to keep himself from falling to the midnight stone. He could barely breathe. Pain flared at the base of his spine and wrapped up his back til it reached the crest of his skull.

"This is it, isn't it? Magic is our only hope...without magic...Christ, it's the only thing that's kept us alive..."

He could almost hear the Old One smile. Cross fought off unconsciousness even as it swept over his eyes like a welcome warmth. He saw faces in the obelisk, distorted and half melted, smeared against the inner walls of the translucent stone.

It is my promised gift to the Ebon Cities, the Old One said. *I created it, but as you surely saw, I didn't know much about it, nor did I know how to destroy it. I am the only one left of that doomed expedition, and by the time I made the sacrifice the rest of the ritual had already been prepared. The act of killing was all that remained. The secrets of the prison were lost, consumed with the souls of my squad.*

But Red found those secrets, Cross thought. Somehow, in her tenure as Thornn's leader and while acting as the voice of the White Mother, Margrave Azazeth had uncovered some vital details about the obelisk, probably buried away in some obscure text or noted in an elliptical reference in a forgotten calculation book. Knight was no mage, and no scholar. He didn't know the first thing about how to destroy the stone. Everyone else in the expedition had died, and only Knight had been brought back to undeath. He probably hadn't known where to look for the information, and, more importantly, he hadn't *needed* it. By the time he wanted to know how to destroy the obelisk it was too late for him to find it... until Margrave came along and handed him the secrets he'd been looking for.

No one knew, Cross realized. People assumed humankind's mastery of magic had been just another byproduct of The Black, another shift in reality to accompany the ancient cities and dread races. *No one knows about the obelisk, or the glade. All this time, the key to our survival, the source of what's kept us in the war for so long has been held in this bastard's hands, and we never even knew it.*

Cross felt sure that if Knight had known how to destroy the obelisk before Red had come along he'd have already done so.

"So..." Cross was on the brink of passing out. He felt a hand on his shoulder, soft and warm. "Why...why am I...?"

"Alive?" Red asked. "Well, just as the obelisk needed a sacrifice to *become*, it requires a sacrifice to be *undone*." Cross looked up at her. It took nearly all his strength. "We had a candidate picked out," Red said playfully. "Things have changed, however."

Snow stood over him. Her once beautiful face was bloodied and bruised. Deep cuts lined her pale skin. Her eyes were hollow and sunken, and innumerable wounds had been inflicted on her forearms and chest. She bore ritual scarifications, fetishes, brandings. She'd been tortured and marked.

"*I've* changed," Snow smiled. "Red was going to make me the sacrifice, but now it's going to be *you*, Eric: a warlock cut off from his own magic. You're just what we need. That's why Red stole your spirit. You'd already lost her once on your own...back in the crypt..."

"Snow..." he stammered.

"So your spirit was still vulnerable," Snow went on. "It was easy for Red to take her from you again." She leaned close. "Margrave has secrets, Eric," she whispered. "She knows how to do things you and I had never dreamed. And now..." Snow stood up and smiled at Red. "She's made you into the perfect sacrifice."

Snow had become something different. It was like someone had stolen her skin and now wore it.

"Snow," Cross stammered. "Listen to yourself..."

She glared at him. There was nothing but darkness behind her familiar eyes. Cross's heart froze.

They broke her, he realized with horror. *She's one of them, and she's not coming back.*

Cross could barely hold on. Tears welled in his eyes. Images of Snow, young and bright and warm and alive with love flashed through his mind. His baby sister was gone.

"I came here for *you*, Snow," he sobbed. "Please..."

It was the last he thing he managed to say before everything went black.

He drifts over cyan seas, passes through clouds of steam and drifts on crystal winds.

He stands in the glade and senses her on the other side of the iron fog. She screams soundlessly. He reaches for her, desperate, but she's pulled into the sky by unseen hands, straight towards the melting silver sun.

I'm sorry, he says, but she can't hear him. She's well and truly gone, and he collapses in the waters, left alone to bear the weight of his failure. It's over.

TWENTY-FOUR
SACRIFICE

Cross woke to the metal screams of a train.

It was a Necronaught, an undead locomotive, a massive and ugly beast of a machine. It soared down an ethereal track, a rail existing in a space between the worlds of the living and the dead. The train seemed to float over the dead rivers, hovering just out of synch with everything else.

The vehicle was a horror to behold, a monstrosity of black iron. The behemoth was all spikes and bones and razor wire, gun turrets and massive wheels greased with human remains, growling engines sounding of screams and smoke which colored the sky with hexed black fumes. The train was twenty cars long; each car was littered with impaled bodies. The Necronaught's whistle cut through the air like a draconic war cry.

Cross stood waiting, a prisoner. His hands were bound in front of him with metal shackles which cut deep into the wrists of his gauntleted hands. He was weary and sick, terrified, resigned and withdrawn.

A pair of black clad undead attended him. Their claws were the size of knives and their lean ebon bodies were encased in leather and steel armor which left their elongated heads exposed. They had wide fanged mouths and oversized white eyes.

War wights.

They waited with Cross on the train platform. More war wights stood near the obelisk, which floated just inches above the ground, lifted by Red's magic so it could easily be pushed.

The Old One, Red and Snow were all there. The station was dilapidated and ancient. The platform was made of rotted wood pitted by acid stains and termite attacks, and the main building listed sharply to one side, ready to collapse.

237

Cross breathed slowly. He had to shut out the pain of losing Snow, the pain of his own futility. He tried to calm himself.

I was wrong. This isn't over yet.

Cold red dust blew across the ground. They were no longer on the island, Cross realized, but south of the necropolis, at what appeared to be the remains of a shattered frontier town overtaken with rust. The train tracks were ages old and had fallen to pieces, and the whole area had been consumed by weeds and red-white ash. The sky was the color of undercooked meat.

The train drew closer. It churned black smoke into the sky. Dead steam blasted from the engine. Cross watched as the foreword crenellation pushed dust and bone from its path and stirred up a maelstrom of debris. Massive wheels cut like saw blades through the ground. The Necronaught ignored the physical tracks there at the station and created its own, and the air turned heavy as the train groaned to a halt in front of the platform. The world bubbled and swelled, and Cross was pushed back by an unseen telekinetic force.

The Necronaught was even more hideous when viewed up close. Its black iron skin leaked crimson fluids which steamed and stained the ground. The windows had been charred black by some forgotten explosion. Deep white markings like war paint had been cast on the exterior of the tank-like shell of the main car. War wights manned gun turrets at the fore and aft of the second and third cars: cylinder guns, nail launchers, ice cannons. The smell of acid stains and burning tar hung so thick in the air Cross nearly choked on it.

The train came to a halt with a grinding snap. A final banshee scream wailed from within the unearthly engine.

The war wights loaded the obelisk onto the train, carefully guiding it onto a large car. Cross was forcefully seized by the arms and hauled to another car closer to the engine. Great iron doors slid open with a bone-jangling groan. The interior of the car was outfitted with a wrought iron cage and a collection of twisted blades, razor chairs, chain straps and needle harnesses, all of which had been hung with disturbing precision on a weapons rack on the far wall. Cross was taken inside – he offered little resistance – where another pair of war wights waited, commanded by a thin lich with short-cropped hair. The lich wore fine silver and grey clothing.

"Happy day," the lich grinned. "I'm Jebedar Krannor. Your host."

"Great to be here," Cross smiled. "You look pretty good for a lich."

"I take care of myself," Krannor giggled.

"A foppish lich? That's new."

Krannor smiled and dealt Cross a backhanded blow that sliced open his face. Blood ran from the cuts, and Cross recoiled at the rotten smell of the lich's hand. The war wight's bone-chilling grip tightened on Cross's arms and forced him into the cage, and the door closed behind him with a redolent slam.

The walls shuddered as the train surged to life. He looked around. Screams issued from massive pipes running along the ceiling, leading, it seemed, to the adjacent cars on either side.

Access tubes, Cross guessed, placed so incorporeal undead could pass through the otherwise magically shielded outer walls of the cars, which looked nigh impenetrable.

The massive iron door started to close. Cross was thankful for the modicum of light provided by electric lamps in the corners of the grim car. He didn't want to be stuck in there in absolute darkness.

A slim human figure slipped into the car. It was Snow.

Cross's hopes lifted. Just for a moment he allowed himself to believe his sister had somehow broken free of Red's control and come to rescue him. That notion was dashed the moment she shot him an icy glare, then stepped up and reported to Krannor.

"You're to refrain from interrogation," she said with the same cold voice she'd used before. "Our respective masters will join us shortly."

I'm sorry, Cross thought. *God, Snow, I'm so sorry.*

The iron door sealed shut with a hiss of dead air and the Necronaught sputtered as its wheels groaned to life. Within moments the vehicle found its rhythm. Everything inside shook, and after less than a minute Cross felt the train speed along at a terrifying pace.

He looked at Snow. She avoided his gaze and stood near Krannor, who busied himself reading through a set of scrolls she'd handed to him.

"Snow," Cross said. He couldn't whisper – the damn train was too loud – so he had to raise his voice to nearly a shout. "Are you all right, Snow?"

She didn't answer. She kept her eyes on Krannor.

"Snow, what happened?"

She refused to look up.

The arms of her cloak had been torn away, revealing deep cuts and a handful of black and blue bite marks. He *knew* what had happened: they'd broken her. It wasn't Red who'd done it, as he'd originally suspected, but the vampires. Snow had been a captive long enough, so they'd had plenty of time. Almost anyone subjected to their treatment would break, no matter how resolute or determined. There was only so much a human could endure, and vampires were absolute in their methods. Once a human was properly broken there was little chance of ever coming back.

A sick feeling rose in his stomach. He couldn't dispel images of what her torture must have been like.

"Snow!?"

"She is not allowed to speak to you at this time," Krannor said coolly. He turned and looked at Cross. "And you are not allowed to speak at all."

"Fuck you."

Cross didn't see the war wight till it struck him. Lengthy claws reached through the bars and raked him across the chest. He gasped in pain. The claw wounds were deep, and burned like he'd been cut with ice. Even his blood felt cold as it ran down his stomach and across his shirt.

"Anything else to say?" Krannor smiled.

"Yes," Cross managed, biting his teeth to block out the pain. "Why did Knight defect from Rath? What's he really up to? I don't believe he's trying to reconcile with the Ebon Cities. It doesn't make any sense."

The lich's smile broadened. This time Cross was ready, and he pulled away from the bars moments before the war wight's claws took him.

Cross's victory was short lived. Krannor leapt through the bars with a dimensional folding, a translocative jump. The lich gripped Cross's throat in a vise-like grip. He felt his windpipe being crushed. Air built up in his lungs, which he pictured filling and bursting like balloons. He had no strength to fight back.

"You should learn respect," the lich smiled.

Cross couldn't answer. He nearly passed out before Krannor finally released him. He crashed to the ground, gasping for breath, wishing the feeling back into his arms and legs.

The Old One and Red were suddenly in the car. Cross wasn't sure when they'd arrived. Red held Snow in her arms like a long-lost daughter, and Snow set her head on Red's shoulder and kept her eyes locked on Cross. She continued to gaze at him with hate, like he'd committed some horrible crime.

Knight's hood was pulled back so Cross could see the ancient vampire's cracked ebon skin, sunken eyes and decaying flesh. His hands ended in jagged yellow claws shaped like a bird's talons, and his long and forked tongue dangled from his fanged mouth like a thrashing eel.

"Is it...time...already?" Cross coughed. He felt the wounds on his chest freezing. The ice was working its way into his blood.

Krannor hauled Cross to his feet and held him a good foot off the ground. Cross was brought to the edge of the cage. A terrible choir of screams bellowed from outside, and through that din Cross just made out the baying of massive hounds.

We're near the Rift already, he thought in dismay. *We'll be in Rath by sundown tomorrow.*

We must prepare you, the Old One told him without words. The vampire opened his taloned hand and revealed a dim black bulb the size of a turnip. The sphere held a spark of green flame deep in its core, like a torch buried in liquid amber. The subtle green shine radiated sickness and power. Cross didn't need his spirit to feel the monstrous arcane potential in the bomb, far too much to all be contained in a single small device.

That one bomb was linked to others. When it exploded, so would they.

Krannor set Cross down and delivered a sharp kick to the back of his leg. He screamed as bones cracked. Blinded with pain, Cross fell to the floor, and would have toppled over if not for Krannor's claw, which painfully dug into the meat of his shoulder.

Hang on, he told himself. *Stay. Finish this.*

A war wight took the orb from Knight and opened the cage door. The bomb glowed brighter the closer it came to Cross. He sensed the power it was linked to, felt it pulse against him like heat. Krannor pulled Cross's head back by his hair, and the wight walked towards him with the orb held level with Cross's face.

They're going to make me swallow it.

"How many?" he asked. "How many of those things are there?" He didn't actually expect an answer, but asking the questions kept him conscious. "There *are* more, aren't there? You hid them all over Rath, I bet. It would have been easy to get vampire spies into a city of vampires to hide them for you, right?" No one answered. *Did I catch them off guard?* he wondered. "How about the obelisk? Are any of the bombs attached to *it*?"

"Wow," Red laughed. "Shut up, you moron, before you make it worse for yourself."

"Worse than getting a pyroclast bomb shoved down my throat?" he shouted. "I'm the trigger, aren't I? That's how it's going to work: when the vampires of Rath sacrifice *me* to destroy the obelisk, all of those linked explosives are going to go off at once. Am I right?" Red's stunned face gave Cross the answer.

The war wight towered over him. Cross smelled sewage and brimstone radiate from the bomb.

"Am I right?!" he shouted again.

Cross knew he was about to die, and tried to prepare himself, tried to draw in a heroic final breath or think a final heroic thought, but all he could think of was his spirit, and what a crime it was he wouldn't get to say goodbye.

To his immense surprise the wight stepped back. Knight shifted in place.

"You were never going to make good with the Ebon Cities, were you?" Cross pressed. His heart pounded wildly. He felt like he was going to be sick. "You set up this whole obelisk business to get them to deal with you, but it's a ruse. When they sacrifice me, the bombs go off, Rath will blow up, the obelisk will blow up...the Ebon Cities will lose one of their strongest cities, and in the same stroke you'll take magic away from humans forever." *God*, he thought, *it's brilliant.* "And you win."

I win.

"So...that's it? You were one of *us*, God damn it! What the hell happened?"

The Old One glared at him with rotted eyes. His face was surrounded by a faint and sickly shine.

Knight hovered towards him. His tattered cloak dragged across the rattling train floor. The car rocked and shook as the Necronaught thundered over the Carrion Rift.

What HAPPENED?! The voice cut through Cross's mind like a hot knife. *I. Became. This. This shell. This disease. Forever hated by both sides of this ridiculous war. I sacrificed my own life to give humankind a chance, and in reward I was doomed to an eternal damnation. I'm one of the enemy! I cannot, and will not, accept vampires...and I cannot forgive the likes of you. So I condemn you. I condemn you both. I condemn you all.*

Knight snatched the pyroclast bomb from the war wight. Krannor yanked Cross's head back.

Cross took them by surprise. He threw all his weight backwards and into Krannor, brought his bound hands up and pushed the lich off balance. Cross lunged at Knight.

Time slowed. The war wight stepped in Cross's path and grabbed his gauntleted hands with its cold steaming claws. Cross screamed as the talons ripped through his wrists. The blades cut him down to the bone, but he pulled back with all his strength and tore his hands free from the gauntlets.

The containment gauntlet covering Cross's necrotically diseased left hand flew apart. Termites of black shadow exploded all over his arms and seared his skin with necrotic chill. Shadows raced up his chest. The cold was so deep it gnawed straight to his bones.

Cross went numb. He knew he only had a moment before he died.

He lashed out. Though robbed of his magic, Cross was covered in raw and destructive arcane power, the magic of the disease he'd been infected with when he'd battled the hound in the forest.

That disease had only one purpose: to annihilate.

And just as he'd done in the forest when he'd faced the hound, Cross grabbed hold of those shifting shadow energies and channeled them with a natural mastery over magic both he and his sister had been born with. He let the darkness swallow him, but at the same time took just enough control to push the black energy in the direction he wanted it to travel: straight into the bomb.

Pain shredded his body. Cross trapped the pyroclast in a shroud of Wormwood energies, in the shadows existing between moments. Darkness soaked him. He folded the shadows around the bomb, sealed it away from its siblings in a cage of utter darkness.

Only one bomb would go off. The bomb on the Necronaught.

Cross's last conscious thoughts were of Snow. He saw her at four years old, her gangly hair a mess thanks to the plum pudding she'd used to cover her face like war paint. He saw her at thirteen, sleeping until noon no matter how bright it was outside or how hot it was or how many times he threw pillows at her while she slept. He saw her as a woman grown, brave and strong, so wanting to help him and do the right thing she made a secret decision which would ultimately lead to her own death.

He thought of her, and his heart died. He hoped she'd feel no pain.

Snow and Red screamed. Knight's eyes went wide with shock. Cross clenched his teeth and pulled his rotting hand back from the moment. He released the pyroclast and allowed the explosion to happen.

The first blast tore away in a wave of acid and flame. Steel and shrapnel exploded as the detonation ruptured the car. Fire roared down the access tubes in the ceiling and into the other cars, racing along until it found the fuel tanks. When the fuel caught the entire train rattled sideways with a caustic blast and flew off course. Cars groaned and crashed. A crescendo of thunder shook the air.

Cross screamed. He stood at the core of the blast.

The cars at the rear of the train buckled, twisted, and rolled into each other. Storms of red ash roared alongside the screaming souls bound to the Necronaught. The bladed locomotive listed forward and tore the ground apart. Exploding fuel launched the cars forward and flipped them end over end.

The Necronaught careened over the edge and fell into the Carrion Rift. It broke apart in the fall and plummeted in sections.

The train met its demise at the nadir of the Rift. A series of metallic blasts echoed across the plains, through the mountain peaks and into the void of the falling night.

He runs through ankle-deep icy waters. The canopy of leaves collapses like green snow. Angry wind whips through the trees and bends the freezing rain. The black mountain stands, ever vigilant.

He's in the glade. In the obelisk.

It must be safe, for us to be here now.

He runs towards the clearing. There are shouts ahead. His body is whole, but he feels faint, like he's fading.

He doesn't have much time. He pushes through the icy canopy of trees.

Red is there, and she runs from him. She's found a way out, a way to escape her death on the train by moving through the obelisk. From there she'll travel somewhere else, to some other safe exit point back in the physical world.

He knows Red can do this. She's uncovered the secrets of this place, after all. She'll doubtless have found a way to break free.

But she runs as if frozen, trapped in the icy flow. Her every step is prolonged, dream-like. She's not meant to be here, and the world in the prison resists her transgression.

He closes the distance between them. She sees him, and runs faster. Neither of them can use their spirits. They are all prisoners in this place.

She'll fall up and into the sky, he realizes, just as spirits do when their time is done. He hears thunder, the approaching rumble of hooves. Red speeds her pace.

He races toward the witch even as a shaft of silver light embraces her from above. She holds up her arms, and her body starts to rise. He tackles her, and they both fall to earth. They struggle half submerged in the platinum waters, roll and splash in the freezing marsh. He holds on tight, gips her hair and forces her face in the water, not even sure if she can drown in this place.

His skin is frozen. He feels himself slipping away, fading. Light pierces his body. He grows translucent.

The unicorns emerge from the trees. Their bloody and jagged horns bear down on the two mages, aimed like a host of lances. Red screams and struggles, but he holds her tight.

Meet the wardens of this prison, he tells her without speaking. They protect the last vestige of our power and our hope. They're the guardians of what you wanted to take away from us.

He looks to the trees. He sees his spirit there, trapped in this cage with no walls, and she watches him. She waits for him.

He realizes how much he loves her.

The horns cut through their bodies like ugly black blades. He and Red are trampled underfoot, their bodies mangled. The silver waters turn red.

They swim in pain. He holds on to her. He'll make sure he doesn't die alone.

Red's broken body folds. She screams as she's drawn up to the eternal sky. She doesn't make it far before her form scatters like a flock of bloody ravens, torn apart as she leaves the safety of the glade.

It didn't work, *the voice of his spirit tells him. He can't tell if she's near or far. Red hasn't escaped.*

He lays on the ground, broken, bleeding and crushed. But he's still there.

He sees his spirit. She emerges from the trees and walks towards him.

I'm sorry. I'm finished. And with me gone, you'll die too.

It's time, *she tells him.* It's the way of things. One goes. Another stays. I want to go.

No.

It's my choice. Not yours.

And so it ends. A unicorn horn pierces her chest. She gasps. Her hands cling to the bloody spike. Even as she dies she looks at him and smiles.

I love you.

A beam of light takes hold of her from above. She's lifted from the glade and up to the silver sky, where she'll forever fall in the company of other lost souls.

Cross woke to a cold and cloudy night.

His back ached like he'd been stabbed, and his joints and muscles were sore and stiff. Every last part of him felt heavy except for his head, which felt stuffed with cotton. But he was whole. The wounds he'd suffered were somehow all gone: the plagued hand, the blade and claw wounds, even the broken leg. All he was left with was fatigue.

A deep chill gripped his skin, and when Cross took a breath he was struck with a fit of coughing that went on for what felt like hours.

He slowly sat up and looked around. He was in the graveyard.

She sent me home.

The industrial fires of Thornn lit the night and turned the clouds copper. The vastness of the Reach stretched out behind him, a dark and endless field of shadowed frost. Just to his right, dangling from the lonely tree, was the featureless doll he and Snow had seen the last time they'd been there. It was the last place they'd visited together before he'd found out she was to be a part of Viper Squad, before she'd accompany him on what would be her first and only trip away from Thornn.

Cross understood what had happened, even if there was no logical reason why he should. Somehow when he'd used the plague on his hand to detonate the bombs and destroy the Necronaught his spirit had found him. She'd broken though the walls of her prison in spite of Margrave's power and made it so he could defeat Red when she tried to escape, right there in that prison of souls.

And then she'd sacrificed herself to rescue his body and soul from doom, and in the process she'd sent him home.

Cross huddled up to fight off the night's chill. He was warm just moments later. Something took him in its spectral hold and smothered him in a glaze of unseen energies. He heard incomprehensible whispers and sensed a presence beside himself.

It was a spirit. But it wasn't her.

Somehow, for reasons he felt sure he'd never fully understand, he'd been given another. He sensed her. She felt entirely alien to him, and he could tell she was just as uncomfortable as he was. She might have even been the slightest bit resentful, even hostile, but the bond which cleaved them together meant he had nothing to fear from her, or she from him.

I don't understand. I'm sorry...you're stuck here with me, stuck with my pain.

Snow...I'm so sorry. I miss you already. I always will.

For a time Cross just sat in the cold and wept. The weight of all he'd lost came crashing down and threatened to crush him. His tears froze in the bitter and uncaring wind.

His spirit tugged at him, impatient. Restless. Somehow familiar.

Could it have been her? Could it have been Snow?

Likely he'd never know. But he could hope.

Whoever his new spirit was, she was with him now, and he hoped in time he'd come to feel for her as he had for the spirit who'd saved his life, who'd been the other half of his soul for as long as he could remember.

How he'd loved her.

EPILOGUE

BEGINNINGS

He walked the streets of Thornn, headed for the graveyard. It had been some weeks since his return. The world seemed strangely the same in so many ways.

But it wasn't the same, and never would be.

Cross had been debriefed and congratulated on a successful mission. There'd been many questions regarding the loss of his squad and the airship that had deployed them into the Wormwood. There were even more questions about Viper Squad's unauthorized engagement in Rhaine, and the fate of that remote town.

In the end, Cross was commended. They gave him a medal, a shiny white platinum ankh on a chain, a symbol of courage and valor. He stuffed it away in a box somewhere and lost the box in his apartment.

There was no talk of reforming Viper Squad. The general consensus was it would be an ill omen to resurrect a unit which had seen all but one of its members killed in action. Elias Pike, a grizzled officer Cross would report to from that point on, informed him had a place on any Squad of his choice.

Cross asked about reassignment, about helping the Southern Claw in a different way. Pike wanted him in the field.

I'm not sure that's where I belong.

Southern Claw scouts confirmed the destruction of the Necronaught bound from Koth to Rath, and arcane reconnaissance verified the presence of an obelisk buried at the bottom of the Carrion Rift. Because the sacrifice hadn't been properly carried out the artifact remained unharmed. Now it was buried somewhere beneath tons of iron, rubble and debris. Better yet, it was unwittingly being defended by shadow hounds and other mutated monstrosities in the Rift, creatures that were hostile to all other things living or dead. Teams would be assembled to recover the obelisk and bring it into Southern Claw hands before the Ebon Cities could acquire it, but in the meantime the source of mankind's magic was perhaps safer it had ever been.

In the end nothing had really changed, at least not in the grand scheme of things. That had been the point, of course, which meant Viper Squad's mission had been a complete success, even with the terrible casualties suffered in the hunt for Margrave Azazeth. She'd ultimately failed, and had been eliminated. The Old One was gone. The vampires of the Ebon Cities had gained no new advantage over the Southern Claw. The outcasts of Koth, in the meantime, remained a threat, and in time they'd have a new leader.

Life went on.

Cross tried to adjust to his spirit, but it was clear from the start things would be difficult between them. She was anxious and headstrong, reckless with abandon. He feared when he'd first have to go into combat with her, or when they'd find themselves in the presence of the recently dead. It was like playing with fire.

In many ways Cross was a novice again. He and his spirit had been together for most of his life, had grown to know each other. She'd been an integral part of him. There was a stranger inside him now. He had to start all over.

Cross knew he'd have to make a decision regarding his future with the Southern Claw. Retirement wasn't out of the question, considering the short life expectancy of warlocks. He hadn't ruled out the possibility of returning to the field, either. His spirit wanted to roam wild and free.

He had nightmares about Snow, trapped in that burning train as it plummeted over the cliff and into a canyon filled with nightmares.

Cross had a grave marker placed for her right next to their mother. The other members of Viper Squad had been interred in a separate section of the graveyard, but Cross managed to get a special plate made to commemorate the squad as a whole, which he placed next to Snow. He wanted to remember them all together.

He stood and looked down at the markers. It was a cold dry day much like the last. The Reach lay flat and frozen to the east, an eye-numbing white waste fading into a horizon of dark clouds.

The sounds of war machinery thundered from the Bonespire to the west. There were rumors the vampires were mobilizing for an attack on Thornn, the first such attack in many months. With Red gone they'd turned their attentions back to traditional means of wiping humankind.

"What am I supposed to do?" he whispered to the freezing wind. His ears and hands were cold thanks to the gnawing chill. It was nearly spring, but there was little way to tell.

Cross's spirit circled the air. Her power lapped against him like waves of cold water. She made him tired all over.

What am I supposed to do?

The wind picked up, causing the Tin Man to rattle in the wind. Cross glanced at it, and then at the other tree, the one he and Snow had looked at when they'd been there last, when her whole life was still ahead of them. Before she'd followed him into war to die.

Cross's eyes caught on something. He walked over to it. The white apple was still there. It had been weeks since he'd last seen it, but it was identical. It was as if the scene when he and Snow had first happened upon the fruit had been frozen in time.

A tiny ice-white spider the same color as the eastern snows crawled across the face of the apple. Cross smiled, and nodded.

"All right," he whispered. "All right."

He watched the spider until it scurried out of sight, then walked back to the city.

ABOUT THE AUTHOR

Steven Montano keeps writing novels in the hopes that one day he'll wake up and actually feel like a real author.   Maybe it'll happen tomorrow.

He lives in Washington State with a beautiful and intelligent wife, two beautiful and talented children, and a backyard badly in need of some love.

Visit Steven's official website, bloodskies.com

www.ingramcontent.com/pod-product-compliance
Lightning Source LLC
Chambersburg PA
CBHW071137170626
46809CB00002B/660